Sean

McCallum

The

Recalcitrant

Stuff of Life

www.Outcast-Press.com

(e-book) ISBN-13: 978-1-7353126-5-1

(print) ISBN-13: 978-1-7353126-5-1

For Claudia,

without whom this book wouldn't exist,

and for Luciana and Liam,

who wouldn't exist without this book

$$Z = Z2 + C$$

- Benoit Mandelbrot

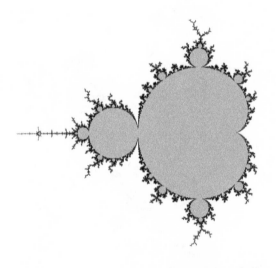

- Mandelbrot Set

"Those melodies come back to me
At times beyond my heartbeat"

- The Tragically Hip
"Escape is at Hand for the
Travellin' Man"

Map of Peru

Table of Contents

Spotify Soundtrack

Prelude
"Blank Maps" – Cold Specks
"Escape is at Hand for the Travellin' Man" – The Tragically Hip
Chapter 1
"Too Sober to Sleep" – Justin Rutledge
"Mr. Tambourine Man (Alternate Take)" – Bob Dylan
Chapter 2
"Unwind Yourself (Remix)" – Marva Whitney
"El Rey de la Puntualidad" –Fania All Stars, Hector Lavoe
"Better Off Without a Wife" – Tom Waits
Chapter 3
"Wheat Kings" – The Tragically Hip
"Legal Age Life at Variety Store" – Rheostatics
Chapter 5
"*Ven Bailalo* (Reggaeton Mix)" – Angel Y Khris
Chapter 6
"Astral Weeks" – Van Morrison
"Caught Me Thinkin" – Bahamas
"Asking for Flowers" – Kathleen Edwards
"Hasn't Hit Me Yet" – Blue Rodeo
Chapter 8
"Smells Like Teen Spirit" – Nirvana
Chapter 9
"Jockey Full of Bourbon" – Tom Waits

Chapter 10
"Love Me Do" – The Beatles
"Against All Odds (Take a Look at Me Now)" – Phil Collins
"Keep On Moving" – Bob Marley & The Wailers
"*Deja la Vida Volar*" – Victor Jara
Chapter 11
"Billie Jean" – Michael Jackson
"Mirror In The Bathroom" – The English Beat

"A Kind of Magic (Live at Wembley '86)" – Queen
"Under Pressure (Live at Wembley '86)" – Queen
"Walk of Life" – Dire Straits
"Vogue"– Madonna
Chapter 12
"Holberg Suite, Op 40: Air (Andante Religioso)" – Edvard Grieg
"Theme From New York, New York" – Frank Sinatra
"Sabotage" – Beastie Boys
"After the Gold Rush" – Neil Young
"Visions of Johanna" – Bob Dylan
"New York City Serenade" – Bruce Springsteen
"This Year's Love" – David Gray
"Concrete Jungle" – Bob Marley & The Wailers
Chapter 13
"Money for Nothing" – Dire Straits
"Sultans of Swing" – Dire Straits
"So Far Away" – Dire Straits
"I Want to Know What Love Is" – Foreigner
"The Waiting" – Tom Petty & The Heartbreakers
"Waltzing Mathilda" – Slim Dusty
"All Day and All of the Night" – The Kinks
"Summertime Blues" – Eddie Cochran
"Do Wah Diddy Diddy" – Manfred Mann
"Sheena Is a Punk Rocker" – Ramones
"You Shook Me All Night Long" – AC/DC
"Baba O'Riley" – The Who
"Gimme Shelter" – The Rolling Stones
"Wooly Bully" – Sam The Sham & The Pharaohs
"It's My Life" – The Animals
"I Fought the Law" – The Clash
"96 Tears" – ? & the Mysterians
"Please Please Me" – The Beatles
Chapter 14
"Pullin Punches" – Arkells
"Bad as They Seem" – Hayden
Small Change (B-Side) – Tom Waits
Chapter 15
"I Will Be There When You Die" – My Morning Jacket
"Salta Salta" – Euforia de Iquitos, Ana Kohler, Erberth

"Don't Worry, Be Happy" – Bobby McFerrin
Chapter 16
"*Surco*" – Gonzalo Vargas, Inkuyo (Andean Pipe Music)
"*Uña*" – J. Mitchberg, U. Ramos, Inkuyo (Andean Pipe Music)
"Maqui Mañay" – Los Sisay (Andean Pipe Music)
"Round Here" – Counting Crows
"American Pie" – Don McLean
"Havana Moon" – Chuck Berry
"Everlong (Live at Roundhouse, London, 2011)" – Foo Fighters
Chapter 17
"Riverboat Fantasy" – David Wilcox
Chapter 18
"I've Got Dreams to Remember" – Otis Redding
Chapter 19
"Cross Road Blues" – Robert Johnson
"Lodi" – Creedence Clearwater Revival (CCR)
Chapter 22
"There's a Hole in the Bucket" – James Heatherington
"Lucky Now" – Ryan Adams
Chapter 23
"Younger Us" – Japandroids
"Hallelujah" – k.d. lang
"You Don't Have to Say You Love Me" – Dusty Springfield
Chapter 24
"Break On Through (To the Other Side)" – The Doors
"Once In A Lifetime" – Talking Heads
"Are You Experienced?" – Jimi Hendrix
"For Those About to Rock, We Salute You!'" – AC/DC
"Welcome to the Jungle" – Guns N' Roses
"Everybody Everybody" – Black Box
"Good Vibrations" – The Beach Boys
"Even When I'm Blue" – Steve Earle
"Hallelujah" – Jeff Buckley
"Medicine (Cures For All)" – Ayahuasca Icaros

1

Rosy – Monday: Iquitos, Peru

"How the fuck did I get here?"

The question hangs in the air long enough to solicit agonizing contemplation. I sit alone in the back of a black-market gentlemen's club the local degenerates will point you to if you spend any length of time in town. The place is about as covert as a seventh grade erection, and the closest thing to a "gentleman" is the guy who scrubs the urinals in the awful, unspeakable morning. It's the place you come if you don't have the stomach for self-mutilation but want the spiritual equivalent. Everyone knows this is nowhere, and—if this joint had a name—that's what it'd be.

I know it's an unhealthy exercise, but I've recently become obsessed with stringing together the sequence of decisions and events that brought me to this or that exact place and time, the present moment of reckoning always a damning indictment of my existence. For example: staring through the smoky haze to a makeshift stage where a girl with a scar on her stomach and a glazed look in her eyes dances, her skin the color of the river as she sways, awkward and serpentine. And I know it's solipsism playing tricks, but it feels like she's dancing just for me.

And then it's down the rabbit hole we go, with the recurring thought that it isn't only the obvious watershed decisions that shape the course of a life: Which college should I attend? Maybe I should quit my job and bum around Europe for a while... What always gets me is the procession of seemingly insignificant decisions, the decisions that don't feel like decisions at all.

I take a long swig of beer, piss-warm in the jungle night.

Those are the moments that really take us down the path: the magazine you flip through in the dentist's office. The parking spot you pass up at the supermarket. The headlines you read at the newsstand before grabbing a Sunday morning coffee... It's a mindfuck of the highest order to retrace that line and weigh the infinite spiderweb junctions where your life could have landed you selling beads on a beach in the South Pacific just as easily as it could have left you with a gun in your mouth.

At the present time, either would be preferable.

The night is sticky and soul-crushing, always, but especially in the miserable hours before the heartbreak of day. When the song ends, the tiny room defaults to a vacuous silence that pushes the boundaries of discomfort. The air is thick with smoke and the musk of sweaty men. A drunk in the corner, *el borracho*, momentarily lifts his head, mumbling incoherently. I look around for the guy who gets the drinks, but he's less than a shadow, nowhere to be found. The TV atop the bar flashes muted images of Bugs Bunny captioned in Spanish.

The girl is alone onstage, motionless as she looks down at an indeterminate spot on the floor. I reach for the Mapacho cigar tucked behind my ear, allowing it to dangle on my lips a moment. I flick my Zippo lighter and inhale deeply, the bristling crackle of still-damp tobacco the only sound in the room.

Unable to withstand the quiet any longer, I tap the neck of my bottle with the lighter, the closest I can bring myself to applause. Mistaking this for an invitation, the girl slowly makes her way to my empty table, pulls up a chair, and sits in naked silence. It's like I'm watching somebody else as I offer her a drag of my cigar. She accepts without a word. I pour half of my beer into a dirty glass and slide it across the table.

"*Cómo te llamas?*"

She smiles. "Aphrodite."

"Aphrodite... That's a hell of a name. I'm Rosy."

A handshake with a naked stripper in a den of depravity somehow seems unnecessarily formal, so I tap her glass with my sweaty bottle. She says something I don't fully understand, but none of it matters. I nod and say *sí* a whole bunch, the exchange somehow a blueprint for my existence.

The conversation goes like a sewing machine from there. With neither of us speaking more than a few token phrases of the other's tongue, the endless misinterpretations fueled by alcohol and wishful thinking allow each culture's expectations of small talk to vanish into the ether.

A ceiling fan spins inconsequentially overhead.

Non-sequiturs be damned, she leans in close to put a hand on my thigh.

For a moment, we stare into each other's eyes.

It's no secret that I've given myself a substantial length of moral rope during this stretch of self-immolation, but that rope seems to have reached its frayed terminus, and bursting to life in its void is the first self-imposed edict I've encountered in this country: I do not go home with Peruvian strippers, no matter how inebriated the two of us are.

I can only shake my head, wishing to hell my conscience would ram its head in the muck again.

I stand to kiss the girl on the forehead, promising to see her around. I throw some money on the table, not giving a single fuck whether she actually hands it to the barman.

On the way out, I wake the drunk in the corner, lightly shaking him and helping him to his feet. The old man is confused, but eventually realizes the hour. We drag ourselves out of the back room, whispering the password to no one as we laugh and climb through the quasi-secret door, weaving through the fake tienda's shelves of dry goods as tiny beams of light shoot through the storefront's rusted door, suspending the sparkling dust. I hoist open the heavy roll-up with a groan, and the two of us—one local looking for a way home, and another far from home and lost in every sense of the word—step into the warm, haunting mist of early morning Iquitos.

The story of modern-day Iquitos begins and ends with its location, deep in the heart of the Peruvian Amazon. This geographic fact attracts a disproportionate number of intrepid backpackers, fugitives, and deadbeat dads ducking their obligations. The remoteness also makes it a monumental pain in the ass to procure virtually anything from the outside world. Lost your passport? Best of luck to you. Want a decent shot of whiskey? Let me introduce you to my friend Jim Beam. How about a ride in an honest-to-goodness automobile? It may sound absurd to imagine an entire city—businessmen, clergymen, and felons alike—tearing around on jerry-rigged choppers, but, like all things, this frenetic frontier dissolves into the schizophrenic canvas of everyday life. The unbearable midday heat? The waking cold-sweat confusion? You get used to anything. Even the hostel's cast iron gates—that once felt so much like incarceration—somehow signify home.

The sun is already burning off the daybreak haze when I ease myself onto The Hideout's front porch. The tables and chairs are made from the cross-sections of giant rainforest trees, their surfaces decorated with the backpacker calligraphy of cigarette scars and stick-letter scrawl. At times like these, drunk and high and more than a little sleep-deprived, I find myself transfixed by the patterns in the wood, staring into the lines created by the unbearable crush of time and the unknowable things of the earth.

I'm not sure how long I've been watching the motorcycles thunder past, when one of the shady locals pokes his head through the gate, hawking jungle tours in broken English through broken teeth. I tell him, "*No, amigo,*" but my tombstone eyes are an invitation. He offers me a medley of chemical drugs that would cause the most hardened adventurer to reconsider his place in the world. I would give my kidney for a bottle of water, but it isn't on the menu today, so I smile and shake my head, my bit part in this degenerate's hustle somehow bestowing a sense of bastardized belonging on the miscreant streets of Iquitos.

As if on cue, The Hideout's proprietor emerges from the kitchen with a cup of steaming instant coffee. He's sporting a stained undershirt and an old pair of gym shorts. Noting my condition, he laughs not-so-under his breath.

"Rough night ashore, kid?"

I exhale audibly, nodding.

Tommy had come to Iquitos from Alaska, his formative years spent working around the world on a variety of cargo ships. His repertoire is replete with tales of being held for ransom by pirates off the west coast of Africa, spending weeks with a harem in Morocco, and eating ant soup on the streets of Bali. Nobody knows what to believe when it comes to Tommy's exploits, but, like every other expat holed up in the Amazon, there's no shortage of rumors speculating on the legal ramifications of him ever returning to his native country. "I remember the days, kid. Those were the fuckin days..."

Tommy lights a cigarette, leaving us sitting in a welcome silence interrupted only by the intermittent roar of the *mototaxis'* sonic artillery. Tommy catches me eyeing the hostel walls with disdain. They're adorned with an array of anaconda skins, alligator jaws, and taxidermic capybaras poached from the jungle. I sense he's about to broach some subject or another, but I'm too tired to dance. I look him square in the eye, daring him to ask.

"So, I was goin' through the books the other day... You know how long you been here?"

I do indeed. Down to the hour. But I plead the fifth.

Tommy shakes his head and sips his coffee before coming in with the big reveal: "Just under nine months." He whistles through his teeth and laughs.

"If you need more money, Tommy—"

"Nah, kid, it ain't the money. You're squared away 'til the end of the month. It's just..."

We're both waiting for the other to blink.

"You know what? Fuck it. None of my business."

I nod and shift my gaze to the street, thankful for the conversation's conclusion.

Amid the silence, Tommy's pet parrot, Lucky, comes waddling onto the front porch. He stands between Tommy and I for a long time, his head moving back and forth between us, as if deciding who to grace with his presence. He eventually jumps onto my table, standing there proudly for the next ten minutes, screeching, "*PUTA!*" at every passerby.

It's the closest I've come to laughing in days.

Tommy finishes his coffee and crushes out his cigarette on my table. He picks up his parrot by its clipped wings, and for a moment, the three of us are incredibly still. I feel the man looking at me, hard, knowing he's incapable of letting it go.

"It's a tough one, kid... No doubt, someone done fucked you up real good... A girl, I bet."

My eyes are hopelessly fixed on the street.

"Yeah, Tom... Somethin' like that..."

Most of my days end this way. The alcohol and the sleep deprivation and the galloping thoughts are a Dervish's whirl of transcendent exhaustion until I crawl back to my room: a tiny, windowless, ground-floor hovel that feels more subterranean than any basement I've ever known. The walls of exposed concrete are barren and cold to the touch. A 100 watt bulb dangles overhead, illuminating the cinder blocks and 2x4s constituting a bookshelf. The stained mattress lies on the floor, covered by a single, unlaundered sheet.

The emptiness feels like an implication.

I strip to my boxers, then turn off the light. My head hits the pillow like a Justin Rutledge hook. A sliver of harsh daylight pushes beneath the door. As my eyes adjust to the darkness, I go through the ritual of counting the cracks in the ceiling.

There's a song running through my head, and I can hear it as if the needle's grinding vinyl in real-time. It's times like these when I feel like a little kid alone in the dark, quietly singing the lyrics, a lullaby and a prayer and a plea all wrapped into one, my voice soft and breaking as I close my eyes and disappear through the smoke rings of my mind...

2

The Deuce – Tuesday: Toronto, Canada

Rush hour traffic crawls past as Stanley "The Deuce" Doucette stands in the faltering afternoon light, vigorously finishing his cigarette. The unrelenting drizzle that sent his crew of laborers home early gifts him plenty of time to get his talk track down. The impending conversation is a slow train coming, and—despite the dread in the pit of his stomach—he knows there's no way around it. He takes one last drag and flicks his cigarette into the slate gray street, leaving the November chill behind as he steps into the warmth of the bar.

The Cloak and Dagger is one of those Toronto institutions that's invisible until some in-the-know *flâneur* drags you there on a foggy night. Little more than a clandestine hallway, the place is all exposed brick and rainy-day mahogany, overworked red velvet and an upright piano. Some of the best nights of The Deuce's life had been spent huddled in one of the tiny booths, a group of buddies solving the world's problems as they hammered home dirty shots of Jägermeister. All while the DJ spins Marva Whitney, then Fania All Stars, as girls with piercings and tattoos splash into their table as they work a disappearing dance floor.

It takes a moment for The Deuce's eyes to drink in the darkness, but there is no mistaking the beer-soaked tang from the night before. The Deuce slides into a well-worn booth with ease. He shakes off the cold and tosses his wet jacket over the bench beside him, ordering a beer and steeling himself for the moment.

He's on his third pint when Ishy walks through the door.

It never ceases to amaze The Deuce whenever he lays eyes on the sidekick of his little cousin, all grown up and decked out in Bay Street attire: Canali suit, Armani overcoat, and a watch that costs more than most people's first-and-last. There's no sign of the kid that used to run around the neighborhood, playing capture the flag until the streetlights came on.

Ishy hangs his jacket on the booth-side hook and takes a seat. "Mr. Doucette?"

"Ishy Lords, good to see ya, my man." The Deuce motions to the girl behind the bar, asking Ishy what he's drinking.

"Bottle of Coors Light, please."

The Deuce shoots a disappointed look. "You know this place has all the best stuff, right? A cask they pump by hand?"

"Can't do it. Need to head back to the office later."

"You fuckin' capitalists. You ever want a spot on my crew, just say the word."

Ishy smiles at the thought. "You know I'm nowhere near man enough for that."

The Deuce gives him a sarcastic once-over, then nods in agreement. "Fuck it. How you doin', bro?"

"I'm good, Deuce. I'm doing really good." There's a pause that lasts too long. Even though Ishy and The Deuce have known each other most of their lives, Rosy has always been their binding tie, the crucial intermediary facilitating all interaction. Some quick math suggests it's been close to a decade since they last sat alone together. There's a reason for that, but they both know this afternoon supersedes those complications.

Mercifully, the waitress arrives with the drinks. They let small talk to carry the day as they wait for the beers to soften the edges. Work. Girls. The fuckin' Leafs. The intervening moments between empty glasses and full clutter with sideways glances and sputtering.

It is during one such lull that The Deuce takes a deep breath. "You know we have to go get him, right?"

Ishy exhales, nodding. He's almost relieved to have the subject broached so they can get down to it.

"...And you know we have to bring him back. No pussyfoot-bitchin' out on this one."

Another deep breath by Ish. "Yeah..."

"Good."

The Deuce nods with slow conviction and drains the last of his beer. He gives the girl behind the bar some sort of predetermined signal, so she brings two shots to the table.

Ishy doesn't bother protesting.

The toast is unspoken as they clink glasses, tequila running down their wrists as they knock back the shots without so much as flinching.

Conversation flows freely from there. Timelines, supplies, vaccinations. More people spill into the bar, ordering pints of local beer and bullshitting about books and politics and music. Two young men come in, carrying Technics and milkcrates filled with vinyl, immediately getting to work on setting up in the corner.

The Deuce orders another round as darkness gathers beyond the windowpane that, for a brief interval, reflects both inside and out.

On paper, the plan is simple: Fly to Peru. Get to Iquitos. Track down Rosy. Drag his ass home. They look at the maps and talk it all through. Ishy is totally onboard, but there's one significant detail he can't get his head around.

"Deuce, can't we just fly into that jungle town? Are the bus trip and boat ride really necessary? You're talking about a hell of a long time in transit."

The Deuce appears to give this some thought. "You may be onto somethin' there, Lordsy. And full disclosure: the only jungle I ever got lost in was between the legs of a Persian one filthy night at The Devil's Martini. But the way I see it, our boy is fucked-up. And as a guy who's been plenty fucked-up, I'm thinkin' we need to get into his headspace, you dig? The kid's gone all Brando in *Apocalypse Now*, and we gotta do everything we can to be fuckin' Martin Sheen down there."

Ishy looks at him skeptically.

"I'm just sayin', don't you wanna see the fuckin' Andes? Don't you wanna see the fuckin' JUNGLE? Anacondas and shit? Fuckin' A-1, you do!"

Ishy laughs and realizes it's true: There's no way he'd ever go to Peru otherwise, so a little jaunt over the mountains and through the Amazon is probably worth the aggravation.

The Deuce orders a final round as a fedora-clad patron takes a stab at the piano, hammering away at a Tom Waits' barroom classic that, through the bar's natural acoustics, is miraculously audible over the clamor of the increasingly intoxicated weekday crowd. As drinks slosh on the table, Ishy concedes that he's past the point of no return. There's no going back to the office. The Deuce slaps him on the back and congratulates him on the decision.

Shortly after, Ishy goes for a piss and takes the opportunity to peek at his BlackBerry. The Deuce settles his tab with the girl behind the bar, then notices her phone number scribbled at the bottom of the bill. The Deuce gives her a wink and a smile, then heads for the ATM in the corner. He takes out some cash and rifles through the receipts left along the ledge, finding no account balances of interest.

When Ish returns to the booth, The Deuce pulls an envelope from his coat pocket and slowly slides it across the table. The gravity of responsibility descends upon them. They sit in silence and stare as if waiting for the packet to speak.

The Deuce finally says, "Friday morning."

Ishy takes a deep breath. "Friday morning."

"You'll be outside your building?"

"Indeed."

The Deuce nods with certainty and slams the last of his beer. "Time to fuck off?"

Ishy can't help but smile at his eloquence. "Yeah, Deuce. Let's make like a baby…"

"Head out, motherfucker. Always."

Ishy and The Deuce step out of The Cloak and Dagger and into the evening, the metallic taste of winter filling their lungs as their breath billows in swirling, slowly dissipating clouds. Ishy blows warmth into his hands as The Deuce lights a cigarette, inhaling deeply.

"Friday," The Deuce emphasizes. "I'll grab you at six."

"Six, it is."

"And Ish?" The Deuce looks Ishmael dead in the eye. With the weight of earnest importance in his voice, he implores, "Fully expectin' you to pull some dirty Peruvian poon down there, so don't forget your fuckin' rubbers, bro."

Ishy laughs, shaking his head. "Friday morning," he assures, stepping into a waiting cab.

The Deuce watches the taxi pull away, taking a final drag on his cigarette before flicking it into the alley and walking towards a streetcar.

3

Rosy – Before: Canada

By now it's impossible to remember the feeling, but the first few months of love unfurling are the closest we ever come to transcendence.

She was flawless in those days, and I was at the peak of my powers while with her. And even though everything I'd ever experienced informed me that she wouldn't stay perfect, and everything I'd ever been suggested that I wouldn't remain impressive—and even though the history of the universe foretold that this relationship wouldn't ever be as good as it was in the beginning—in those first few months, it sure as hell seemed like things might just stay that way forever.

Katrina was an actress. And yeah, I know, aren't we all in the beginning? But from the moment she took the stage that night at the Berkeley, I knew she was the one.

It was one of those dazzling evenings in late May when the warmth of the afternoon lingers long enough to cradle the city at dusk, summer having announced itself in the smell of fresh cut grass and sight of girls in halter tops, the peel-back of the Dome's lid and fact that the Jays are only a game-and-a-half back.

One of my old college pals had called me at the office at 4:30 on a Thursday, and, fuck, it'd been forever since I'd seen him. He was pushing the hard sell, pleading that he required my expertise as the sounding board for a deadline-fueled piece on contemporary stage adaptations of Canadian novels. He even promised an extra ticket and first round at the hopping mad King East patio he was hunkered down at.

McConvey and I had been thick-as-thieves since the early days at school, where we bonded over Bushmills and books, drinking and debating them in my dive bar dorm until the wee hours, much to the dismay of my roommate, Ishy Lords. Degree in hand and living in the city, McConvey was one of those eternally interesting guys who improve with age. While I spent my days calculating density coefficients for the city's rapid transit expansion, McConvey was eking out a living writing reviews of emerging rock bands for the local alt-weekly. More than a small part of me envied his struggling artist experience, and the chance to ride along for the night and offer my common man's take was too intoxicating to pass up.

I caught up with him just after six, the two of us tapping glasses and tipping back pints of Tankhouse Ale in the glorious afternoon sunshine, where we busted each other's balls and chatted up the pretty girls in summer dresses. We crushed three beers apiece and split the tab, eventually escaping the back alley patio, and walking the four blocks over to the Berkeley Street Theatre, where the weathered bricks were awash in slanted, golden light. Someone in the gathering crowd sparked a joint and we all smiled, the undeniable feeling of summer alive in the dusk.

Theater can be tiresome and—if we're being honest—most dramatic productions are atrocious. But in the rare instance that theater is good, there's nothing better. This play had all the makings of greatness even before she stepped onstage: a flawed god, a more flawed Noah, blind cats and blue brothers, a benevolent lady-Lucifer, and plenty of rain. She was in the role of Emma, enchanting, playful, beautiful, and in complete command. By the time she appeared naked in front of the packed, enraptured house—innocently submerging full-frontal into a warm bath prior to her tragic encounter with a unicorn—all bets were off.

I couldn't stop whispering about her, raving endlessly at intermission as we knocked back Heinekens, and then again during the standing ovation. When McConvey realized that I wasn't going to shut the fuck up, he took me backstage under the guise of an interview. He was laudatory and she was responsive. I was deer-in-the-headlights, but sometimes that quality of utterly exposed uncool does the trick. Thank fuck for McConvey, who had the wherewithal to suggest we grab a drink.

He and I stood in the alley behind the Theatre, smoking Du Maurier cigarettes while she changed into her Thursday night attire. Then the three of us hightailed it to an Annex back-alley bar, where we talked feverishly about music and art and the city over melting candles—until McConvey slipped out the back, leaving Kat and I alone to drink Amsterdam Lager well after the chairs were stacked and the lights flicked on.

It wasn't even awkward in the morning. That was enough for me.

There were so many things I loved about her in those early days. The way her lips moved ever so slightly when she read to herself. How she kissed me on the cheek before crossing the street, playfully saying, "Just in case!" The way she examined her hands pressed against mine, wondering what the hands of our children would look like. The little tells were too plentiful to list, but they were ours and ours alone.

The nights she'd stay at my place, we'd wake up early and stand on my little balcony overlooking the quiet, leafy street, sipping coffee in oblivious contentment. Sometimes, she'd surprise me at work in the afternoon and we'd walk through Nathan Phillips Square, stopping to feed pigeons near the reflecting pool. Whenever I'd return to the office, all the guys would wink and confide what a lucky son-of-a-bitch I was. And yeah, on occasion, she'd show slight signs of being batshit crazy, but that's why I wanted to be there.

She was already living with me by the time my birthday rolled around, and we had a raucous, little shindig at our second-story walk-up. Everyone was there: Ishy, The Deuce, McConvey, the guys we'd grown up with and the girls whose hearts we'd broken. We played the music loud and late and when the neighbors called the police, we cranked it another notch. We hot-boxed the living room to a hazy state, and The Deuce made sweet love to a strange girl on my desk. Kat had gone to the trouble of getting a cake, but when you're 26 nobody thinks of candles, so she lit a pack of cigarettes and jammed the filters into the buttercream, so I'd have something smoldering to huff and puff at. It was everything a guy could ask for.

Late in the summer, Kat proposed that we do a little camping. I had always been a fan of driving to Grand Bend with a group of friends, day drinking at the beach and sitting around a crackling fire with the radio playing The Tragically Hip and Rheostatics, talking deep into the night as the moon hung somewhere beyond the pines. But what Kat had in mind was different: a five-day, unguided portage through Northern Ontario. The kind of trip that requires special gear, topographic maps, and the ability to read a compass. The kind of trip you could die on.

We were young and stupid and crazy in the early days of love, so I agreed without a second thought.

Early on a Thursday, we loaded our gear into a couple of backpacks and filled a small cooler with cold cuts, potato salad, and booze before setting out for Algonquin Park. Some four hours later, we reached a nameless access point, where we unloaded then walked off into the bush, overstuffed packs on our backs and a rental canoe held high above our heads.

In retrospect, I should have inquired earlier. But I guess when the girl you're newly dating suggests that you take a five-day canoe trip, you operate under assumptions. For instance, you assume she possesses some of the skills germane to surviving in the woods. Or you assume she has—at the very least—spent a night in a tent.

It wasn't until we hiked 300 meters through the dense brush and launched our canoe into the crystal-cool waters of the lake, that the consequences of these assumptions manifested. As we paddled from shore, our oars licking the water in the near-silence that accompanies solitude, I took a deep breath, finally appreciating the perfection of this timeless place. I looked at Kat, a *Field & Stream* vision of back-country competence settled at the front of the canoe, and asked, "Where to now?"

I'll never forget the blank look she gave me.

"I don't know."

I laughed. "What do you mean you don't know?"

She looked like she thought I was playing coy. "I thought you knew where we're going."

I looked at her, awaiting a punchline. "You're joking, right?"

Now it was her turn to laugh, uneasy. "Nooooo. What made you think I know how to do this sort of thing?"

We looked at one another in dumbstruck befuddlement until I found myself yelling in disbelief, "Because it was your idea to come here!"

We went silent. Then she began laughing hysterically.

When Kat finally pulled herself together, she confided that, ever since she was a little girl, she wanted to go on a wilderness excursion, that her dad had always promised to take her here, but never followed through. She assumed that, as a *guy*, I'd know what to do.

The two of us burst out laughing, understanding that her sexism and my lack of rugged masculinity had left us sitting in the middle of the lake, holding a map we didn't know how to read.

We were resilient and crazy and carefree in those days, believing that no problem was greater than the story it left behind, and that a robust sex life could take care of everything else.

The laughter gave way to desire to prove my manhood, and it wasn't long before I began tearing away Kat's clothes, the great outdoors working its magic as I went at her with ferocity, the act reminiscent of that old joke about cheap American beer being a lot like sex in a canoe: It's fucking close to water. When we gave each other all we had, we leaned back in the boat and looked up into the perfect, blue sky.

Kat, still spectacularly naked, crawled to the cooler and pulled out a bottle of whiskey, amber and dripping with icy goodness. We spent the next two hours in that canoe, passing the bottle back-and-forth as sunlight shone down on our glistening bodies. Before the sun set, the whiskey was gone and we were rowing to shore, searching for a place to camp.

We tried stringing up a tent, but the act devolved into something more primal, and it wasn't long before we were making love on a big, warm slab of Muskoka granite as frenzied mosquitoes had their way with our flesh. When we finished, I doused some damp logs with lighter fluid and flicked a few matches into what would become a roaring bonfire for us to huddle naked under a sleeping bag by. As the stars winked above, we ate pretzels and carved off hunks of salami with a pocketknife. The night was perfect and the air so invigorating that we gave into the uncontrollable desire to explore our most natural selves one last time, miraculously finding our way to the tent that remained in an incomplete state of erection.

We slept late into the morning and awoke to find that some wildlife had paid us a visit. Drunk, spent, and utterly content, we had slept through the invasion. After a breakfast of instant coffee and granola, we packed our gear into the canoe and went out onto the water, spending most of the day paddling around, exploring the hidden nooks and coves created by jagged rocks and fallen birch trees that disappeared into the cool, black water. Occasionally, we pulled our canoe ashore so we could swim naked and fuck on sun-soaked rocks in the day's glorious light.

In the afternoon, I dropped my fishing line to see if anything would bite. With every intoxicating tug, I'd reel the line until I was removing a fish from the hook and smiling for a photo Kat would take with her vintage Polaroid. We threw every pike and smallmouth bass back, neither of us having the faintest clue on how to gut or fry a fish.

It must have been close to four when we determined that our best course would be to get back to the car, hoping to find one of those classy Muskoka cabins with hot showers and bearskin rugs to spent the night on.

And those were our true intentions, swear to God. But then we happened upon the humans.

It's strange to consider the dichotomy of life in an urban setting, versus existence in the vast expanse of nature. Because living in a city, surrounded by and bumping into thousands of people every day, we never think of the miracle of happenstance: the endless possibilities in each encounter, the lives unlived, individuals and stories undiscovered in passing... We rarely stop to consider that any brush could be with our soulmate. A best friend. Someone to share life-altering experiences.

But, unlike city life, when on a lake in the wilds of Algonquin, one needn't be confronted with the existential crisis of unrealized potential. Especially while my girlfriend and I screamed for and frantically paddled toward the three young men who happened to be calmly navigating their canoe in our direction.

The young men were from Peterborough, and, upon our encounter, three facts became apparent:

They were experienced outdoorsmen.

They were barely old enough to shave.

They were stoned out of their minds.

We asked their names and told them ours. They invited Kat and I to smoke a joint and we agreed without hesitation. They had beef jerky and cold beer, and we had half a bottle of Jäger. We passed these provisions between canoes, talking about the lake and outdoor survival, Pachamama and the utter lunacy of our clusterfuck expedition. We were laughing our asses off as we got more stoned, the shadows growing long as golden light sparkled on the water. We were in no rush to track down that elusive Muskoka cabin, and—just when it seemed there would be a lull in the conversation—one of those Peterborough kids reached into their pocket and pulled out a ball of opium.

I'd never even seen opium before, let alone known it was possible to produce a baseball-size orb. But there it was, plain as day. The kid took a look at it, then winked at me. He tossed it over to Kat and encouraged us to have at it.

The rest of the evening was a reckless, glorious blur. We made it to shore, and, with the help of our Peterborough trio, set up some semblance of a camp. We squirted the last of my lighter fluid onto a pile of brush that saw us chanting and dancing naked in the moonlight until we could stand no longer. It was beautiful chaos. Without any concept of time, I crawled to the tent where I found Kat fingers-deep in herself, panting and moaning and ruthlessly pleasuring herself as she awaited my arrival.

When it was all over, strangely but unmistakably, I was able to reclaim a moment of complete clarity. I dragged myself from the tent and found one of those great Muskoka rocks that descend at a gentle slope, disappearing into the black stillness of a Northern Ontario lake. I was all alone and had the last of a small joint tucked behind my ear. I sparked it and inhaled deeply, looking up into the infinite stars that revealed themselves in a way that felt like spiritual awakening.

Sitting on that rock, I was overcome by the realization that I was immersed in a universe that was a living, breathing entity. That the expansion of the universe rushing away from me at the speed of light was the exhale and one day, 14 billion years from now, that universe would *in*hale. And when it did, all the things in that universe would contract and come rushing back, and we would live this life all over again, exactly as it was transpiring, but in reverse—people walking in a way that would appear backwards to our current selves, absorbing written words into our pens as a means of internalizing knowledge, drawing in furling clouds of smoke before blowing it back into the crushed filter of a joint manifesting itself from ash—the theories and laws of gravity and physics and equations working inversely and in perfectly beautiful symmetry.

Light and darkness. Yin and yang. The Big Bang and the Big Crunch.

As I sat there on that slab of rock, finishing the last of my tiny joint, I wondered if it was in that penultimate moment of exhale—when the heavens have expanded to the furthest point they ever will—is that the moment our universe finally tickles the other, mirrored universe?

I took one last drag and changed my trajectory, trying to figure out just how many breaths I'd taken in this lifetime, and exactly how many times I'd wind up fucking Kat in the dirt.

4

Vanessa – Tuesday: Florida, USA

Nov. 8th, 2011
Somewhere above the Keys

I should probably begin by asking a favor. Dear Reader, should you happen upon this personal journal, it would be wonderful for your karma to stop reading and return this book of observations and self-reflection to:

Vanessa Van Dyne
505 West 122nd Street
New York, NY
10027

As I write this, I'm sitting on an airplane, on my way to Lima, Peru. Am I flying away from something? Probably. Am I flying towards something? Almost certainly. What that something is, it's impossible to know. I'm hoping by the time these pages are filled, I'll have a better understanding.

Three weeks ago, I took an indefinite leave from school. I should be clear that I have no intention of dropping out, and that this sojourn is temporary. But the need to step away from my life is very much real, privileged as it may seem. The only way I can describe it is to say that I felt some force tugging me, telling me to exit Manhattan and the cushy college scene. My parents don't know about this pivot yet and for the time being I plan to keep it that way. The fact that they don't know I'm heading to Peru is a little unnerving, but I'm hopeful they'll one day understand... Or at least get over it.

So, does this compulsion to put school on hold and use my student loans to explore the Amazon and visit the shaman have anything to do with love? Well... Doesn't it always?

Am I hoping to cure my existential loneliness? HA!

The truth is, I have no idea what I'm doing. I'm 22 years old, and—although it would be an overstatement to say I've lost my way—I *have* lost the motivation to do the things as I've always done them. School was fine, a totally normal college experience. But, for a few months, I haven't been able to shake the feeling that New York and Columbia can no longer give me what I need, that maybe I should be learning new things, and that I should be learning them in a different way.

And then there were the boys I'd grown tired of. Tired of waiting for them to grow up. Tired of TAs trying to get into my pants when they should be more concerned about their receding hairlines.

It's kind of absurd when you think about how we end up with the people we end up with... Maybe I'm alone in this, but I've always sought someone who was the exact opposite of the person I just broke up with... As if the replacement's oppositeness will somehow be enough... I bounce from failed relationship to imminently failing relationship, like a pinball in an arcade, careening down a path of compounding mistakes that carry me further from the person I'm supposed to be with. The disappointments have been jading and scarring to the point that I'm not sure what I'm supposed to be looking for or feeling anymore.

Okay, therapy session almost over. Just one more metaphysical question:

Is love a function of the body, or of the soul?

Is love a chemical reaction in the brain? Is it a scent, or a taste, the feel of someone's touch? Or is it two lost souls searching for one another until they finally reunite, the moment of connection indisputable as they grapple to one another at long last and for all of eternity?

I used to be fun, I swear.

Back to the here and now. Why Peru? Why the Amazon? Why the need to see a shaman? Why ayahuasca?

And what will the ayahuasca ceremony be like? Will I come out on the other side like I've just been dipped in the Ganges, washed clean of all sin?

Will I be a new person? A different person?

I've read that an ayahuasca ceremony is the closest we come to experiencing death. This terrifies me. The emptiness. The loneliness. The infinite nothingness... But it also excites me. A large part of me is ravenously curious about the moment just before you die.

I've become obsessed with the idea that, in the moment before the lights go out, we finally grasp the true meaning of life. That, in that instant, as we hang over the precipice with our life flashing before our eyes, we experience the interconnectedness of all living things, we finally understand the meaning of space and time. We are somehow made conscious of all knowledge and possibility... I can't help but wonder, as I look obliteration square in the eye, whether I will be granted a glimpse of that understanding.

Whatever the reasons—unknown and unspoken, conscious and unconscious—it feels like something is pulling me to Peru, to Iquitos, and to ayahuasca.

I know that momentum is determined by multiplying the mass of an object and the velocity it's travelling. In my case, direction is due south at about 900 miles per hour, and the magnitude is this nagging loneliness that sits heavy in my heart.

There's no turning back.

Okay, last thought for the night. I am about 150 pages into Proust's *In Search of Lost Time* and I can't get this passage out of my head:

> *"But when from a long-distant past nothing subsists, after the people are dead, after the things are broken and scattered, taste and smell alone, more fragile but more enduring, more immaterial, more persistent, more faithful, remain poised a long time, like souls remembering, waiting, hoping amid the ruins of all the rest, and bear unflinchingly, in the tiny and almost impalpable drop of their essence, the vast structure of recollection."*

I am mesmerized by the notion that souls can remember and wait, after nothing subsists and amid the ruins of all the rest... Does this really happen?

I have no idea what I'm in for when I reach the shaman. I have no idea what I'm going to see, what I'm going to feel, and what

I'm going to learn while in the clutches of ayahuasca. But I can't wait to taste what lies beyond the pale, if only for a moment.

This is beginning to feel like a late-night drive into the existential wilderness. Probably best that I get some sleep. Next stop? Lima, and the purgatory of an airport layover. Then Iquitos.

5

Rosy – Wednesday: Iquitos, Peru

There are zero bridges spanning the Amazon River.

For more than 4,000 miles, the Amazon winds through cities like Macapá (population 368,000) and Manaus (population over 2 million), emptying close to 3.5 billion gallons into the Atlantic every minute. At points, the river is 11 miles wide and contains an island the size of Switzerland. The area of the Amazon basin is similar to that of the continental US, has more than 3,000 varieties of fish, and is home to a third of all bird species.

In a world of global integration and exponentially expanding telecommunications, 24-hour news service, Skype, Siri, Instagram, and wireless internet humming from every Starbucks on the planet, explorers are still discovering uncontacted tribes deep within the Amazon. And each year when the full moon crosses the equator, the river experiences a phenomenon known as Pororoca, where, through the conflicting power of the river and the ocean, a massive tidal wave travels inland against the river's current at 50 km/h, providing surfers the opportunity to ride the world's longest wave as it breaks for more than two hours on its way upstream.

Yet, despite this and an infinite array of natural wonders, I'm most astonished by this extraordinary fact: to this day, not a single man-made crossing links one side to the other.

I awake in the damp coolness of my room, the hostel quiet in the emptiness of late afternoon. My mouth is ragged, and my breath tastes so much like death that it frightens me. I slip on a pair of shorts and walk into the crumbling courtyard at the rear of the building, the hot sun shining on my naked back as I brush my teeth at an outdoor sink. I remember the early days in Iquitos, when I was cautious enough to use bottled water for everything. Those days are long gone now, and I rinse my mouth with the tepid jungle water without a second thought. Back in my room, I throw on an old T-shirt and sandals, then slip out of The Hideout to disappear into the hot noise of Putumayo.

As I make my way to the Plaza de Armas, I pass rows of men inexplicably sitting at desks and banging away at typewriters in the middle of the sidewalk, the infinite monkey theorem in full effect. Before reaching the Plaza, a group of schoolchildren come skipping up the sidewalk, all pleated skirts and button-up shirts, smiling unabashed gap-toothed smiles, the chorus of "Hello! Hello!" quickly changing to "Hello, *gringo!*" as they pass, uproarious laughter coming from all as they run with glee. I can't help but smile, recounting what it felt like to be innocently audacious and carefree.

The town square is relatively quiet, populated by the usual cast of iniquitous Iquiteños hanging around the fountain, hustling backpackers with their selective brand of Gringlish. Some elderly locals try to keep cool by sitting on park benches under swaying palms. A man in a backwards Yankees cap pedals through on his Dickie Dee-style bicycle, yelling, "*Shambo! Shambo!*" as he hawks fruitsicles from his cooler. The scene encapsulates Iquitos in all its glory, but I have places to be.

An old saying is that you know you've reached the Belen Market when you're stepping over piles of trash and by the time I hit the squalor, most vendors are clearing out, leaving the day's remnants to the dogs. The stench of the place on a sweltering afternoon defies description, but cholera seems like a decent starting point. Women swat flies from raw meat, while naked babies and dirty toddlers look on disinterestedly. I find myself unable to turn away as a man breaks the neck of a chicken like a child might snap a twig.

Head down and senses overwhelmed, I walk to the stall I've been seeking: a rickety booth with a couple sanded planks constituting a counter.

Griselda, the elderly proprietor of this little nook, is missing almost all her teeth, but, what she lacks in dental hygiene, she makes up for in product, which consists of the most remarkable collection fruits, vegetables, roots, eggs, saps, powders, berries, dried insects, and spices a person could fit into a six-foot space. A few months back, I didn't have a clue what 95% of the stuff was, but there was something magnetic about this old lady. I'd asked her for something to ease my pain, and even though she didn't speak English, she concocted something so god-awful that it had to be good for me. Since then, on days I've felt as despondent and near-dead as today, it was instinct to pay her a visit. I even made a point of learning a few words to describe my condition.

"Hola, Griselda... Resaca."

She smiles that beautiful, toothless grin. "*Señor, señor,*" she playfully scolds, filling her filthy blender with a stupefying combination of wilting flowers and ominous leaves.

I glance at the stall next to hers. The old man who runs the operation is a purveyor of exotic animals, with baby sloths and shimmering pythons on display, as well as cages filled with birds that dangle overhead, their feathers a rainbow of divinely inspired colors. I peek down into a bucket on the tabletop and see a dozen tiny alligators climbing over one another as they gasp and struggle for space.

The old man smiles. "You want monkey for make friend?" The monkey on his shoulder squeals and flashes its teeth.

I smile at the thought. "*No, gracias.*"

"No monkey? *Esta bien.* You want for see cock?"

I say nothing, stunned.

"Fight cock. You want for to see fighting cock? *Pelea de gallos?*"

I laugh. "Cockfight. Fuck. I thought you meant... Nah, man. I think I'm all set."

But the old man persists, taking a leaflet from his pocket and sliding it across the table. "*Sí.* Cockfight. *Mañana en la noche.* You come for to see." Still somewhat embarrassed, I stuff the flyer into my pocket as Griselda hands me her herbal brew.

I raise the glass and give her a wink, taking my medicine in a few deep gulps, the cool, salty earthiness causing my stomach to cramp and heave. There are traces of disgusting noni fruit and sour oranges, but I can't identify anything else. As is often the case, I have a feeling she's given me something intended to cure more than a hangover, but I don't pry, dropping three soles on the planks of Griselda's stall, thanking her for providing me with the good stuff, and assuring her I'll see her tomorrow.

My first visits to Belen were filled with suspicion. I was leery of the kids looking me in the eye then walking too close, following me through the Market, along the streets and down the alleys. It made my heart race as I picked up the pace. Like any stranger in a strange place, it was impossible not to feel sized up, like there was a group of bleary-eyed 12-year-olds around every corner, brandishing knives and intending to take something from a world that never handed them a thing. But over the months, I learned that most of the hoodlums were innocent. They were young, inquisitive, and unashamed. They didn't know they weren't supposed to stare, and they couldn't fathom that following an outsider at a distance could make them skittish. Invariably, their curiosity dwindled, and they found something more interesting to observe. My conscience gnawed at me for assuming the worst—but not enough so that I'll unclench my fists while traveling down narrowing, garbage-strewn streets.

I reach the point where the Río Itaya floodwaters meet the streets of Belen. With filth lapping the sidewalk, I approach a man in a *llevo-llevo* and explain where I want him to take me. Understanding that no tourist in their right mind would request such a destination, the man forgoes the gouge-the-gringo dance and quotes a fair price. I hand him five soles and carefully step into his makeshift canoe.

Belen has been euphemistically referred to as the "Venice of the Amazon," but beyond the fact that water flows through its streets for most of the year, those cities might as well be in different constellations.

There is neither artifice nor façade in Belen. The barrio sits in a floodplain of the Itaya River and is home to roughly 7,000 people. Most inhabitants are newly arrived from the jungle, looking for a better life in the city. The houses are constructed with scrap wood and balsa logs pilfered from plantain rafts, the roofs thatch and rusty, corrugated steel. The more stable homes are built one or two stories off the ground, but most are little more than covered rafts, tiny shacks tethered to wooden poles, rising and falling with the floodwaters.

Like all immigrant shantytowns, Belen has a litany of problems: poverty, illiteracy, sexual abuse, teenage pregnancy, kids who consume Peruvian moonshine in broad daylight, people who shit in the water they drink… In the dry season, when most of the houses lay haphazard in the mud, the dusty streets are rife with disease, and there is little to distract Belen inhabitants from the condition of their existence. In the dry season, the pursuit of happiness seems an ignoble farce. The pursuit of life itself is all-consuming.

But in the wet season, as water levels rise, so do the houses—and along with them, the spirits and living conditions. Relatively speaking, it is a time of plenty. As the floodplain swells, Belen transforms from the silhouette of broken dreams to an auspicious, floating marvel.

The water taxi takes me away from Belen Market, past the giant Amazon water lilies, and to a neighborhood of floating houses. There is a woman washing clothes on her front porch while her daughter splashes by her side. We drift past a floating gas station with a cat slumbering atop one of its pumps while chickens cluck from an adjacent roof. We pass a soccer field submerged six feet, kids doing backflips from the goal's crossbar, laughing and squealing as they splash into the water below.

The driver guides our vessel to a non-descript shack, where he ties off onto a beam. I climb out of the canoe and step onto the porch, indicating that I'll return in a minute or two. As always, the door is open, and I step inside.

Freddie is in his late 60s and seated at the tiny kitchen table with his wooden cutting board, surrounded by tobacco leaves and a bowl of water. His wife kneels over a charcoal fire, stirring a pot of rice and inspecting the morsels of skewered meat, which, despite their suspect origins, smell absolutely delicious.

Freddie finishes rolling his cigar before acknowledging me. *"Amigo, buenas."*

"Buenas, señor. Cómo estas?"

"Bien, bien."

Our conversation never deviates from the script. I smile and wave at Ida.

"Mapacho hoy dia, amigo?"

"Sí, señor. Mapacho. Gracias."

Mapacho cigars, although relatively unknown outside Peru, are a big deal in Iquitos, and none are better than the hand-rolled variety Freddie makes out here on the floodwaters. Crafted from potent jungle tobacco, Mapacho cigars have significant cultural and spiritual meaning for Amazonians. The sacred connotations have never done much for me, but I love the way they smoke, tasting unlike anything I've ever burned, packing a massive nicotine punch, and mellowing me in a way weed and alcohol never can.

And there is no disputing the charm in paying Freddie and Ida a visit. I stand in their kitchen, marveling at the way Freddie works: His hands have absorbed so much of the tobacco over the decades, it's impossible to distinguish where his fingers end and the leaves begin. He's an artist in every sense of the word.

When Freddie finishes, he holds the cigar in the slanted afternoon light for inspection. He stands to hand me the offering. *"Tres soles, amigo."*

As always, I slip him a five and implore him to keep it.

By the time the skiff reaches dry land back at Belen Market, the sun has dipped beneath the horizon. I pay the driver, happy to set foot on firm ground again. Understanding that the Market is no place for a gringo after dark, I navigate the labyrinthine alleyways with urgency and into the bustle of Jirón Próspero.

Próspero in warm twilight is the Yonge Street Saturday night of youth, the aphrodisiac dusk that captures what it means to be alive. The rickshaw mototaxis dart through the streets, their headlights glowing in the haze. The sidewalks bustle as open-air storefronts blare reggaetón music, salespeople half-dance as they peddle knockoff Nikes and black-market Breitlings. The smell of chicken and charcoal from a nearby stand and a girl in a dimly lit doorway ask if I'm looking for a friend.

For a guy who hasn't much felt like living lately, there are few places that make me feel as alive as Próspero in the sublime parenthesis between day and dark.

By the time I make it back to the Plaza de Armas, the sky is all purple and rose, the smell of fresh popcorn filling the air as a man sells small bags from a cart for one sol. Well-dressed families gather in front of the church for evening mass as children chase one another in the square. Teenagers lean against the fountain, doing their best to look hard, while women sit on blankets spread across the sidewalk, pushing crafts and clothing to all who pass. At the stoplight, one man juggles bowling pins while another eats fire. I wait for a break in the action to cross the street, dancing through light beams cast by idling mototaxis, finding my way into the little internet café I've come to adopt as my own.

It has been weeks since I've been to this place, but nothing ever seems to change: the air hot and thick with the smell of youth, the room bathed in fluorescent light, the humming glow of video games and Facebook pages pulsating on computer screens. There's a young Romeo locked away in one of the telephone booths, talking dirty and sweet to his girl in Pucallpa. The proprietor drinks from a bottle of Coca-Cola while perusing his Hi5 network. I take a seat at the only available computer and stare ahead, unable to decipher the next move.

Sensing my indecision, the girl sitting next to me leans in close, asking if I need any help. She smells of watermelon Bubblicious and wears nothing but tiny shorts and a bikini top.

"No, I'm okay. I'm just trying to decide where to start."

"You should start with email. This is the first thing I look at when I am in the computer. What is your name?"

"Ummm, my name's Roosevelt. Rosy."

"*Hola,* Rosy. I am Gali."

"Nice to meet you, Gali." I make a move like I'm ready to check my email, but she's undeterred.

"Is it okay for to practice my English with you, Rosy?"

I chuckle in resignation. "Yeah. Sure. That'd be fine."

"*Bien.* Because I am wanting to show you something." She turns her monitor in my direction and begins clicking through countless photos, showcasing herself in stages of undress with a variety of traveler types. "This is my friend, Mark. He is from New Zealand. And this is my friend, Dragen. He is from Croatia. And this is my friend, Allister. He is from United States... In curious, where do you reside from, Rosy?"

I've seen a lot of crazy shit in this place, but this is a whole new level of audacity. "I'm from Canada, Gali."

"Oh, I have many friends in Canada! Let me show you."

As she tracks down more evidence of her popularity, I log into my email.

The internet is notoriously slow in Iquitos, and as the page loads, the girl taps my shoulder. "This is my friend, Gaston. He is from Quebec. This photo is from when we are in the nature reserve." As is the case in almost every photo, she sports a bikini top. "And this is my friend, Steve. He is from Calgary. He is VERY nice." It goes on and on.

By the time I'm able to redirect my attention, the contents of my inbox fixes its gaze on me. I sit for an indeterminate amount of time, staring into the screen's soft glow, unable to move.

It's all there in the messages left unread: **"We NEED to talk to you," "How Are You?" "[No Subject]," "Call Me... PLEASE!"**

It might have been hours. Or maybe only a second. It is impossible to know. With my head twitching, I finally blink. As if by instinct, I click the "Delete All" tab, shut off the monitor, and walk into the Iquitos night without so much as acknowledging the endlessly chattering nymphet.

6

Rosy – Before: Canada

"I want you to know that you don't gotta stay. If we're not gonna make it, it's gotta be *you* that gets out, 'cause I'm not capable. I'm fuckin' Irish. I'll deal with somethin' bein' wrong for the rest of my life."

Kat and I were sitting on the couch with a bottle of wine late one Friday night, watching a rented DVD of *The Departed*. When Matt Damon turned to that girl from *Up In The Air* and whispered those words, the temperature in the room changed ever so slightly, the subject matter hitting a little too close to home. Kat and I exchanged a nervous half-look of recognition, silently agreeing to never speak of this moment again.

I probably asked her to move in too soon.

I *definitely* asked her to move in too soon.

Like all bad decisions, it seemed not only like a good idea, but the *best* idea at the time. We were young and in love, running on instinct and lust, virtually inseparable our first few months together. I was also completely broke, and the idea of rent relief sounded *pretty* attractive. And yes, I know that financial instability is an ill-advised justification for premature cohabitation, but I was in my mid-20s and operating under the idiotic premise that everything works out in the end.

If I'm being honest, there was an additional catalyst beyond irrational optimism and economic uncertainty that led to this unholy arrangement. When I first met Kat, she was living with a roommate I abhorred: a viciously obnoxious foul-weather friend from theater school. This roommate thrived on chaos and misery, and whenever Kat came to my place after a night on the town with her, she would be more fucked-up than ever, reeking of cigarettes and tequila and God knows what else. And yes, considering my life choices, I understand the severe hypocrisy of taking a holier-than-thou stance on getting wasted. But when it came to Kat's roommate, I always felt like she was bringing Kat along for these kamikaze missions just to prove she could.

It was about control, and I was losing.

So, Kat moved into my Wallace Avenue walk-up sometime in August—suspect motives and flawed logic be damned. We had only known each other for four months, but I figured I was willing to live with the unforeseen consequences, and fully prepared to go down with the ship.

You learn a lot about a person when you move in together. This is especially true when they're essentially a stranger with whom your only point of reference is their insatiable libido.

One of the first things I discovered about Kat was that she had no friends back home, childhood or otherwise. This was shocking to me, and starkly contrasting my life. I had known my two closest friends, Ishy and The Deuce, before I could reach the sink for a drink of water, the two of them shaping me like family members.

Kat's lack of lifelong companions seemed innocuous early on, as I rationalized that she probably discovered more interesting people in college. It was also possible that I was the anomaly in this dichotomy, and that not everyone dug the idea of living out an episode of *The Wonder Years* for all their days. It was only when Kat began to begrudge me for these friendships—becoming clingy and bitter and pouty whenever I wanted to hang with my buddies— that I began to question whether it was normal to have precisely zero friends that go back five years.

Her resentment culminated one night after one of my high school buddies had come to our place. Doug had just borrowed some money from his boss so he could buy an engagement ring from a Koreatown jeweler and propose the following weekend at his girlfriend's family cottage, north of the city. He brought the ring along to show me and was absolutely beaming with pride when he opened the little velvet box.

It was a pretty special moment, and we both got a little misty-eyed, thinking about him as a married man, and maybe someday a father. I poured us some Bushmills and put my arm around him in that awkward way guys are never really comfortable with, and the two of us got wondrously drunk at my kitchen table, listening to Van Morrison records and talking about the old times until he fell down the stairs and into a cab at three in the morning.

There was a house party the following evening, and it happened that Doug and his soon-to-be-proposed-to girlfriend were in attendance, along with Kat and her loathsome ex-roommate. As was often the case, Kat and her former roomie were out of control, acting like a couple high schoolers at their first party, drinking and smoking and hamming it up in a way that even my degenerate cast of pals recognized as a play for attention. The shrieking and cackling and off-color jokes made it seem as though they were on a mission to mock our quaint, little get-together, but all of that was simply a prologue to the moment Kat and her crony tracked down Doug's future fiancé, so they could ask her and the entire party, in shrill, drunken unison, "WOULDN'T IT BE AMAZING IF DOUG PROPOSED TO YOU AT THE COTTAGE NEXT WEEKEND?"

There were five long seconds of silence.

It was the closest I'd ever come to striking a human being.

I took a deep breath. We all took a deep breath. Then we acted as if the incident never happened. I promptly left the party to walk home alone—a two hour hike, when factoring the three establishments I stopped in to knock back angry shots of whiskey, vowing to never again be in the same vicinity as Kat's ex-roommate. I texted my buddy to drunkenly apologize, and like it always is with old friends, the episode was water off a duck's back. Doug and his girlfriend were engaged the following weekend, and we all found a way to move on—almost.

I couldn't let the episode slip.

Things were never quite the same between Kat and me. We grew distant over the next few months. We hung out with my friends a lot. We occasionally went out for dinner. We had a few drinks and a little sex. We drove out to Simcoe to see her family every couple of months. We fought a little more often and a little more viciously and—if you were counting the hours—we were probably spending less time together. Despite her increasingly irritating pleas for us to up our alone time together, I rationalized this was merely the evolution of a maturing relationship.

One night I came home late after getting drinks with some coworkers, only to find an old milkcrate of mine sitting on the coffee table. The red crate—stolen from the back of a Dairy Queen days before setting out for university—was one of many bulky, burdensome items I'd grown fond of lugging from apartment to apartment around the city.

Kat was sitting cross-legged on the floor, her body language speaking of an anger that frightened me. She was puffing on a cigarette, an obvious fuck-you lobbed in my direction, knowing full-well how much I hated smoking indoors.

Having never had the resources to purchase a camera of my own and before the ubiquity of smartphones, I'd been at the mercy of ex-girlfriends for photos of my formative years. A typical roll of film would include shots of me and whichever girl I was dating, and a whole whack of images of my buddies and me doing debaucherous things in various states of inebriation, including multiple portraits of The Deuce's genitals. Most of the time, those wonderful ex-girlfriends of mine were kind enough to print an extra roll for my archives.

Truth was, I'd never looked through those photos when moving, and I certainly hadn't considered what a new love interest might make of me "stashing" dozens of adorable snaps of former conquests. But, seeing Kat there on the floor, surrounded by what amounted to my "greatest hits of romances past," I had a feeling I was about to learn exactly what such a girlfriend might think.

"Are you still fucking any of these girls?"

I gasped, then laughed. "Are you serious?"

"Yes. I am asking you a serious, legitimate question, and I would like a serious, legitimate answer. ARE. YOU. FUCKING. ANY. OF. THESE. GIRLS?"

"Holy fuck…"

"Holy fuck WHAT?"

"What's the matter with you?"

"Just answer the FUCKING QUESTION!" Kat always seemed to be seething beneath the surface. It was this smoldering rage that frightened me most.

"No. I am not fucking any of those girls."

"Then would you mind explaining why you have these photos in our house? Why you have been hiding these photos from me, in our house? What, do you... *jerk off* to them when I'm not around? Is that why you keep them? So you can jerk off to your ex-girlfriends every time I leave the house?"

"No. I do not jerk off to those photos."

"Then why the FUCK do you still have them?"

I couldn't even look at her. My mind was a Molotov cocktail of anger, pity, and shame.

"Tell me. Just tell me why. Why do you have them?"

"I don't know. I never got rid of them. I didn't know I had them. I couldn't even tell you the last time I went through them."

She must have known I was lying. She always did. "Well, now you know. So, you can get rid of them."

"I'm not getting rid of them."

"Excuse me?"

"I said I'm not getting rid of them. I'll get rid of them sometime, but I'm not getting rid of them now."

"Would you mind explaining to me why you'd wait to get rid of them? What do you want, some *time alone* with them first?"

"No, I don't want to have some time alone with them. I just don't like to be bullied into—"

"Into what? Into doing something you don't want to do? You know what? You want to keep these? Fine. Let's keep them. In fact..." In one swift motion, she grabbed a handful of photos and stormed into the kitchen for a roll of Scotch tape.

"What the fuck are you doing?" I followed her as she marched down the hall.

"You want to keep these photos in our house? Be my fucking guest. But you can't hide them from me. If these bitches are *so important* to you, let's put them on display!" She flung open our bedroom door and violently ripped the tape from the roll. Haphazardly, she plastered photos all over our bedroom wall. "Do you like that? Is this what you had in mind? Now you can beat off to these whores every night, you FUCKING ASSHOLE!"

"You're crazy. Honestly. What the fuck is going on in your head?"

"You're saying that my feelings are *invalid*? Is that what you're saying? Are you saying that I shouldn't be feeling this way? That I shouldn't be upset about the fact that my boyfriend—who I *live with*—still wants to fuck his ex-girlfriends!"

I laughed pitifully. "You know what? I'm gone. I'm outta here." I turned and began walking away.

"Where the fuck are you going?"

As I made my way down the hall, I said, "Away from you." When I got to the bottom of the stairs, I blurted out a diagnosis of my love life: "This is so fucked-up."

I don't remember whether I called The Deuce or just bumped into him at The Dakota Tavern, but we wound up in a dark corner, drinking Steam Whistles and shots of Jack Daniel's while The Bahamas grooved and reverberated through three tremendous sets, closing it down with a song about a guy who comes to realize that everything is his fault.

We clanged glasses far too enthusiastically, reveling in our self-inflicted misery. For all his womanizing and idiotic machismo, The Deuce could be a surprisingly good listener, capable even of offering decent advice. He told me I was welcome to crash at his place. I spent that foggy night on The Deuce's couch, and after going to work smelling like a distillery the next day, I returned to my apartment shortly after six. I knew that Kat would be gone by then, tending bar at a local watering hole, serving desperate down-on-their-luck regulars.

What I found when I walked through the door was the spine-tingling stuff of Adrian Lyne thrillers.

In the front hall laid a pile of photos of Kat and me. Pictures that had previously been curated, framed, and tastefully set throughout the apartment were now bent and crumpled and tossed on the floor.

Hanging on the wall was a frame that had hosted one such photo, but now encased a photograph of my most recent ex and me. The photo had been taken a few years back at a Maple Leafs' road playoff game. We were surrounded by a bunch of rowdy, tailgating Torontonians, reveling in the cheap beer and the Carolina sunshine of a long May weekend. I was wearing my 1960s Dave Keon jersey, and my ex and I were draped in a Canadian flag, flanked by thousands of like-minded Leafs fans who made the trip south. Dangling from the frame were the remnants of the Canadian flag and my autographed jersey, both of which had been strung up like the entrails of a medieval peasant convicted of high treason.

Kat's iPod was plugged into my stereo, playing a song just for me. It was Kathleen Edwards' "Asking for Flowers" set on repeat, hauntingly quiet, the refrain echoing over and over as I slowly made my way down the hall:

> *"Every pill I took in vain*
> *Every meal for you I made*
> *Every bill I went and paid*
> *Every card I signed my name*
> *Every time I poured my heart out*
> *Every threat you made to move out*
> *Every cruel word you let just slip out*
> *Every cruel word you let just slip out..."*

Hanging on the wall outside the bathroom was another photograph in an ill-fitting frame. This snapshot depicted a college ex and me posing in front of a beach sunset in Grand Bend. It was Canada Day, 1999. A group of us had piled into a van and driven down to celebrate Canada's birthday on the strip. We hit all the legendary joints that afternoon: Coco's and Gables and Sanders on the Beach, then crashed random cottage parties until we were kicked out of them all. We wound up huddled, sleeping on the beach until dawn. I was wearing a terrible Hawaiian shirt, and that shirt succumbed to a similar fate as my priceless Leafs jersey. The Hawaiian was doused in Kat's perfume, then cut into long strands she'd taped to the wall to spell "ASSHOLE" in Aloha technicolor.

A feeling rushed over me, and I realized Kat could have skipped work to observe me making these grisly discoveries from somewhere in the apartment. I stood very still, then nervously called out a couple times. When there was no response, I took a deep breath and made my way to my home office. The door was closed, but adorned by another crooked frame, this one containing a photo of a female friend I had known since grade school. We were 19 and had been up in Muskoka one August weekend with a bunch of friends. After basking in the afternoon sun on a weathered dock, talking about everything in the world that seemed important at the time, the group of us had ventured into town to catch Blue Rodeo at

The KEE to Bala. The photo had been taken under the hand-painted marquis with the full moon hanging low, and, by the time Jim Cuddy took the stage, I could have sworn I was in love, though I never once tried to kiss her.

The photo came from one of those wind-up disposable cameras, the film laboriously brought to a Shoppers Drug Mart for developing. It was the only keepsake I had from that glorious weekend. Today, it was accented by fragments of my collection of Blue Rodeo CDs, their pulverized pieces taped to the door, sharp and shiv-like as they shimmered my reflection in a mosaic of jealous insanity.

A chill ran down my spine. I was dreading what awaited on the other side of the door.

I took a deep breath and turned the handle.

It's difficult to describe what races through your mind the moment you smell burning flesh. After a panic-stricken beat, I noticed a photo from when I was 16, posing with my eleventh grade girlfriend in my mom's backyard on a sweltering June afternoon, hours before prom. I was wearing a rented tuxedo, a pair of cowboy boots, and a haircut that embodied everything wrong with the '90s. The tux had long since been returned, presumably to be sullied and vomited on at a later date, but those cowboy boots—a prized pair of Tony Lamas that my mom had saved up for and purchased on her one and only trip to visit her sister in El Paso—those had been all mine. They were snakeskin and leather, so singular and magnificent that I only wore them on the rarest of occasions, the kicks never failing to draw attention in all the right ways. They were of such fine craftsmanship that they would have been virtually impossible to destroy with a simple kitchen knife or pair of scissors.

But, as it turned out, they were not immune to the effects of massively increasing incalescence. Having been roasted in the embers of my charcoal grill, those boots now sat in a scorched heap, unrecognizable as they propped up the photo of my virginal high school sweetheart and me, the two of us at the apex of adolescent awkwardness.

I shook my head and gathered the remains of my melted boots.

Then I got the fuck out of the house.

7

Vanessa – Wednesday: Peru

Nov. 9th, 2011

I have arrived in Iquitos. This place is surreal and manic and unbelievable, and I mean that in the best way.

But before Iquitos, there was Lima. I arrived in the capital in the middle of the night and, truth be told, I hadn't planned on leaving the airport, having heard the city is noisy and dangerous, not worth one's time. But a couple of hours spent on a concrete floor can be an amazing source of motivation, so, at the hint of dawn, I stashed my bag in a locker and headed for an ad hoc tour.

It was 6:30 in the morning when I found a cabdriver I was fairly certain wouldn't assault me (a guy at the taxi stand vouched for him, so there's that)! I heard that Centro Lima is a little sketchy for tourists but figured I should at least check it out while in town, so asked the driver to take me to the Plaza de Armas.

How do I describe the taxis in Lima? I have been in some busted-up rides, but never cars *this* shitty. The doors were wired shut with coat hangers, the seats torn to shreds, every window cracked, and toxic levels of exhaust spewed from every car... and the drivers! They make right-hand turns from the left-hand lane like it's performance art: reckless abandon meets chaos theory!

It took us about 30 minutes to get to the Plaza de Armas and when we arrived the place was... fine? I don't know. Maybe the yellow walls of the Municipal Palace are more impressive under sunny skies, but, shrouded in early morning fog, the whole place just seems cold, gray, and unaffecting.

Yet something pulled me to the salty breezes of the Pacific, so I snapped a few photos and jumped back in the cab, hightailing it to the Miraflores District of Lima.

My cabbie was an older gentleman who had learned a few token English phrases by watching *Friends* and *Seinfeld*, so was able to point out a few of his favorite places to me: the National

Soccer Stadium where he lived and died by the team, the magic water fountain park where kids splashed in amazement, and the church where all his children were baptized. We zigzagged through that crazy city until we finally got to Parque Kennedy in the heart of Miraflores.

Even though it was early, the park was alive with vendors selling freshly squeezed orange juice, *triples* (triple-decker sandwiches with avocado, tomato, and egg), and *turrónes* (sugary cakes). Artists were beginning to set up on the sidewalk, displaying their originals. (Anyone need a painting of Machu Picchu?) But the main attraction was the hundreds of stray cats lounging on the grass. Apparently, people began dropping their unwanted felines off at the church near the park years ago, and the kind parishioners took mercy on the little darlings.

I eventually bought one of the sugary cakes and a cup of coffee, then found a place on the church steps where I could sit and smoke and read my book, petting every kitten that came into orbit. It was a long way from sleeping on the floor at Jorge Chávez Airport, and a pretty perfect morning, all things considered.

When I got the itch to move, I strolled along the beautiful streets, past tiny bars and cafés on Calle Berlin, then down Bolognesi, to a pretty little park that doubled as a roundabout in the heart of an intersection. I stopped at a *sanguchería Criolla*, where I had a *lomo saltado* sandwich with French fries made from purple potatoes. I sat out on the patio with an Inca Kola and watched the madness of Lima go by.

After lunch, I meandered to Parque del Amor at the edge of the golden sunset cliffs that overlook the Pacific. I was invigorated by the first taste of ocean air. The restorative qualities of seaside living have been well-documented, and there is no disputing that I felt better, energized, and alert as I took a deep breath, thankful for the cleansing negative ions in the salty breeze.

I sat on one of the beautiful concrete mosaic benches lining the Malecón walkway, with its towering palms and lavish floral gardens, taking in the splendor of Delfin's most famous sculpture, El Beso. El Parque del Amor is a make out destination, and the endless views of the Pacific ensure there are no shortage of couples—native or tourist—attempting to reignite romance with a grass-rolling kiss. Alone but not lonely, I did my best not to stare, diverting my end-of-chapter gazes to the surfers bobbing like tiny shark fins hundreds of feet below, or the paragliders sailing in slow-motion above and beyond. The soothing heartbeat of the crashing waves below very nearly lulled me to sleep.

In Search of Lost Time, indeed.

I jumped in a taxi around 3:30, not knowing it would take more than an hour to get back to the airport. This was cutting it way too close, and there were a few gridlocked moments I was certain I'd miss my flight. But fortune favors the naïve, and I had just enough time to grab my pack and catch my flight.

With a window seat, I watched Lima disappear into the hardscrabble desert foothills, which gave way to the mud and green of the Andes, then the snow-capped summits of the Cordillera Blanca. The sun was setting somewhere over the Pacific as we crested the mountains, washing the entire landscape in beautiful, pink light. From 30,000 feet, you'd swear you could see God.

Stepping out of the airport and into Iquitos at night was sheer madness. The blast of oppressive heat even with the sun long gone felt like getting punched in the face. I was instantly swarmed by 15-year-old taxi drivers shouting in broken English and smiling in a way that made my skin crawl. It wasn't until I was able to break from the mob scene that I realized the taxis were actually motorcycle rickshaws! I ultimately settled on a prepubescent kid who had a tiny statue of Jesus hanging from his rear-view mirror.

What can I even say about my first whirlwind mototaxi through Iquitos? The smells were so raw and heavy and real, the air soaked with humidity, earthy vegetation, and a hint of woodsmoke. Every now and then, I would catch a whiff of some beautiful frying meat, only to have it lost in a lungful of motorcycle exhaust.

The acoustic experience was as astounding as the olfactory adventure, the ride as raucous and roaring as any I'd ever been on. The music, the horns, the sirens, and all the people in the streets: Everything is cranked to 10. Even my driver was getting in on the action, yipping and whistling at everything in sight.

I witnessed entire families riding a single motorcycle: young father driving, mother on the back, toddler squeezed between, and a BABY in the mother's arms... Again, they were all on one *motorcycle*... and none of them wore helmets!

The energy of Iquitos is intoxicating. This place is pulsating and absolutely dripping with sex. The sticky-hot jungle isolation, the dark skin, the thumping music... Maybe it's all in my head, but I get the sense that everyone's making eyes with everyone on every corner.

And the GAS STATIONS! Even the girls working the gas stations are decked out in the tiniest booty shorts, flashing their coochies as they pump petrol for the horny, teenage taxi boys!

All of it is ridiculous and unforgettable and amazing.

The hostel I'm staying at is called The Hideout. I'd read about it on Tripadvisor and heard the proprietor is an ex-pat American with a taste for big-game jungle hunting. The décor isn't exactly my thing—too many dead animals on the walls—but there's a cute front porch that doubles as a common area. Upon arrival, that front porch was filled with a boisterous group of friendly Europeans: always a good sign in a hostel!

The guy who runs the place is a little creepy but left me alone after showing me to my room. I joined the Euros down on the porch for a beer (Iquiteños) while they regaled me with stories of the best places they've been:

Montañita – a postcard Pacific beach town in Ecuador.

Salar de Uyuni – salt flats and pink lagoons with windswept desert landscapes from another planet.

Potosí – a functioning silver mine in Bolivia where they let you blow shit up with homemade dynamite.

I never cease to be amazed by the quantity of alcohol the average British male can consume, and this group did their reputation proud. They were a great hang and made me feel right at home. After an hour or so, they determined it was time to hit the sweaty *discotecas* in the main square. They tried to drag me along, but the past 36 hours have left me totally spent, and I wanted nothing more than to sit on my bed and write in this journal.

Which brings me to now: alone and a little tipsy in a sweltering dorm, thrilled and excited and exhausted to be here.

Buenas noches.

8

Rosy – Before: Canada

Kat and I never truly got over the *Fatal Attraction*-style photo incident, but we learned to bury it deep enough to get by, the closing bars of "Smells Like Teen Spirit" providing a mantra for our relationship: denial.

I spent a few days at The Deuce's in the immediate aftermath, but Kat was persistent in calling and apologizing. I got the sense that she felt genuine remorse and, truth be told, The Deuce's place was a fucking pigsty with no telling how much DNA resided on the couch I laid my weary head. All my stuff was back at the apartment, and the idea of breaking up just seemed like way too much... work? So, for those underwhelming and indefensible reasons, I decided to go back to Kat.

The subsequent months unfolded with relative calm. I had my work and friends, and she began taking yoga classes. As a means of concession and coming to my senses, I threw away most of the ex-girlfriend photos, choosing to hold on to a select few for reasons I still can't explain. On weekends, we stayed up late and went for brunch at 3PM at a hipster place on Dupont Avenue. Our sex life waxed and waned, but I assumed that was normal. We danced around talk of the future and never spoke in absolutes.

We existed in an indefinite holding pattern, but still... There was the incessant pull of an uncomfortable feeling.

One night, with the streets soaked in April rain, I found myself unable to go home. I had been playing hockey with Ishy, The Deuce, and most of the guys we'd grown up with. We wound up sitting around the dressing room, ripe with the unmistakable musk of hockey gear as we drank cold cans of beer and busted balls. Like always, The Deuce was standing naked far too long, speaking of sexual conquest in barrooms and bathrooms and Bathurst Street basements. Ishy and I typically rode together so one of us could crush a few extra tallboys, and it was well past midnight by the time we pulled out of the parking lot.

I drove from George Bell Arena back downtown to drop Ishy off at his King Street condo, talking the entire way about the weekend and the coming summer and whether Ishy would ever ask his cute office admin out for a drink. When we got to Ishy's, he shook my hand and grabbed his gear, then knocked on the trunk as goodbye. I sat parked out front a long time, watching him go into the lobby of his building, then staring into the street. When I pulled away from the curb, I didn't go home.

I drove through Chinatown and crisscrossed Kensington Market, where the deserted streets looked like they belonged to a different city. I crawled along Dundas to Lansdowne and imagined what it might be like to live there and go salsa dancing at the Lula Lounge every Saturday night. I drove through the Junction as a freight train rumbled overhead. I meandered through High Park and looked out over Grenadier Pond, the frogs groaning in mesmerizing synchronicity. I drove down residential city streets, the puddles reflecting moonlight, the grassy, leafy smell of spring thrilling and soothing and heartbreaking all at once.

I drove all night long, sad and terrified and unable to explain why. I parked in the shadow of a big tree in front of my childhood home, staring into the void of deserted street, looking for an answer that never came.

It was after four when I dragged myself home. Kat had fallen asleep, her worried text messages unanswered. I crept into the house and slipped into bed, careful not to wake her.

Like most struggling couples, we fought more than we should have, but these disagreements ended in screaming, crying, and her throwing objects in my direction. It didn't matter the subject—the fights were always about deeper issues we didn't discuss: my unwillingness to commit and inability to admit it. How I couldn't mask the desire to be elsewhere while spending time with my "significant other." How she'd never speak of her deep-rooted insecurities and scars from her past.

Those were the things we were really fighting about, but they manifested into arguments about which movie to watch, and what it meant when someone looked at their phone mid-conversation. Days later, we wouldn't remember the reasons. We'd only remember the hurt, and the feeling that we would probably never understand each other.

I'm not sure if it had been happening all along, but I recognized a pattern in the frequency of our altercations. The first time I connected the dots was when we were trying to get out the door for my mom's 55th birthday dinner. We were already 45 minutes late and if we dove any deeper into whatever grievance she had raised, we'd miss the dinner completely. Despite our obvious time constraints, Kat stood in the living room with tears streaming, very much on the verge of detonating. I was left with no choice but to give in to whatever she demanded, admit that I was wrong and promise to be better next time, all in the name of getting the fuck out of the house so we could get to my mom's birthday party.

The calculated confrontations continued throughout the year, and always at times where I couldn't do anything but acquiesce: when I was trying to leave to play in my men's league hockey final; when my buddies were parked out front, waiting on me to drive to Buffalo for the Bills-Dolphins game; when Kat and I were going to meet my boss and his wife for dinner at Canoe. In each instance, I had to capitulate, the two of us acutely aware the flipside would spell some big social or professional faux pas.

My friends referred to her technique as "hostage-taking."

The second-to-last premeditated hostage situation occurred in my car, on our way to Doug's wedding rehearsal—the same Doug whose proposal had been all but sabotaged by Kat the previous year. The rehearsal was an hour outside the city and *once again* we were tight on time. We were somewhere near Orangeville when Kat started in on some nameless injustice, turning on the theatrics in an instant as she screamed and smashed her fists against the window. Mascara bled down her face as she asked if I even cared about her feelings, demanding that I stop the car so she could liberate herself from me once and for all.

As much I wanted to, there was no way I could leave her by the road at nightfall. And there was no chance I'd turn around to drive her all the way back to the city... Meaning I was euchred again. She knew exactly which levers to pull and when, and I had no choice but to submit.

In the end, I admitted I was a terrible human being and somehow committed to a trip out west to visit one of her college friends. It was the only way to ensure we made the rehearsal dinner on time—which we did, but not before she said she loved me and sucked me off as we wound through the rolling hills of Hockley Valley.

With a little distance, it's obvious now that I was no Prince Charming to Kat. I was petty and resentful and internalized almost all my frustration. Every slight or snub, every time she did something thoughtless or lazy—all of it was begrudged and suppressed and never forgotten, until it boiled over, and I'd unload on her for the slightest transgression.

I was immature and more than a little insensitive to her feelings and mental wellbeing. I spent way too much time with people outside our relationship, and I probably bullied her into spending a disproportionate amount of time with my friends and family. I hated most of her theater school acquaintances and made no effort to hide my disdain in their presence. Maybe worst of all, I'd sulk and bitch through most of the quality time she worked so hard for us to have.

I was a complete asshole most of the time we spent together, but especially at the end.

And then there was Jasmine.

Jasmine began working in the city's planning department earlier that summer, and I knew the moment I laid eyes on her that I was in trouble. My relationship was in a death spiral, and this new girl was everything Kat wasn't: young and well-read, fit and exotic, riding a bicycle to work every day. She didn't inflict her mood swings and misery on me, she didn't scream at me for staying out late with my friends. She hung on my every word, and I ate it up.

Nothing happened. Of course, nothing happened. But it wasn't unusual for Jasmine and I to eat lunch in the park or go for drinks after work with a big group of colleagues. Sometimes I'd walk her back to the subway and sometimes I'd ride with her all the way to her stop. She once invited me up to her place for a nightcap, but I knew the temptation was too great, and graciously declined. In her orbit, I was polite and thoughtful, a true gentleman. In short, I was the person I should have been with Kat.

There was more than one occasion my mind wandered to a fictional time where Jazz and I existed in some East End loft, all exposed brick and ductwork, wooden beams and polished concrete floors. It wasn't uncommon to find myself alone in my apartment with my dick in my hand, visions of Jazz in sultry disgrace overtaking my head.

The totality of it all was the super fucking obvious canary in the coalmine, but I was too stupid to admit it and too gutless to act on it. Deep down, I knew I owed it to Kat and myself to get us off this sinking ship, but I didn't have the stomach to do it.

Come July, Kat and I were heading west to visit her college friend, driving my Volkswagen TDI through Detroit into Chicago, where we sat in the bleachers at Wrigley and danced the night away on North Halsted. We awoke early and drove through Madison, Eau Claire, and Minneapolis before chasing the legend of Chuck Klosterman in *Fargo Rock City*. We drove through the badlands of North Dakota and weaved through Montana: Billings and Bozeman and Butte, then Great Falls and Sunburst and Sweet Grass because it sounded like poetry on the map.

We crossed the border back into Canada and dug for dinosaur bones in Drumheller, cruising into Calgary as the sun was setting just before 10 on a Saturday night. We lit up the Red Mile with Kat's small contingent of theater school friends until the sun came up, sleeping through the next day on thrift store couches in a dimly lit apartment. We went out again the following night, two-stepping 'til our feet hurt with the gaggle of bartenders and service industry types who inhabited the likes of Cowboys and Knoxville's in Stampede City.

We spent the next few days living a bohemian Rocky Mountain dream, buying western plaid and ill-fitting cowboy hats from a Southend pawn shop, and eating at Earls and Booker's BBQ, often drunk in the glorious midday sun. One afternoon, with her friends at work, Kat pulled me into the shower and gave herself to me completely. Her cries for more careened off the tiles, reminding me ever so briefly of the old times.

We decided to head into the mountains to find some of that fresh air and natural beauty we'd heard so much about, driving into

Banff and setting up camp just outside town, pitching our tent for four dazzling nights. Infinitely more prepared than we had been on our first foray into the wilderness, we spent the days trekking and climbing, following maps that seemed like they belonged to another century. We hiked to Paradise Valley and Bourgeau Lake, swimming naked in the icy waters and warming ourselves in the sun. We hiked through Johnston Canyon and up to the Lake Agnes Tea House so we could look out over that breathtaking body of water while sipping steaming green tea. We walked into town and ate at fantastic restaurants serving hearty Canadian fare: venison and duck, bison and bone marrow. We drank strong local beer at bars with vintage ski posters, the staff wearing toques and plaid. Late at night, we'd return to our campsite and sit around a crackling fire, gazing up at the sky as we passed a tightly spun joint, eventually climbing into our tiny tent to make love and fall asleep in the cool mountain air while the stars twinkled above.

On our last day, we hiked to Bow Glacier Falls to take in the beauty from below, then continued up the mountain to gaze at one of the most spectacular views: a massive glacier that seemed to recede into the distance forever, the truth of this revealed only from our vantage point, where the ice-melt waterfall cascaded into a perfectly serene and indescribably blue mountain lake. Kat and I stood there a long time, transfixed by the river being born into that perfect perpetual moment.

Getting back down was lengthy and difficult. We followed the rocky river back to Bow Lake before walking most of its circumference and eventually reaching the car. The drive into town was slow and it was nearly dark by the time we reached our campsite. Kat turned in early, so I built a fire, hypnotized by its dancing, narcotic rhythms as darkness crept closer.

In the morning, we packed our gear without saying much. We headed back to Calgary for one uneventful night before saying goodbye to Kat's friends and climbing into the car for the three-day journey back to Toronto. The drive across Saskatchewan and Manitoba's golden prairies was surprisingly quiet and—after a forgettable night in a rundown motel on the outskirts of Winnipeg—we traversed the Great Lakes in one 24-hour marathon stretch. Most of it passed, unspeaking, as Kat slept against the window, my only company the glow of the dashboard and the fading signal searching for CBC Radio. With the predawn civil twilight unveiling a misty haze, I pulled into a deserted beach an hour outside Sault Ste. Marie and dipped my weary bones into the life-affirming waters of Lake Superior. I swam out as far as I could and floated on my back, watching the sun come up. It was solitary and magical, and when I came back to shore, I dried off and climbed into the driver's seat, knowing unequivocally I could make it home in one shot.

By the time we were fighting Toronto traffic, it was understood that Kat and I were somehow no longer on speaking terms. I chalked it up to road weariness and assumed things would be fine after a hot shower and some pad thai from our favorite spot. But once we got back to the apartment, Kat was interested in neither, turning in for the night without a word.

After a cold beer and the first four innings of the Jays game, I fell into bed and slept like the dead. I awoke early the next morning and hit up my favorite Bloor Street coffee joint for a strong Americano and to read the newspaper in peace. Kat was still asleep when I returned an hour-and-a-half later, and when I tried to interest her in a little Sunday fun, she lashed out and advised I leave her the fuck alone.

I nodded, slightly wounded by the outburst. I grabbed my car keys and drove down to Queen and Ossington to shoot hoops with the City Hall interns who ran a pickup game on Shaw Street. It was when I arrived back at the apartment, tired and sore and dripping with sweat, that I found Kat sitting alone by the window. In tears.

My first thought was that there had been a death in her family. I slowly moved towards her and sat on the arm of the chair, putting my hand on her shoulder and rubbing her back as I gently asked what had happened.

She continued to look out the window.

"Is everything okay?"

"Everything is fine."

"Are you sure? Because it really doesn't look like everything is fine."

"It's stupid. I'm really just mad at myself more than anything." She shook her head, a tear rolling down her cheek. "I can't believe how stupid I was..."

I took a deep breath. "Come on now. Don't be like that. Tell me what's wrong."

"I don't want to talk, okay? Please, just leave me alone."

I exhaled frustration but continued to sit by her side. I eventually took another deep breath and went to get myself a glass of water. But I couldn't leave it alone. I made my way back, her tears streaming all over again.

"Honestly, Kat, you need to tell me what's wrong. This is starting to freak me out a little."

She just shook her head.

I laughed bitterly. "Ever since we left Calgary, something has been up with you. Is it something I did? Something I said?"

She turned and looked at me with daggers in her eyes. "No, you *did* nothing."

Now we were getting somewhere.

After a long silence, she said, "I don't know... For some reason, I just felt like, when we were in Banff... I thought you were going to *propose* to me."

I could not believe what she'd said. I took a second to consider what I'd heard. Then I burst out laughing.

In retrospect, my reaction was probably a little insensitive.

Her face was all abhorrence and wounded disbelief.

"Honestly... I'm sorry, but where did you get that idea? Do you really think, with our relationship being as fucked-up as it is, that we're at a place where marriage is remotely possible?"

She was no longer crying.

I was too fucking stupid to realize that was a bad thing.

"I mean, I'm sorry if you thought that, but we're nowhere close. I just... Really? Marriage? That's actually pretty funny." I chuckled again, shaking my head before announcing I was hitting the shower. Removing my shirt as I made my way down the hall, I barely gave the conversation another thought.

9

Ishy – Thursday: Toronto, Canada

Hours after meeting with The Deuce, Ishy lets his memory wander back to the immediate aftermath, when Rosy gave him his apartment keys and made one request: "Sell every last item ASAP and deposit the money directly into my savings account."

Ishy knew better than to ask why.

The big-ticket items were easy to unload. Rosy's new leather couch and loveseat fetched a grand. His flatscreen TV brought in $600. If there's anything Ishy learned from working in equities, it's that you can always find a market if the price is right. A pair of greys from the now-extinct Maple Leaf Gardens brought in $2,300. His stereo system netted $1,700. His entire wardrobe went to the Salvation Army.

The liquidation was a nightly ritual for Ishy. He'd finish work around 6:30, then make his way to a rundown warehouse on Dupont Street, where Rosy's remaining possessions were stored. In that poorly lit alley, Ishy would rendezvous with strangers who responded too quickly to his Craigslist ad, the dusty storage unit becoming more barren each visit. In every other facet of life, Ishy was calculating the odds, hedging every bet, taking the safest option. But, on these nights—with no emotional attachment and not caring whether he sold this or that item to whichever haggler was trying to pay a penny less than the previously agreed price—on these nights, he got to exude the "I don't give a fuck" swagger he'd always dreamed of. And it felt fantastic.

But there were a few items Ishy knew he could never sell:

Rosy's hockey equipment. It was understood that a late-night pickup game with close buddies had immeasurable regenerative properties, and there was no way Ishy would deny Rosy that chance once he found his way home. Rosy also kept a nice collection of single malt scotch and Irish whiskey in his fully stocked honor bar, but there were a few bottles he cherished above the rest: a bottle of Bruichladdich earmarked for that first ride along the St. Clair R.O.W., and a bottle of 18-year Macallan he put away for the day—should he ever be so lucky—his first child was born. In his hasty instructions, Rosy implored Ishy to get rid of everything, but Ishy knew some things transcended conventional significance.

Lastly, there were Rosy's album and book collection. Ishy determined that Rosy simply worked too hard, invested too much time, energy, and love—too much of himself—into tracking down, devouring, and recommending them. Ultimately, there wasn't a price in the world worth discarding them.

The night before Ishy and The Deuce are scheduled to fly into Lima, Ishy finds himself alone in the office, a copy of *Lonely Planet Peru* atop his desk. His computer screen blinks the "Out of Office" autoreply he revised countless times, the image casting a dull glow across the stack of papers he constantly reshuffles to assure everything is in order. A week is nothing in the world of investment banking, but it is also everything. He's gone over his checklist half a dozen times but can't bring himself to leave.

The previous night, on the advice of a mail clerk with Buddy Holly glasses and skinny jeans, Ishy ventured over to a hipster video store off Queen Street West. Reared on the alphabetical simplicity of fluorescent chain establishments, Ishy was out of his element. Tom Waits seeped through the speakers as he waded through confounding sub-genres like "film noir," "Korean horror," and "girls with guns." He browsed the aisles in a futile attempt to familiarize himself with arthouse canon. There wasn't a hope in Hell he'd find the recommended disc on his own, but he was convinced the people who worked these bohemian haunts were elitist snobs who'd mock him for knowing less than them, like Jack Black in *High Fidelity*—except with an ironic moustache.

After nearly walking out empty-handed, Ishy mustered the courage to ask the film school grad with an eyebrow ring if he had a copy of Werner Herzog's *Fitzcarraldo*.

"I do have it," the kid said. "But I'll only lend it out on one condition."

Nothing would've surprised Ishy at that point. "Lay it on me."

"You have to rent *The Burden of Dreams* along with it, and you have to promise to watch it immediately after. It's the Les Blank documentary about the making of the movie. It will blow your fucking mind."

And it did.

Back at his desk, running through the inventory of all the things he's read and seen about Peru over the past three days, it is the sound of the cleaning lady's footsteps that convince Ishy it's time to head home.

As he stands to put on his overcoat, the woman smiles. "*Señor Ishmael*. How are ju this night?"

"I'm doing well, Rita. How about yourself?

"I am no complains, *señor*. I see that ju ees working late once again."

"Paying the bills. You know how it is. How're the girls?"

"*Mis hijas estan excelente, gracias*. They still are talk with the choco-latte *grande* you give for the *cumpleaños*."

Ishy smiles, imagining Rita's two young daughters tearing into the giant Toblerone he gifted them. "It was my pleasure." He turns off his monitor and notices her eyeing the book on his desk.

"*Señor Ishmael*, ju ees planning a vacations to Perú, yes?"

"Actually, yeah. I'm heading there first thing tomorrow."

"*Mañana*? I am so happy for ju, *señor*. I am certain ju will love Perú."

There's a momentary silence as Ishy considers his stupendous ignorance. "Wait, Rita. Where is it that you're from?"

"I come from Perú. I am born in Lima. That is where ju is flying to, yes?"

"Yeah," Ishy says, incredulous. "Lima. Tomorrow."

"*Hablas Español, verdad?*"

Shame flushes his cheeks. "Actually, no. I-I don't speak any Spanish."

"Do not be worry, *señor*. *Las Peruanas* will be happy to meet ju. *Las mujeres del Perú les gustan los gringos!*"

Ishy laughs bashfully. "Well, that's not actually the reason I'm going down there."

"I will give you these advise, *señor*. If ju see a *Peruana* and ju is wanting to makes some conversations, please say at her, '*Me gustan tus aretes.*'"

"May goostan toos arrett-ess?"

"*Sí. Me gustan tus aretes.* The meaning ees: 'I like your earrings.' It is what my husband say to me when we meet."

Ishy chuckles. "May goostan toos arrett-ess. Got it. That's perfect. Thanks, Rita."

Grabbing his *Lonely Planet* from the desk, he catches himself. "Hey, what can I bring back for the girls? Surely, there's something from the motherland they'd like to have."

"Do not be worry about those things, *señor*. Just be worry about safety, do not be getting sick, and have a good time. *Cuídate, por favor.*"

"I'll be sure to do that. Thanks, Rita."

As is the case at the end of almost every workday, Ishy says goodnight and leaves to the sound of Rita's vacuum tirelessly maneuvering around his desk.

The only explanation I can muster for catching a mototaxi to the outskirts of Iquitos is an unspeakable curiosity that draws me through the warm darkness. It is close to midnight when the driver stops near an abandoned soccer stadium and points down a dimly lit laneway. I hear drunken shouting as I wander down the alley, hesitating before crossing the threshold and stepping into a crowded room.

The ceiling is low and the lighting poor, the room thick with smoke and rife with the tang of booze and sweaty men. I remove the Mapacho cigar from behind my ear and light it, seeking out the lady in the corner selling bottles of Iquiteña from a metal horse trough. I drink half the beer in one swig, then exhale deeply. There appears to be little action in the way of cockfighting, and, as if sensing my confusion, the beer lady gruffly says, "*Medio tiempo.*" For reasons I can't explain, I muscle through the crowd for a better view.

The pit is smaller than I imagined, with sheets of plywood enclosing the ring and a thin layer of sand coating the concrete floor. I lean against the boards for a few minutes, smoking and drinking and listening to the spittle-slinging, rapid-fire Spanish of drunken lowlifes, which, I realize with satisfying self-loathing, I can now be included among.

I contemplate paying the lady at the trough another visit when an appreciable buzz envelopes the room. The murmur gives way to a roar, followed by the crush of humanity as the mob clamors for better positioning.

Unannounced, two men enter the pit, each carrying a gigantic rooster. Their plumes are unlike anything I've ever seen: fiery and shimmering and terrifying; the birds looking as though they've been put on this earth just to tear each other to pieces. Each man takes his bird to a side of the pit and ties a blade to its left leg with binder twine. One of the men readies his bird so close to me that I could reach out and touch it.

Money excitedly changes hands, and as the referee enters the ring, the crowd quiets. One man blows air into his rooster's beak in a ritualized pre-suscitation to steady him for battle. The owners place their birds on the floor, and the referee rings a little bell to signify the beginning of the fight.

For a moment, the roosters seem indifferent, clucking and prancing around in their corners. Then there's the sudden shriek of frenzied action, arms flapping and feathers flying in a rolling blur of violence. A broken wing. A dislocated leg. The howling squawk of survival.

The birds lunge furiously at one another in a cloud of dust, their knives glinting as they leap over one another in a tumbling, frantic wheel. The action moves toward me and all I want is to turn away. Like a bad dream, the press of bloodthirsty spectators intensifies, and I find myself pinned against the boards. It's happening so fast but unfolding in slow-motion.

As one bird flails against a wall, I see into its eyes. The terror. The disbelief. The inevitability. The other attacks with a savage wrath, its blade plunging into the chest of the cornered bird, the wounded's wings flapping in furious desperation, blood smattering everywhere.

The drunken crowd erupts as the winning cock stands over the convulsing body of the other, plucking its eye out not two feet from where I stand. The growing lump in my throat is the truth.

It isn't until the unfortunate bird's owner comes to drag its body away that I notice the blood on my hands. It is all too real, too familiar. I am sick to my stomach, retching as the bilious taste climbs into my throat.

I don't remember how I escaped the chaos, but with the roar still echoing, I am back on the street, walking through the night. I have no fucking clue where I am, but I know I need to be gone.

It is after 3AM when I reach the Plaza de Armas. The stillness of the square is jarring. I sit on a bench, mesmerized by the murmur of insects, the misty night air sweet with earthy perfume. A pair of mototaxi drivers have their rickshaws parked on the corner and speak in hushed tones. I have no idea what to do with myself but understand I'm in no condition to face The Hideout just yet.

In existential distress and with nowhere else to turn, I'm drawn to the southwest corner of the Plaza, where, through the still palms, the Iglesia Matriz's neo-Gothic cathedral is bathed in soft light, beckoning me.

I open the heavy wooden doors and step inside. Having escaped the humidity of the Iquitos night, the church feels cool and clean. My steps are heavy as I find my way into the nave. I stand for a long time in the aisle, taking in the beauty as fans silently turn overhead. I take a seat near the back, careful not to kick the kneeler.

I remain in that rickety pew for a long time, trying to void my mind of all thought, but the harder I try, the more ardently images bully their way in. At long last, I rest my head and allow the memories to consume me, inadvertently contemplating time and space, and how badly the collision of the two can fuck you up.

I knew it all along. I must have.

In the months leading up to the end, Katrina and I were at loose ends. And although communication had always been an issue with us, we devolved into corresponding almost exclusively through text messages:

> **I'll be home at 10**
> **can u pick something up 4 dinner**
> **where r u?**

To this day, I have no plausible explanation for why or how some of these messages got lost in time and space. It was fucked-up and alarming at the best of times, relationship-destroying and sanity-threatening at the worst. Sometimes the messages would arrive at their destination hours after being sent, sometimes days later... Most people didn't believe me, but I swear there were some messages that never made it to her phone at all, messages that just vanished into the ether.

As one might expect, this had a way of putting the screws to our increasingly fragile relationship. A delayed request to pick up a sandwich would leave the other feeling unappreciated and hurt. A lost message intended to inform the other they would be home late would make the other suspicious and worried and angry. These orphaned messages doused our brushfire problems with gasoline, and Kat became increasingly vocal about the dysfunction in our relationship, airing our dirty laundry to anyone who'd listen. It wasn't uncommon for me to come into the apartment and find her on the phone with her sister or mother, discussing all the ways I'd let her down, her revulsion pervading every conversation.

Everyone knew we had deep-rooted issues, and everyone in her life was under the impression I was to blame. She was controlling the narrative, *again*.

I didn't want to be there.

The decision to attend or not attend was eating me up, but, in the end, I knew I had to be at that church.

Everyone was there, and it was hell to sit through. Hell for me. Hell for her parents. Hell for everyone who'd ever known or loved her.

All their eyes were on me, convicting me in staggered, sickening leers. All of them wondering in whispers, assuming in absolutes. It was my fault, and they knew it. I could have helped her, but I didn't. Only the most compassionate of them made any attempt to speak to me or provide any measure of comfort. And yeah, my friends were there for me, but it was only my mom, sitting stoically by my side, who didn't believe I was entirely to blame.

Even with the February freeze, the church was hot and suffocating, the air stale and choked in misery. I had been drinking pretty dangerously in the days leading up to the funeral, and the devastating flowers and violent perfume were making me nauseous. I felt as though I was going to faint in the pew.

By the time they started the service, I was in a cold sweat, no doubt looking the part of a despicable scumbag for everyone to point a finger at. In all the guilt and soul-searching and self-loathing I had been forced to confront in the fog of that morning, the last thing on my mind was switching off my phone.

In the sickening silence of that church, and halfway through The Beatitudes, it erupted with that unmistakable *ping* of a text message.

I couldn't breathe. All eyes were upon me, burning holes in the back of my head as they glared with contempt and condemnation and disgust.

I was gutted. Something inside of me broke. The capacity to give a fuck about what others might think or believe now belonged to another universe.

When the prayer ended, as if in a trance, I went for my phone. My mom tried to stop me, but it was too late.

The text was from Katrina. It simply read:

why didnt u love me enough?

10

Vanessa – Thursday: Iquitos, Peru

Nov. 10th, 2011

I saw a funeral in Iquitos today. I was walking through the town's main square as mourners were milling outside a church. The service just ended, and people were hugging one another with tears in their eyes. I don't know what came over me, but I felt compelled to go inside.

The casket was sitting there in the sanctuary, and I couldn't keep myself from looking. The body belonged to an older man, someone who looked as though he'd lived a good enough life and had experienced a peaceful death. Standing over the body, I couldn't reconcile the fact that this man surely endured so much over the course of his life: that he had seen and done so many things, loved and been loved, had his heart broken numerous times. He'd experienced an existence distinct from any other in the history of the universe... And yet, as I stood there looking at his lifeless body, there was nothing remotely lifelike about it. This man would never tell another story. He'd never share any of the wisdom he'd gathered from his time on earth. He would never feel, or have the ability to make others feel, again.

The finality of nothingness is astonishing.

It got me thinking about when my dad and aunts and uncles decided my grandma was too confused to live alone in her house, and it was time to move her to a nursing home overlooking the East River. They just up and sold the house she and my granddad lived in for 60 years, the house that my dad and his brothers and sisters had grown up in, the house we'd spent every Christmas Eve in, caroling and dancing as the fire roared in the living room and us kids bounced on the couches, waiting for Santa to come...

Her children were somehow anointed her arbiters, sorting through an entire life of memories meticulously preserved for reasons only my grandma would ever fully understand.

After the house was finally stripped of everything that had made it a home, it was sold, and a new family was set to move in.

I remember going over to that old brownstone for the last time and being taken aback by the stillness and desolation. As I stood in that empty house, all I could think was: Some family is going to move in tomorrow, and they will NEVER know how important this place was, how much fun we had, how this was the center of the universe and the place where it always came together, how this place embodied what it meant to BE... And then, in the blink of an eye, it's nothing more than an empty space, and no one besides me and a few others would have the faintest idea it ever meant anything at all.

That was how I felt when I saw that lifeless, lonely body in the quiet, Iquitos church.

Deep breath.

That realization rattled me a while. I took a long walk along the Malecón to get my head right, staring off into the Amazon and watching life go by. It's hard to explain, but the river has a way of centering you, of putting things into perspective. You realize that time is short, little more than a flash of light.

I bought an Inca Kola and spent the afternoon walking the streets of Iquitos: Arica, Nauta, Loreto. I passed an absurd restaurant where the waitresses wore Texas Longhorns cheerleader outfits. I also discovered places that seemed totally unique to a jungle frontier town: street-side food stands selling fresh juice and sweet fried dough. Banks with armed guards where the open doors blast icy air out into the street. Motorcycle repair shops with shirtless young men hanging around. Concrete buildings in various states of construction and deconstruction with virtually no safety precautions to speak of (I saw a building with a missing wall that still had a family living inside! I was literally looking into their second-story bedroom from the street).

And then there were the tiles!

When Iquitos was a booming rubber town, the barons had an infatuation with artisanal Spanish tile. I have been told the *azulejos* are a sign of wealth and prosperity, so those beautiful, glazed tiles cover every surface in Iquitos. The brilliant, intricate patterns in yellow and royal blue speak to the former affluence and stand in stark contrast to the poverty that defines the city today.

    I had been walking for close to two hours and was ready to head back to the hostel when I made the ultimate unexpected discovery: a record store... in Iquitos!

    This storefront was like most others in Iquitos: barred windows and concrete walls. But the guy running the joint was spinning a Spanish edition of a Beatles album (*Por Favor, Yo*), and had a cat named Mauricio that rubbed against my legs while I flipped through obscure salsa discs. The place was dark and cool and had the funky universal record store smell of dusty cardboard and stale cigarettes. It was absolutely perfect.

    Like every other record store, it had copious amounts of '80s mass production (I'm looking at you, Phil Collins!), and heavy doses of Dire Straits and Queen. But I eventually found some South American albums I'd never seen before. I asked the dude for a recommendation. He pulled out something by Victor Jara and gave it a spin. The disc was an original pressing, scratchy and well-listened to. I didn't have a clue what the poet was singing, but it sounded powerful and the clerk got all quiet and misty-eyed. That was all the endorsement I needed.

    (It was only back at the hostel that the Euros informed me Victor Jara had been such an important political voice that, when Pinochet overthrew the Socialist Party of Chile in 1973, soldiers imprisoned Jara the next morning. They kept him captive in the National Soccer Stadium, broke his fingers and cut out his tongue so his voice would never be heard again.)

    Beyond the haunting cries of Victor Jara, I opted for some reggae. Call me sappy, but I'd been hearing so much Bob Marley down here (the universal language of wayward backpackers) that I had to splurge on *Soul Revolution*. I probably couldn't afford it, and it'll be a bitch dragging those two albums in and out of the jungle, but that's the price you pay when it comes to vinyl.

    In fact, that might be the best thing about vinyl. And that was my second revelation of the day.

    As I carried those records through Iquitos, I thought about what a labor of love listening to vinyl is: how you have to listen to the album without skipping songs, how you have to get up every 20 minutes to flip the disc to the B-side. Even owning vinyl is hard work. Albums take up space, collect dust and—when you move from apartment to apartment—you have to jam those heavy things into milk crates and drag them down the block through heat and rain and snow... That's the price you pay for the things that matter.

Because the things you work hardest for wind up being the things you love most. I've heard people say that's why, beyond all the obvious reasons, people love their kids so much: because you must invest so much time and energy and work into them. Because they're *worth* it.

And it might sound crazy, but it feels the same with vinyl. I'll take charm over perfection any day. And I'll take the significance and the memories created by the blisters, the sweat, and the inconvenience of tracking down and holding onto those physical things—things you can actually see and touch and smell—relics of a time when you had to hit the streets and talk to people and slip them some cash if you wanted to feel and be moved by music.

And that's why I'll always remember I found Victor Jara's *Geografía* and Bob Marley's *Soul Revolution* in that hole-in-the-wall record store down a sweltering Iquitos back alley.

Okay, full stop on the metaphysical introspection. It must be the homesickness getting to me. Time to be present.

4:13AM: I am making note of this to be sure it actually happened. I'm a little drunk and a little stoned and spent too much time on the porch with the Euros tonight. I was the last one awake and contemplating sleep when a guy I've never seen before came into the hostel, looking like he'd seen a ghost. He was all alone. He walked right past me and didn't say a word.

I can't explain it, but I am concerned for his well-being.

As for my own well-being, I need to get to bed. Out, out, brief candle.

11

The Deuce – Friday: Toronto, Canada

"This airport security is bullshit."

It is 6:30 in the morning and The Deuce is not so much hungover as he is completely intoxicated. Still, from last night's decision to catch an obscure alt-country outfit at the Horseshoe Tavern before joining his co-workers at an adult entertainment establishment that proves to be more ill-advised by the minute.

"I don't know how the fuck I spent $500 last night."

Ishy Lords is doing his best to ignore his travel companion, but The Deuce will not be denied.

"Strippers are my kryptonite, man. You gotta make sure you keep 'em away from me in Peru. I swear to God, if I get locked into one of those Bermuda Triangles down there, I'll never make it out alive." He laughs boisterously, but the young families and elderly travelers in the line are not impressed. "Fuck me, Lords… If I knew I was gonna be so thirsty this morning, I woulda drank more last night. I am fuckin' PARCHED."

Ishy tries to shush him, but it is no use.

"Honestly, whose dick do I gotta suck around here to get a glass of water?"

A sweet old lady takes mercy on everyone by passing back a bottle of water.

The Deuce is grateful to the point of obnoxiousness, demanding the lady's name and then announcing to the entire line, "Betty, you are a beautiful human being. EVERYONE? You need to know that BETTY RULES!"

When they reach the security checkpoint, The Deuce turns to Ishy and asks, "Hey, what do you call a black man that flies an airplane?"

It is one of those surreal moments where the entire place seems to fall silent. Ishy should have known it was a mistake to travel to South America with someone like The Deuce. He looks imploringly to the African American security official, practically begging the man to detain him.

After a beat too long, The Deuce slaps Ishy on the back, and says, "A PILOT, you fuckin' RACIST!" He throws his head back and howls as the blood drains from Ishy's cheeks and security subjects them to an additional search.

By some stroke of divine intervention, The Deuce makes it through customs and is deemed fit to fly. The strong coffee and warm donuts in the waiting area do little in the way of sobering him up, with The Deuce providing horrifyingly off-color stream of consciousness commentary on all things air travel.

It isn't until The Deuce is sound asleep on the plane that Ishy can relax. He orders an orange juice from the flight attendant and pulls out his copy of Malcolm Gladwell's *Outliers*, losing himself in the book so deeply that he doesn't think to look out the window until they touch down in Miami.

The stopover has a quick turnaround, and at their new gate, Ishy informs The Deuce that he needs to check in at work. Ishy throws his pack on the seat next to The Deuce and puts his phone to his ear, walking away without asking if he'd mind watching his stuff. After three hours of fitful sleep on the airplane, this gesture pisses off The Deuce to no end. He sits for a long time, brooding over Ishy's white-collar arrogance before deciding it's time for a smoke, not caring one way or the other if Ishy's pack grows legs.

When The Deuce returns three cigarettes later, Ishy is sitting with his backpack on his lap, a large coffee and a Cuban sandwich extended as a kind of peace offering. The Deuce feels a brief wave of guilt rush over him, mustering a half-hearted apology about needing to find a bathroom, but Ishy waves it off. They sit in something approximating silence for the next hour, sipping coffee and looking on as the gate's waiting area swells with happy Latinos.

Ishy and The Deuce board without incident, and it isn't until they're high above the Caribbean Sea that The Deuce regains his old form. After having spent most of the day in a hungover fog, The Deuce suddenly sits up straight and slaps himself in the face, proclaiming that the interval for "sleeping it off" is officially closed. "We're on our way to fuckin' Peru, man. We need to get us some of those free in-flight drinks, STAT."

Ishy chuckles. "Free drinks?"

The Deuce nods. "Yeah. I love those little fuckin' bottles they give you. Makes me feel like I'm in the movies."

"Have you ever been on an airplane before?"

"Fuckin' guy... I dated a stewardess. Mile-high club, son."

Ishy shakes his head. "I hate to break it to you, Deuce, but they don't really do the free drink thing anymore. Maybe if we were up in first class, or in 1970, but not back here with the great unwashed. Trust me. I fly all the time for work."

"*You fly all the time for work*. What the fuck does that even *mean?* Hey, you see that little cutie making her way down the aisle?"

Ishy follows The Deuce's gaze, acknowledging the existence of the flight attendant.

"Ten bucks says she comps me this first beer."

Ishy smirks. "Too easy. I'll give you 2-to-1 odds."

"Done. Watch and learn, son."

As the flight attendant reaches their row, The Deuce flashes an irresistible smile.

"*Disculpe, señorita. Sería mucha molestia si le pido una cerveza?*"

The girl smiles and pours an ice-cold Corona into a plastic cup, handing it to The Deuce.

"*Muchas gracias, amiga.*"

"*De nada, amigo.*" She gives him a wink before moving to the next row.

Ishy looks like a kid whose uncle just pulled a quarter from behind his ear. "You speak Spanish?"

"I'm a *roofer*. The fuck language you think we speak up there?" The Deuce takes a long sip, smacks his lips, then insists that, by his calculation, this is probably the most refreshing beverage he's ever tasted. He extends a hand, palm up, waiting to collect. "Look around, Ish. Every one of these motherfuckers is sippin' whiskey or some shit like that. You ever seen this many people get shit-faced on your work flights? Acourse the drinks are free!" The Deuce makes a production out of testing Ishy's $20, snapping it a couple times and holding it up to the light for inspection before ramming it into his pocket. "This ain't no business trip. Can't be Bolivious to the particulars."

Ishy is disconsolate for being bested by someone he considers an intellectual inferior. His sullen look prompts The Deuce to howl with delight. His roar increases with each of Ishy's failed attempts to garner the flight attendant's attention, who seems to be making a game out of ignoring him. By her third pass, the flight attendant and The Deuce determine that Ishy has suffered enough. With The Deuce's subtle nod, she looks his way. Ishy sheepishly asks for a Coors Light, and The Deuce orders a double gin and tonic in a way that leaves the attendant blushing.

The plane is one of those older models where communal TVs come down from the ceiling, and the in-flight movie is *The 40-Year-Old Virgin*. Ishy initially thinks this is a controversial choice, considering the cultural diversity and number of small children aboard, but based on the laughter from The Deuce and Peruvians alike, it turns out that Seth Rogen talking about his dick is funny in any language.

While Steve Carell gets his chest waxed, Ishy diligently flips through his *Lonely Planet* guide to double- and triple-check his facts. The conversion rate on money. The average temperature in November. The neighborhoods they're most likely to get robbed in. He turns to the full-color, two-page map of Peru and finds himself staring in amazement: at the thousands of kilometers of beaches along the Pacific coast, the snow-capped mountains of the Cordillera Blanca, the vast arid deserts to the south, and the deep cobalt blue of Lake Titicaca. But of all the terrain, what he marvels at most is the sheer nothingness surrounding Iquitos. Looking at the scaled map, their destination is little more than a dot in an abyss of jungle, flanked by muddy rivers that snake through an entire page of Amazon green.

It is one thing to contemplate vast isolation from the comfort of your King Street condominium; it is another thing to contemplate it while facing the imminence of firsthand experience.

Ishy leans back and takes a deep breath, sliding the book over to The Deuce. "You ever see a map that looks like this?"

The Deuce briefly glances. "Like what?"

Ishy points in the vicinity of Iquitos. "With this much empty space."

The Deuce takes a closer look. "Whole lotta nothin' out there."

Ishy exhales deeply, whispering, "Fuck me."

The Deuce takes the guide to study the map more closely. Ishy notices him concentrating hard, as if visualizing what a slow trip down the Amazon might entail. After some time, The Deuce nods, somehow convinced that they're up for whatever lies ahead.

As The Deuce flips through the *Lonely Planet*, it becomes apparent that this is the first such guide The Deuce has ever come across. Ishy can't help but feel a small sense of pride at the interest he takes in it.

After some time, The Deuce announces, "I think I got it."

"Got what?"

The Deuce wears a big, shit-eating grin. "Listen to this: 'This long-established clubbing haunt plays all the crowd-pleasing favorites and has a well-deserved reputation as a travelers' pick-up joint. Tequila Rocks.' Done and done."

Ishy shakes his head. "Come on, Deuce. You really wanna go all the way to Lima and end up at the local frat house?"

"Did you even hear what I said? 'Well-deserved reputation as a travelers' pick-up joint!' Fuck, Lords. How long has it been since you got your dick wet?"

Ishy laughs, embarrassed. "Too long... You don't even want to know." He punctuates this drought with a sip of beer.

"More than a month?"

Ishy spits his drink all over the seat in front of him, making The Deuce squeal. Regaining his composure while frantically wiping the seat with napkins, Ishy confirms, "Yes, Stan. Most certainly more than a month."

The Deuce considers this dry spell, then asks, "Why don't you just join one of those internet dating sites? Those things are supposed to be a goldmine for pussy."

Ishy takes a long sip. If he's being honest, the thought of meeting a woman online is a little unnerving. "I don't know. I guess you could say I prefer to meet women the analog way."

The Deuce shoots him a confused look. "I once dated a chick who was into that."

Before Ishy can make the connection, The Deuce holds his glass high in the air, calling out, "*Señorita?*" When the attendant arrives, he says, "*Una cerveza para mi amigo el maricón, y un whiskey para mi... Triple, por favor!*"

Ishy looks at him with disgust. "A triple? Really?"

The Deuce slips the flight attendant Ishy's $20 and proudly announces, "Anything less would be uncivilized."

As is almost always the case, The Deuce's good vibes have a way of reaching everyone in his orbit, the sweet glow of alcohol eroding the bounds of social diffidence, and it isn't long before a group huddles around him, laughing and drinking and sharing their best stories. There are a few gringos in the mix, but most are expat Peruvians triumphantly returning home, only adding fuel to the crackling festivities. When the twinkling lights of Lima emerge from the darkness beneath, a Limean in his early 30s gives them a bar recommendation, cautioning, "Be careful out there: Peru has many beautiful women you could fall in love with."

As the plane touches down, it's accompanied by a round of applause, the Peruvians stopping only to cross themselves in thanks. The Deuce, catching Ishy's eye, winks knowingly.

T.S. Eliot wrote that the first condition of understanding a foreign country is to smell it. But it might be said that the first condition of understanding Lima, Peru, is to sit in the backseat of a taxi as it makes its way from the airport to Miraflores on a Friday night.

Ishy and The Deuce are swarmed by cab drivers the moment they step beyond the airport's sliding-glass doors. Unshaven men persist with an endless barrage of "Taxi, *amigo*? Taxi? American, yes?" After checking and double-checking their pockets, they tumble into a backseat with overflowing ashtrays and duct-taped doors. The windshield is cracked, and the seatbelts don't buckle, but the windows roll down and the driver blasts reggaeton beats as they race away.

Ishy and The Deuce's eyes dart from the street bustle to one another as they giddily laugh, unable to believe the smell of diesel and earth and ocean, the noise, the billboards, the lights, the chaos. Traffic is bumper-to-bumper with horns blaring as cars jerk and jockey for position, eating up every available space. A kid juggles fire at an intersection. Stray dogs travel in packs along the sidewalk. An old lady meanders dangerously through the traffic, selling Coca-Cola and cigarettes to outstretched hands.

The streetscape is a looping canvas of neon-lit *pollo a la brasa* joints, glittering casinos, and *Chifas* with names like Who Wah and Jackie Chan. Men huddle on the corner, equal parts jovial and menacing as they sip beer in front of caged-window tiendas while girls in electric sex miniskirts parade with Latina sass through the warm, dark, narcotic Limean night. Meat-grilling on the sidewalk, men barking bootleg DVDs, concrete shoebox apartments that seem toddler-stacked, clothes hanging from lines tethered to balconies, soccer highlights flickering across every TV screen... All of it is an unforgettable feast for the senses.

At one point, their taxi rear-ends another at a stoplight, and both drivers simply wave it off. No insurance, no inspection, no exchange, no problem. In a single exhilarating cab ride, Ishy and The Deuce know they've never been to a place that feels so alive.

The taxi drops them off in front of The Happy Llama Hostel in Miraflores. Avenida Larco, the district's main drag, is hopping with action as Ishy and The Deuce haul their backpacks across the sidewalk and up the long, narrow flight of stairs that constitute the hostel's entrance.

The girl at the front desk greets them with a beautiful smile. Making no attempt at Spanish, Ishy explains that they have reservations under the names Lords and Doucette.

The girl smiles again. "We do not have so many reservations in this place. You are very... How do you say...?"

"Anal-retentive?" The Deuce offers.

"*Prepared*, I think is the word."

"That's exactly right," The Deuce exclaims. "Our little Boy Scout is always prepared!"

Ishy and the girl exchange a knowing look as she takes their passports and shows them to their dorm room.

As the girl heads back to the desk, The Deuce throws his pack on the bottom bunk and says they require cervezas without delay. Citing the little tienda he'd taken note of on the corner, he disappears before giving Ishy a chance to tag along.

Ishy takes the opportunity to dig through his backpack for a clean shirt, shorts, and sandals. After splashing some water on his face, he looks around. The Happy Llama is a quintessential Limean party hostel with the common area overlooking Parque Kennedy. The huge windows are open, filling the place with street noise, and there's a big communal bar with a pool table and foosball. The room's only occupant is a sketchy dreadlocked dude in his underwear. He's splayed across a battered futon, smoking while watching *Die Hard* on the big screen. He nods vaguely in Ishy's direction and makes a half-hearted effort to make space, but Ishy urges him not to get up, wandering over to the window to breathe in the distant sea breeze. Looking down at the street, Ishy wonders how long he'll have to stand there before making it obvious he's vacating the room simply because of the dirtbag's presence.

The girl at the front desk is preoccupied with the computer so doesn't immediately notice Ishy. Her hair is jet black and a length that seems exotic as it falls around her bare shoulders. She bites her lip ever so slightly in concentration, and the intimacy of this glimpse melts Ishy's heart. When she looks up, he smiles, half-embarrassed, and improvises a question regarding check-out procedures before retreating to the safety of his room.

The Deuce eventually bursts through the door, carrying a plastic bag with clanging bottles. "Holy fuck. This place is crazy. There's like a thousand stray cats in the park there, and I gotta say, a park full of pussy is a great fuckin' omen if I ever saw one." The Deuce goes into his bag and produces a 750ml bottle. "Look. This giant beer costs a *buck*. And look at THIS!" He goes into the bag and pulls out a pack of cigarettes. "Lucky Strikes! You can't even get these fuckin' things in Canada. Less than two bucks a pack!"

He lights a cigarette right there and cracks open the beers, handing a Brahma to Ishy before realizing, "Hey, what are you doin' in the room anyway? Let's go shoot some pool, bro. It's Friday night in fuckin' Lima!"

He's out of the room before Ishy can warn him about the near-naked hippie, but it doesn't matter, because, by the time Ishy finds his way back to the common area, The Deuce is already bosom buddies with the guy.

"Hey, Ish, you meet José yet? He's from fuckin' Bogotá. How awesome is that?"

Ishy smiles weakly and sips his beer as The Deuce peppers the guy with questions about cocaine production and drug cartels and soccer riots until José signals *no más* and mutters something about needing a shower.

For the next hour, The Deuce runs Ishy all over the table to the tune of five soles per 8-ball, the stereo playing Michael Jackson and The English Beat. It's strange that the hostel's bar isn't stocked with any staff or alcohol, but neither Ishy nor The Deuce mind, as there's something indescribably South American about popping into the little tienda on the corner for big bottles of cold beer every half-hour.

It's close to 11PM when The Deuce announces, "I believe it is time to procure some snatch."

Despite all The Deuce's sophomoric antics, Ishy can't help but laugh at his phrasing. Sporting a decent Brahma glow, Ishy surprises himself by suggesting, "Why don't we ask the girl at the front desk? I'm sure she'll be able to point your dick in the right direction."

"That's a good call, Lordsy. If memory serves, she's a little coffee 'n' cream cutie. Go warm her up for me. I gotta take a mad piss."

With his confidence bolstered by the big Peruvian beers, Ishy makes his way to the front desk. The girl is still sitting at the computer. She smiles and waves, saying, "*Hola.*"

Ishy smiles and waves, saying, "*Hola*" back.

"This is your first time en Lima, *sí*? Your friend and you?"

"*Sí*. We flew in tonight. This place is *muy, muy* crazy. So loud and... Latin American."

She nods. "And you will go out to the bars now, *sí*?"

"*Sí*. I was going to ask you... We have no idea where we're going. Is there a bar around here you recommend?"

"There are many bars in Miraflores. What kind of bar you are wanting to go?"

The Deuce bulldozes into the room. "We're lookin' for a place we can score a little 'taaaang! You know..." He rapidly pumps his fist, communicating what he considers to be the international sign for sex.

Ishy's ears burn. "No... We're— We just want to go someplace someone like you might go."

"*Claro*," she says, pointing behind her. "Across Parque Kennedy, there is La Calle de las pizzas. Es how you say... a street that is bars?"

Ishy smiles. "A street full of bars. Perfect."

"*Sí. Muchas gringas borrachas para tu amigo*," she says, winking. Her eyes rest upon him an extra beat.

"Hey," Ishy says. "We don't even know your name yet. Como tay yammas?"

The Deuce shoots Ishy a confused look.

She smiles beautifully. "*Mi nombre es Lucía.*"

"Lucia. That's a pretty name." Before he even knows what's happening, Ishy declares, "May goostan toos arrett-ess."

Lucia's eyes shimmer as she blushes. She quickly tucks a strand of hair behind her ear. "*Ah, sí? Que lindo eres...*"

Ishy isn't entirely sure what she's saying, but there's no mistaking the meaning. He leans in close, lowering his voice, "At what time do you finish working here?"

"I am finished at one, but Rolando, the other worker, he comes early some nights, so I can often leave in *media noche*."

"Perfect. Will you come meet us? At the bar in the street of bars?"

She considers this proposition for a moment and smiles coyly. "*Sí*, Mister Eeshmayal from Canada. I will think about it."

Ishy nods slowly. "Alright. I'm gonna write down my phone number for you, so you can find us." Ishy scribbles his cell on the back of a hostel business card and slides it across the desk. "I hope I can see you later."

"*Yo tambien.*"

Stepping into the night, The Deuce jumps up and down, incredulous with excitement. "What the fuck was that? *Cómo te llamas?* And that other thing you said? That was like the fuckin' Jedi mind trick!"

Ishy doesn't have the heart to tell him he'd been practicing Rita's maxim for the past 24 hours and been rifling through a Spanish phrase book he'd come across at the hostel. "What can I say, Stanley? I'm a regular Don Juan down here."

The Deuce howls at the moon, grabbing Ishy in a headlock and practically skipping across the park.

There is no mistaking La Calle de las Pizzas when they arrive. It is literally an alley of bars, teeming with aggressive proprietors promising free pisco sours to every gringo in sight. There are countless ultra-friendly Peruvian women who may or may not be "professionals," and loud music pulsating from every direction. The flashing neon lights are offensive, overwhelming, and awesome. After a quick tour of the alley, Ishy and The Deuce duck into a little watering hole closest to Parque Kennedy.

The room is thick with smoke, the music Queen's "Under Pressure." Ishy is only half-joking when he asks The Deuce which section he prefers: smoking or extra smoking. As their eyes adjust to the haze, they notice that every TV displays a Wembley Stadium crowd eating out of Freddie Mercury's outstretched hand. Neither Ishy nor The Deuce have ever been to an establishment that plays music videos in conjunction with the tunes, but it does the trick, the place bursting with travelers and Peruvians alike.

Grabbing a wobbly table in the corner, Ishy and The Deuce are welcomed by a waitress who promptly puts down a 1 liter *jarra* of ice-cold beer. They neglect to mention they hadn't actually ordered this Godsend, clinking glasses as beer sloshes over the table and hits the absolute fucking spot.

The Deuce sparks a cigarette and sits back to absorb the scene. "This place is the tits, man. I mean, look! There's a jukebox for music videos! That's the greatest fuckin' thing I ever saw."

As if on cue, the keyboard intro of Dire Straits' "Walk of Life" comes pouring through, and the entire bar is treated to a montage of '80s baseball bloopers, somehow instilling a sense of pride in Ishy and The Deuce for their North American lineage.

By the time the second *jarra* comes around, they are on top of the world. Ishy can barely contain his smile as a group of girls scream and dance in a place where tables used to be, Madonna striking a pose on every TV. The nostalgia of the music and the joy of the moment stir some memories in Ishy, and he finds himself asking in a throttled yell, "Hey, Deuce, you ever run into an old crush?"

"Fuck yeah. In high school, I wanted to crush every girl. Run into 'em all the time these days."

Ishy laughs. "Nah, not girls you wanted to sleep with. Girls you had *feelings* for."

"Feelings? Sure. That too."

"For me, it was Mandy Flanagan." Ishy motions to the video on the screen. "She fucking loved Madonna. We were really good friends, but I always hoped we'd be more... The timing was never right, you know? She always had a boyfriend and—in the rare instances she didn't—I would miraculously be dating someone."

The Deuce lights another cigarette.

"I remember being at this party with her in grade 10. We were drinking in the way 15-year-olds do and wound up sitting on the steps of the backyard deck, just the two of us. I had my arm around her to keep her warm, and there was a full moon hanging low in the sky... It was the perfect moment to make my move, right? That was my chance... But I couldn't bring myself to do it."

The Deuce is shaking his head in disgust. "What a fuckin' pussy you are, Lords."

"Guess I figured there would be other opportunities. I was dating some forgettable girl, and faithfulness or loyalty or something wouldn't allow me to make that move, even though everything in my 15-year-old body was urging me..."

"...to give 'er the ol' Jolly Roger?"

Ishy nods as if it would have been possible. "I ran into her last week for the first time in about 10 years."

The Deuce perks up. "Oh yeah? How'd she look?"

"She looked fucking great, man. Better than ever. But here's the thing: She's married to this French guy, Francois, or something, and he's just... I mean, I'm not saying I'm George Clooney or anything, but I've got more going on than that fucking guy, you know? And it's like... All those times I hesitated to let her know how I felt because I was afraid that she wouldn't feel the same, or she was out of my league, or I didn't want to hurt anyone's feelings... and then she ends up with some fucking *French douche bag?*"

The Deuce laughs his ass off and though Ishy is still disgusted with his 15-year-old self, he can't help but guffaw. The Deuce puts an arm around Ishy and says, "You shoulda fucked her at that party, dude. Fortune favors the brave. Always. Allow me to demonstrate. You see that girl over there?" The Deuce points his glass past the dancing drunk girls to where the object of his affection stands alone at the bar.

Ishy takes a long swig of beer. "Which? The blonde?"

The Deuce nods defiantly. "That little surfer girl. She's coming home with me tonight. Fact." He slams the rest of his beer and springs from the seat, making his way through the smoky haze.

The girl is devastating up close, with a body that could make you forget who you are for a very long time. But The Deuce is undaunted. He's seen this movie before: a girl so breathtakingly beautiful that guys are too intimidated or too drunk to charm. But The Deuce happens to be residing in the sweet spot in-between. Stepping up to the bar, he motions for the tender to bring him *dos cervezas*. He matter-of-factly turns and asks, "What's your name?"

Without looking, she answers with an accent, "Simone."

"Tell me, Simone, What does a guy like me need to do to bring a girl like you home tonight?"

She turns to him, smiling coyly. "Buy me a drink. Sing me a song. Take me as I come, 'cause I can't stay long."

For the first time in his life, The Deuce is speechless.

She motions to the two large bottles of Cusqueña on the bar. "One of those for me, mate?"

"What can I say? I'm a loser at the top of my game."

She grabs both bottles and hands him one, tapping the neck of hers to his. "I have to go to Máncora tomorrow... I hope that isn't a problem."

The Deuce nods. "They don't call me One Night Stan for nothin'."

"Well then," taking him by the hand, she says, "if you're planning to shag me within an inch of my life, I guess you'd better introduce me to you friends."

The Deuce follows her gaze across the room, through the noise and myriad drunken, bouncing bodies, only to be momentarily overcome with the feeling of paternal pride as his eyes settle upon Lucia, sitting at the table next to Ish.

12

Before: Aug. 14ᵗʰ, 2003

Lower Manhattan

The thing about a power outage is that we assume the power will come back on. We assume that the world we've come to accept as absolute, with systems we've taken for granted, will be restored. We assume that there is an inverse correlation between the duration without electricity and the moment that electricity will return. But if one happens to be stuck on an elevator the moment the grid separates, our understanding of time begins to bend in unanticipated ways.

Ishy spends fractions of that first second subconsciously calculating his chances of survival, and the next three seconds believing that he's going to die. Acutely aware that this building is only two blocks and 23 months removed from the World Trade Center attack, he takes an indefinable amount of time to consider whether this might be another act of terrorism.

He takes a few deep breaths. He spends 10 seconds looking at his phone, before realizing there's no reception in these brutalist concrete elevator banks. He looks at his watch: 4:11PM. He spends 30 seconds taking in his surroundings, to truly look at the people he's sharing this surreal space with. There is fear on their faces. Ishy makes eye contact and raises his eyebrows to some, as if to say, *Can you believe this?*

He takes the next 15 seconds to determine their position within the elevator shaft.

Someone makes a joke that isn't funny, but everyone laughs because this is a situation that demands levity in any form. Someone starts yelling, "Hello! *Helloooooooo!*" while hoisting himself up to bang on the ceiling.

Ishy takes the next four uneasy minutes to become uncomfortably aware of how claustrophobic an elevator is when you're trying not to think this exact thought.

Someone spends 45 futile seconds trying and re-trying the call button. Then he presses the alarm. Incessant ringing begins.

For 20 seconds, Ishy wonders if there's a security camera, whether the cameras work when the power is out, and how discernable this group's panic would be in grainy black-and-white. He takes 135 seconds to avoid thinking about the time dissipating from his life, then considers this: If matter can be neither created nor destroyed, what happens to time when it disappears?

Ishy smacks himself in the face and mutters something about getting a grip. He wonders how hot it can get in an elevator with eight people stuck somewhere between the 18th and 19th floor on a 90-degree day in New York City, about how much oxygen is in one of these little boxes, and if the cracks in the door allow sufficient air circulation. He debates removing his suit jacket.

Intervals of time begin to lose shape, becoming more fluid and less defined. He wonders how long it will be until someone freaks out. As if on cue, a lady he recognizes starts unraveling. Her breathing is erratic. She mumbles some mantra that's failing her in her hour of need. She kneels on the floor and puts her head between her knees.

Ishy knows that if he sees this woman again, it will never be the same. He looks at his watch. They've been stuck for a full 43 minutes. He considers the possibility that the power might not come back at all.

And this is precisely when the group begins to make things happen.

Ishy isn't the one to suggest it, but he's unequivocally onboard. He thinks to press the STOP button just in case, but people are already pressing against the elevator's back wall. So, Ishy and some goon from the trading floor go to work prying open the doors, not giving a single fuck whether this might disable or disconnect the elevator from its cables. The trading floor hooligan speaks for the entire group when he says, "I'd rather die than spend another fucking second in this tinderbox coffin."

It doesn't take much effort once they've shattered the glass ceiling between "Do not, under any circumstances, compromise the operating and safety integrity of the elevator," and "We're getting the fuck out of here!" They pry open the doors and help one another climb onto the 19th floor, find the emergency stairwell, then descend in relative calm before spilling out into the bedlam of Vesey Street.

Ishy can't get away from the building fast enough. After putting a couple blocks between himself and his office, he checks his phone again, only to find there's no signal. He looks at his watch and notes it's 5:13: the heart of rush hour.

The West Side Highway is an absurdist comedy about 50,000 people in 50,000 cars trying to access a closed tunnel on the hottest day of the year. Gridlock. Cars idling. The look of defeat in the eyes of every driver. People yelling and cursing and honking horns. A man in a BMW shakes his head as his engine overheats, his designer shirt suctioned with sweat to his arm as it dangles out the window.

Some people gather around a parked car, listening to news on the radio. In an act comically out of character, Ishy nods towards a black man in soaked coveralls and asks, "What's the word?"

"Power gone clear to Canada, my man."

Ishy's heart sinks.

There's a payphone on the corner, but the line of people waiting to use it is a dozen deep. He absolutely needs to check on his girlfriend, Samantha, in Toronto to ensure that she's alright. He's still wracked with guilt from taking this job in New York after she accepted an internship in Toronto, leaving her alone in a city where she knows virtually no one.

But the despondency on the faces of those waiting to use the phone is impossible to ignore. Standing in the sweltering street, still in his suit after having spent the worst part of an hour trapped with stifling, recycled air and sweaty bodies, something inside says he needs to get moving. Before realizing he's shirking his responsibilities, Ishy finds himself running away from that phone booth as he dances between unmoving traffic.

Toronto

The Deuce has been sleeping for close to three hours, the soft summer breeze tickling the curtains that hung across his window. From the quiet darkness of his basement apartment on Macklem Avenue, he's oblivious to the fact that his city is immersed in the biggest blackout North America has ever seen.

Lower Manhattan

Six blocks from his office, Ishy finds a street vendor selling bottles of water. He purchases two, knocking each back in a single tilt. He thanks the man and takes a deep breath, feeling the humanity slowly seeping back in. He considers the condition of his suit jacket—the only decent one he's ever owned—now soaked through with sweat.

Ishy fondly remembers the day his father took him to buy it before moving to New York. The two of them rode the subway down to the Harry Rosen on Bloor Street and spent the afternoon talking to the salesman about how important it is for an aspiring business tycoon to have a quality sport coat, how to wear it and with what, the meticulous measurements. While the tailor fixed it just so, Ishy and his dad had gone to a little café in Yorkville, where Lamborghinis and Ferraris lined the block. It didn't register at the time, but, standing on the corner now, Ishy recognizes the day as a rite of passage between father and son before setting out to make his way in the world.

As they sipped cappuccinos in that café, the advice his dad had given him was: "Will it to fruition and be ruthless in pursuit."

Ishy had vowed that afternoon to learn the ropes, hence his temporary New York state of mind, and his summer spent apprenticing with Wall Street douchebags no one would let within a hundred yards of their sister.

And now, on this day, even though he's aware how ridiculous it is to wear a jacket in the sweltering heat, Ishy simply cannot bring himself to take it off. Like a security blanket with a thread that goes all the way back to Toronto, Ishy convinces himself that, as crazy as this whole day is, it isn't crazy enough to abandon the one material item that keeps him tethered to his dad.

At the best of times, Canal Street is a fish-smelling whorehouse clusterfuck, but today it's unlike anything Ishy has ever seen. Bodies mingling with Detroit steel in the kind of street chaos typically reserved for the squalid metropolises of Southeast Asia. City buses that New Yorkers would typically thumb their nose at suddenly inundate with humanity. Lunatics atop milk crates preach about the afterlife. A barefoot bum directs traffic in the middle of the street, waving some cars through while giving others the STOP hand. The flapping of his scraggly hair accentuates his vigor. Ishy doesn't know what's more impressive: that this guy has the confidence to control Broadway traffic, or that no driver questions his frantic commands.

Ishy turns up Mercer Street. The glittering spires of the Chrysler Building and art gallery streetscape pull him north. The thrill of cobblestone keeps him going as he walks in the middle of the street, simply because he can.

As he rounds NYU, he runs through rudimentary calculations: If there are 20 blocks in a mile, and he's 163 blocks from his apartment, he has just over eight miles of hiking ahead. Eight miles in the blistering heat, assuming he can walk a straight line all the way home. Ishy chuckles, shaking his head. If there's anything he's learned this afternoon, it's that straight lines exist in theory alone, and Woody Allen had it right in saying, "If you want to make God laugh, tell him about your plans."

As if on cue, Ishy notices a parade of taxis parked along Washington Place. Intrigued by the sight, he hangs a left, following the line of empty cars. As he makes his way through the park, to his utter disbelief, he comes across a young man seated at a baby grand piano, right there in the middle of the sidewalk. Like a scene out of a movie, the man plays the most peaceful music Ishy has ever heard. Ishy stands awestruck in the shade with a small gathering of people. They listen intently, sharing this serene gift of music and moment amid the chaos of a powerless city. The woman beside him pulls a tissue from her purse to dab her eyes.

When the man finishes, there are polite applause and whispers of congratulations. Ishy digs into his pocket for a dollar, approaching the piano and dropping the money into the man's briefcase. As he does so, Ishy says, "That was quite something. Do you mind my asking what the name of that piece was?"

"Not at all." The young man glances at his sheet music. "It looks like 'Air #4' by Edvard Grieg."

Ishy slowly nodded, making a mental note. "Thanks, man. Beautiful stuff." With a smile, he walks up to Washington Square Fountain, no longer spouting but indubitably present. Amidst bare-chested children and chattering cabbies, Ishy joins the cast of New

Yorkers by removing his suit jacket, shoes, and socks, placing them along the ledge. He wades knee-deep into the chill, dunking his head into the water.

After luxuriating in the cool a few minutes, Ishy dries his feet, slips on his shoes, grabs his suit jacket, and exits the park at West 4th Street. He feels the pull of disorientation that befalls every tourist and fledgling New Yorker wandering the disjointed West Village streets. Regardless of whether he's walking the most direct path, Ishy decides the tree-lined streets and stately brownstones cast in slanted afternoon light are too picturesque to abandon. From late nights spent on the couch with Samantha and her housemates, Ishy recognizes this neighborhood as the stomping grounds of Carrie Bradshaw, and although he secretly loves every block of it, his feet begin to scream, and he feels—for the first time in his young life—in *need* of a beer.

Cue the Frank Sinatra as he turns a corner and stumbles upon a group in business attire, disheveled and drinking directly from bottles as they sit on stoops. The entire scene is carefree in a way Ishy has always unknowingly yearned for. He approaches the rowdy group and notices three speakeasy steps carved out of the sidewalk, descending to a door hidden between two brownstones.

Ishy smiles as he makes his way down the stairs, walking through a propped door with CANNERY ROW scrawled above. It takes him a moment to adjust to the subterranean darkness, but the space soon reveals itself as long and narrow with a low, cozy ceiling. The bar runs the length of the room with a few tiny tables scattered near the back. A couple of small candles flicker next to bottles of whiskey lined like trophies. The walls are hung with black-and-white photos depicting a 1930s Monterey, and a shelf along the ceiling houses vintage canned goods, their labels showing the full spectrum of colors and non-perishable preferences of a generation, from Early June Peas to Eatwell Mackerel. The sawdust strewn across the floor only partially eliminates the tack of spilled beer. In the corner is a dusty bookshelf displaying many great works of American fiction. It's the kind of place you could lose yourself and your problems, maybe for a little while, maybe forever.

The room is empty but for the barkeep, who catches Ishy's gaze.

Noticing a phone on the wall behind him, Ishy reaches for his wallet. "Does your phone work?"

"Amazingly, yeah. Nothin' on tap, no A/C, freezer's dyin' a slow death, but the phone works clear as a bell."

Ishy places a bill on the bar. "I'll give you $20 if I can borrow your phone two minutes. Honestly, man, I'm dying here."

The bartender smiles. "Put the money away. It's all yours."

Ishy scampers behind the bar like he's been granted access behind the velvet rope. After dialing Samantha on the old rotary, the call redirects to a message indicating that all circuits are down, followed by a busy signal. Ishy laughs through the word, "Fuck." He tries again, knowing her cell is as useless as his. He dials his parents, but the phone just rings.

He considers his options. His first thought is his oldest and most reliable friend, but Rosy is in England for the summer, studying London's urban plan as part of a university exchange program. And all Ishy's Toronto-based co-workers are young, urban cell users, off the grid, and undoubtedly soaking in the jovial chaos of their own powerless city.

Ishy only knows one other landline by heart, and it's as last-ditch desperate as it gets. He can't believe he's spinning the dial, even as the rotary wheel twists in reverse.

"Sun-Storm 2003, MUTHAFUCKAAAAA!"

Ishy only shakes his head. "Hello, Deuce."

"Ish-man? Where the fuck you at?"

"Some bar in the West Village."

"Like your style, my man. Little out of character for you, but maybe you're learnin' a thing or two down there."

"Listen, Deuce, I need you to do me a huge favor."

Silence.

"Deuce?"

"...Yeah, man."

Ishy takes a deep breath. "I need you to go to Samantha's. I need you to check on her. She doesn't really know anyone in the city. I just want you to go over and make sure she's alright." The request hangs in the air a beat too long.

"You got it, dawg. Shoot me her address. I'll get on my steed."

Ishy places the phone back in its perch and feels physical relief. He exhales and forces a smile, nodding to the bartender and mumbling thanks. He crosses back over to the patron's side and orders a Coors Light before walking into the vibrato of the street. He finds a place on the steps between people as they take turns buying rounds of increasingly sweaty beers and watching the spectacle of the sun setting over a powerless Manhattan.

The West Village scene is unreal: An old Malibu with the ragtop rolled back blasts salsa music while barefoot women dance in the street, foregoing their torturous heels for tequila sours and a taste of New York that only exists in movies. Wall Street brokers do their best *Fresh Prince* impressions, wearing their ties as headbands, throwing a football around West 4th, and calling out to one another like they go way back beyond this afternoon. Some kids open a fire hydrant and everyone, young and old, takes turns dousing their heads and wetting their toes in the gathering pool. Some dudes drag down barrel drums from a hidden rooftop so they can grill on the street, bringing the wistful smell of charcoal as they announce, "Everythin' must go. Ain't no meat that won't be eat."

All the while, the sky puts on the oldest show ever known, transforming into spellbinding shades of pink and pumpkin, the brownstones and blacktop drinking in the light, the west eventually divulging in the gathering dusk like an iron rod left too long in a fire.

When the sun is buried and gone, Ishy is treated to a chargrilled steak on hunks of fresh bread, two hotdogs dipped in mustard, seven bottles of gloriously warm beer, and the most electrifying bout of human contact he's ever experienced. The people he shared the sunset with say their goodbyes and vow to stay in touch, scribbling their numbers and Hotmail addresses on the inside of Cannery Row matchbooks. An older gentleman sets his hand on Ishy's shoulder and Ishy chokes back tears. The man laughs and does the same, then Ishy sets off into the night, meandering toward 7th Avenue before heading north.

Toronto

It's been years since The Deuce dusted off his skateboard. The reasons are obvious and plentiful: He's 24 and in possession of a valid driver's license. But there's no denying his regret for relinquishing the youthful habit. And so, with no better way to track down Ishy's girl, The Deuce digs out his old Metropolitan with a naked woman painted on the deck. He slips on a pair of torn Chuck Taylors and hit the blistering streets, the Beasties blasting on loop from the boombox in his head.

Swerving around sweaty pedestrians and eerily stopped-in-place streetcars, The Deuce winds through asphalt cracks and trolley tracks, wheels rumbling along College and Dundas, youth rediscovered on a wooden deck. He roars past Ossington Avenue and Trinity-Bellwoods to the foot of Kensington Market.

There's no rush, so now seems a good time to test if he can keep up with the locals. He shreds with the groms at the Bathurst Street skate park and—after showing him how much he'd forgotten over the years—they invite him to sit on the warm curb. The Deuce tells stories of what this place was like in the '90s, the group of them smoking cigarettes and playing Hacky Sack while taking in the last of the sun as it disappeared behind the Chinatown semis.

The Deuce hops back on his board and backtracks the last half mile stretch of Dundas Street, where families in plastic chairs line the sidewalk, the noodle joints yielding to Little Portugal's flower shops and Virgin Mary shrines. Devoid of electricity and A/C, the crowd at The Communist's Daughter spills onto the street, appropriating the corner and annexing the streetcar frozen mid-turn. The Deuce scorches down Ossington Avenue, where mechanics in dirty coveralls sit on stacks of tires, drinking homemade wine from grease-stained jars.

The Deuce locates the address, a three-story walk-up cornering a graffitied alley. He looks up at the vacant, unlit windows. Even though he's certain Ishy's girl is inside, he can't bring himself to knock on her door in the grainy light of dusk.

He makes tracks over to Dovercourt Road, with its Victorian houses, towering elms, and the Cuban place with a leafy patio set back from the street, so he could smoke and drink *cerveza fria* in contemplative silence as the night gathers soft and slow.

Midtown

Since stumbling away from Cannery Row and escaping the West Village, Ishy cracks off the blocks with exacting efficiency, heading north along 7th Avenue and stopping only to knock back waters two-at-a-time. With darkness now set in, he sees hotels roping off sections of sidewalk for the overflow of stranded patrons. The sight of well-to-do homeowners from Oyster Bay and Westchester County preparing to spend the night on the street makes Ishy wonder if this blackout could be permanent, that in some messed up and yet-to-be-revealed way, this could be the new world order. The thought, fleeting as it is, changes his perception.

Ernest Hemmingway wrote that it's awfully easy to be hard-boiled about everything in the daytime, but at night it's another thing entirely. Now that Ishy considers it, Gotham's darkness is a little disconcerting: walking the gauntlet of towers as shadows, the headlights of cars disproportionately bright as they silhouette pedestrians with slasher flick abruptness. The people on the afternoon streets looked good-natured, but, as they all fade to black, they draw inward, huddling in groups and speaking in hushed tones. In the absence of cell phone distraction and flashing light fluorescence, the senses become acutely attuned, and it isn't so easy to be boisterous in the glorious Bowery style.

Ishy catches snippets of conversations:

"My knees are gettin' shaky, you know?"

"Gotta drink more watta."

"What's the longest you figure you can go without coffee?"

"Feels like I'mma get fucked outta somethin' at some point."

It isn't until Ishy hears a lady remarking that she can't believe she's looking up at the stars from Times Square that he realizes he's standing at the Crossroads of the World. He stops. Above the *Phantom of the Opera* billboards and beyond the darkened screens, the sky is brilliant with galaxies speckled like pixie dust across a velvet canvas.

"Apparently though, on August 14th, you can see Mars."

Ishy takes a seat on the curb, hands on his knees. It's hard to believe this is the same place that inspired Richard Price to write his famous "keys on the jizz-soaked peepshow floor" passage, or where Ishy went his first day in NYC.

On that warm afternoon in May, Ishy had rushed to the subway, giddy with anticipation. As if drawn there by human kinetic energy, he hopped off at 42nd Street and climbed the steps into the awe-inspiring afternoon chaos of Times Square. Mouth agape, he bought himself an "I (heart) NY" T-shirt and some Nuts 4 Nuts honey roasters, settling on The Olive Garden like a tourist to gorge on all-you-can-eat soup, salad, and breadsticks with a view of the pandemonium below. That unforgettable Saturday had been only three months ago, but it felt like another lifetime.

After popping into the ESPN Zone, he took the subway uptown. As the train jerked through 120 tunneled blocks, nearly to the northernmost tip of Manhattan, Ishy had grown tired staring out the window. At first, all he saw was the darkness of the tunnel, the closeness of the walls and the earth as it screamed past.

When the train emerged from underground and into the Manhattan Valley Viaduct, afternoon light poured in: blinding, warm, welcoming, and unpleasant all at once. It was only when the train went back underground at 135th Street that Ishy noticed he was not only staring into the darkness, but into the light; he was staring *outside* at the walls of blackened earth, and *inside* at the reflection the window, the darkness, and the light were creating. He was mesmerized by this discovery, and realized that, if he concentrated, he could simultaneously see the darkness and the light, the tunnel and the train, the outside and the inside. He was staring out into the darkness from inside the light, like magic.

Toronto

It's well after 10PM when The Deuce stumbles away from the Cuban joint, determining he's had two too many beverages. So, with his old Metropolitan under his arm, The Deuce walks three blocks back to Ossington Avenue.

Before gentrification, this was not the neighborhood you wanted to be stranded in at night. As The Deuce walks the dark, deserted streets, he begins to appreciate the frantic concern of Ishy's phone call.

Samantha's building is one of those urban, turn-of-the-century Toronto walk-ups with commercial storefronts yielding to nondescript doors. The main door The Deuce is searching for is locked, and the intercom for her unit—like everything else along the eastern seaboard—is dead. The Deuce exhales audibly, whispers, "Fuck me," and walks back onto the sidewalk to gather pebbles. Not having a clue which apartment is hers, he tosses tiny rocks at every third-floor window like he's back in high school, trying to score some tail.

The combination of open windows and The Deuce's drunken motor skills results in a handful of pebbles pelting the bedroom of a large man in a stained undershirt, who kindly asks The Deuce to fuck off. With the law of unintended consequences in full effect, the commotion draws everyone to their windows. Scanning the silhouettes, The Deuce recognizes her shadow.

"Samantha?"

"Who is that?"

"It's Stan. Ish's buddy. The Deuce?"

Five seconds of silence. Then, "What're you doing here?"

The Deuce starts to laugh as he realizes how bizarre turning up on her sidewalk must look. "Ahhh, I'm not really sure. Ish asked me to check on you. You know, see how you're doing?"

More silence.

Nobody has vacated their windows. In the absence of television, this exchange must constitute high drama. "So, ahhh. Do you mind if I come up for a minute?"

As he says it, the door to Samantha's building swings open with a young man heading into the night. The Deuce catches the door before it locks shut, shouting behind him, "Don't *worry*, I got it!" He climbs the creaky stairs, his Zippo lighting the way. Knocking with unaccustomed formality on 3B, he hears the click of the lock, Samantha opening the door with a degree of caution.

The Deuce always finds it thrilling to enter a young lady's apartment for the first time, and tonight is no exception. Candles flicker on the kitchen table and a few others yawn from the window ledge. The soft light falls perfectly around her.

It has been close to a year since The Deuce has seen her: a night out in Kingston with Ishy, Rosy, and some college buddies, where they drank until closing at a Princess Street dive, romping back through the wet, autumn streets and depositing into the house occupied by Samantha and her smokeshow housemates. Rosy, Ishy, and The Deuce had sat on the floor, listening to Neil Young, Bob Dylan, and early Springsteen records as they debated the merits of rock and roll lyrics versus contemporary poetry at increasing levels of volume and vulgarity. The Deuce vaguely recalled Samantha and her housemates looking at them in captivated horror and morbid curiosity. The night ended with The Deuce falling into bed with one of Samantha's housemates, but not before Rosy and he Sharpied across the wall what they believed to be the most profound revelation they would ever know: **Walk tall... Or, baby, don't walk at all...**

Tonight, she wears a white halter top and grade-A booty shorts, her blond hair tied up and sweat glistening on her fit, little body. The Deuce absorbs it in an instant: the warm candlelight, the verdant breeze coming through the open windows, the blackout vibe of uncertainty, the taste of pheromones mixed with the unmistakable scent of a girl's apartment, a summer almost spent.

He knows he's in trouble.

They exchange pleasantries: "This blackout is pretty fuckin' crazy" and "You managin' to keep cool?" He explains that Ishy can't get a hold of her but wants to ensure she's alright. Once the small talk evaporates, there's silence. It's long, intended, and palpable. In the absence of anything else, The Deuce asks Samantha if she has anything to drink.

"What did you have in mind?"

"Anything flammable."

She says she has white wine in the refrigerator, so he opens it and pours a couple glasses.

"How you diggin' Toronto?"

The apartment is a blast furnace.

"You ever hit up Sweaty Betty's? Decent little joint down the street here."

She's as closed off as any girl he can remember.

"I ever tell you about the time Ishy and I drove to Montreal to get some poutine?"

He's sweating his ass off. After 15 minutes, he asks if there's any place cooler they can go.

They climb out her bedroom window and onto the fire escape, bottle of wine in hand. It's the ideal place for small departures, the night air like a spot in the shade and lilacs on the breeze. They sit on the metal steps for a long time, the sky winking like fireflies.

Eventually, The Deuce asks, "So how'd you end up in Toronto, anyway? I mean, don't get me wrong, I love it here, but Montreal in the summertime is the fuckin' tits: Peel Pub, Schwartz's, Super Sex... What the hell could be better than that?"

Samantha laughs. "Well, for starters, nobody from Montreal actually goes to the Peel Pub. The thought of smoked meat makes me want to vomit. And if I was looking to subject myself to STDs and the female exploitation in the establishments you Ontario boys frequent, I'd at least have the decency to do so at Wanda's."

The Deuce nods, impressed.

Samantha takes a quick sip. "But the truth? I came here because I wanted to be with Ishmael."

The Deuce whistles, long and descending. "Damn, girl. I don't know what's worse: the fact that you abandoned La Belle Province to hang with Ish, or that your boy jumped ship." He shakes his head, then goes to his pocket for cigarettes. He feels her eyes as he pulls them out, so he offers one.

She knows she shouldn't, but rules don't apply on a night like this.

His lighter illuminates the scene, and the two of them lean back, smoking in contemplation.

After a while, The Deuce asks, "So how did it all go down, exactly? With you and Ish livin' in foreign cities? How the fuck did that conversation go?"

Samantha nods. "Believe it or not, that wasn't the plan I contrived. My hope was that the two of us would be living here together. For some reason, I felt like we should see if this relationship was going somewhere beyond university life. I figured being out here in the real world—if that's what you call this—would be a whole other thing... So I came to Toronto during reading week and was able to land a summer job at Nesbitt Burns. I assumed Ishmael would have his choice of internships." There's another long pause.

"And New York?"

Samantha choses her words carefully. "I didn't even know he was applying down there."

The Deuce nods knowingly. He grabs the bottle of wine and pours her another glass.

Harlem

The Upper East Side is a breeze, like life up there always seems. Ishy decides to eschew Central Park for the relative safety of Madison Avenue. He hums along at the breakneck pace of a block a minute, not stopping until he reaches 110th Street, less than an hour after leaving Times Square.

He has been carrying his suit jacket since the West Village, but now he puts it on to make himself look bigger and tougher. He moves his wallet to his front pocket because he knows he isn't. He keeps his head down and his footwork swift, not daring to look anyone in the eye. As a gangly, 21-year-old Canadian walking the unlit streets of Harlem, he's terrified.

His anxious ramble up Madison Avenue brings him to Marcus Garvey Park, and a moonlit basketball game in the shadows of Mount Morris. In the absence of electricity, it's hard to beat a rim-rattling street game on a hot, sticky night. Ishy guesses there are close to 500 people taking in the action, their fingers peeking through chain-link. Ishy knows he sticks out as a white guy, but carves out a spot along the fence, nonetheless.

The action on the court is fast and furious: a veritable highlight reel of "Skip to My Lou" handles and no-look passes. The trash talk makes one cooler simply by witnessing it, and it's interrupted only by the roar of the crowd after thunderous dunks and Mutombo-style rejections. After a particularly violent flush, the man next to Ishy turns to give him a stank-face nod of approval. This small gesture makes Ishy feel more like a New Yorker than he could ever articulate.

It isn't long before one team closes out the other on a long, chain-clanging two. As the players slap sweaty palms, Ishy makes his way over to the drinking fountain. As the water cools his parched throat, a little girl saunters beside him, curiously watching this outsider drink long and deep. When he finishes, he looks down and remarks how good the water tastes.

The little girl, suddenly shy, scampers back to the bench, climbing onto her father's knee. Ishy hears her ask, "Daddy, what makes water?"

The man smiles. "I'll have to think about that one, kiddo."

Ishy stands there with his hands behind his head, fingers locked in a pose that lets him rest and half-stretch. He's close enough to hear their quiet conversation, drawn to it, as if catching a glimpse of his future.

The little girl looks up at her dad and asks, "What's thinking made of?"

This one really throws the man for a loop and Ishy smiles. The man sees it and gives him a welcoming look.

Ishy nods in the little girl's direction. "Cute kid."

The man laughs with pride. "She's somethin'." He makes space on the bench. "Grab a seat. You look like you could use it."

In a million years, Ishy would never have imagined taking up a stranger's seat invite after midnight, but this day exists beyond those parameters. He concedes that he could use such a seat.

He sits at the end of the bench, his body weary and grateful for the rest. The dad still has the little girl on his knee. His wife sits beside them with a baby in her arms, and she smiles warmly in his direction. "Some day, huh?"

"I've never seen anything like it."

She nods. "When I was a little girl, this is how I remember summer being. Everyone outside all the time, together, talking late into the night with no place else to be."

The notion dips Ishy in deep pools of nostalgia, but before he can formulate the words to explain his childhood, the little girl pipes up again.

"Mommy, when you were a little girl, where was I?"

Ishy laughs, apologizing.

The mother takes a deep breath, and says, "I guess you were in my tummy."

The little girl hasn't even thought it through when she points at her baby brother and asks, "But where was Liam?"

The mother gives her husband a knowing look and sheepishly says, "I guess he was in my tummy, too."

The little girl's eyes open as wide as the moon. "TOGETHER? WHAAAAAT? And I was kicking him and pushing him!"

The mother and father burst out laughing, and the mother adds, "Yes, when I was a little girl, you were both in there together. But you were both very small."

"VERY small," echoes the dad, laughing some more.

Ishy shakes his head and half-whispers about how awesome this all is: the curiosity, the questions, the way the world appears to a three-year-old.

The five of them savor the night as they look up at the stars. In the distance, Ishy can hear the delighted squeals of kids as they splash in the swimming pool beyond the courts.

After a time, Ishy gets to his feet and says, "Well, I still have a long walk ahead of me."

"Where to?"

"163rd."

The dad exhales. "Best of luck, my man."

"Thanks. And thanks for the seat. I really needed that. You have a beautiful family."

"Thanks for saying so." The dad looks at his daughter. "Say goodbye, Lulu."

The little girl clumsily waves. "Bye-bye."

Ishy feels his heart melt, followed by a dull ache in his throat. He waves goodbye and turns to leave. As he does so, he hears the little girl ask, "Daddy, what is light made of?"

The dad sighs, long and laborious. "A shadow's shadow is the light, young lady."

Toronto

Alone on the fire escape under that pincushion sky, Samantha and The Deuce near the point of plausible deniability. She sits close enough to feel the heat pulsing through his body and considers resting her head on his shoulder.

"How long you and Ish been together, anyway?"

"Two-and-a-half years."

The Deuce thinks for a moment. "Isn't it a little fucked-up that you and I barely ever had a conversation until tonight?"

Samantha gives him a look somewhere between coy and contemplation. "I wouldn't exactly call it fucked-up. Self-preservation, maybe."

The Deuce raises his eyebrows.

"I've seen you in action with the ladies. Heard the stories, witnessed the carnage."

"What? Your roommate?"

"Yes. Getting to know my roommate in the Biblical sense didn't help, but believe me, your reputation preceded you."

The Deuce shoots her a sideways look.

"Ishmael and Roosevelt have been known to chronicle your exploits."

The Deuce tries imagining to what extent they'd enlightened her.

"There was also a girl by the name of Vicki LaFontaine."

He thinks a moment. "Rings a bell. Western University girl, right? Saugeen Hall?"

"That's the one."

He smiles as the memory cascades back. "She was a little demon in the sack."

"She's also my cousin. And you were her first."

There's a long silence. The Deuce finally admits, "If I had to guess, I'd say she wasn't altogether thrilled by the post-coital treatment, huh?"

Samantha laughs bitterly. "That would be an understatement." After some time, she says, "Do you know what all my friends call you?"

"They can call me anytime." His ego knows no bounds.

"When you're *not* around?"

"Hit me with it."

"The Douche."

Stanley Doucette bursts out laughing. "*Shiiiiit.* The Douche? That's cold, girl... Fair, probably accurate, but cold." He continues to laugh heartily. When he finishes, the space between them fills with a quiet unease and the prospect of eye contact.

Samantha clears her throat, asks if he wants more wine.

"Absa-fuckin-lutely"

She climbs through the window, leaving The Deuce with his thoughts. He marvels at the predicament. He's been the headliner in this production too many times not to know where it leads. Vulnerable girl. Extenuating circumstances. Perfect summer night. Plenty of cheap wine.

He's in the process of reciting that scene from *Pulp Fiction* where John Travolta is alone in Marsellus Wallace's bathroom—"So... You're gonna go out there and you're gonna say, 'Goodnight, I've had a very lovely evening.' Walk out the door. Get in the car. Go home. Jerk off. And that's all you're gonna do"—when Samantha climbs back onto the fire escape, $8 bottle in hand.

She unscrews the cap and hands it to him.

The Deuce doesn't hesitate, taking a long swig. "I kiss the bottle and it tastes like more."

Samantha smiles and takes a swig of her own. She looks at him now. "Correct me if I'm wrong, but didn't you used to be a hockey player or something?"

He nods, taking back the bottle.

"Ishy goes on and on about what it was like to watch you play when you were younger. Sometimes, I think he has a crush on you. What is it about hockey that gives you boys a little tickle in your trousers?"

The Deuce takes another sip. "Don't even get me started on that one. I could sit here all night and wax poetic about the sound your skates make when they dig into the ice, or the thrill of an odd-man rush. The way a slapshot echoes off the boards in an empty rink at six in the morning... But, at the end of the day, I think it's just the team showers that do it for us."

Samantha laughs and feigns disgust before reclaiming the bottle. "I'm serious. Even growing up in Montreal, I never understood the obsession you guys have with hockey."

The Deuce nods. "I think it's just something that gets passed down from parents to their kids. All those early mornings together, long drives across frozen landscapes with just the two of you in the car, the time it takes to put on your equipment when you're a little kid. The memories are built-in, you know? A cold rink and a Tim Horton's coffee... It's the one constant while everything else changes."

"So, what happened with you? Ishy tells me you barely play anymore."

The Deuce takes out his cigarettes again, this time digging out a perfectly rolled joint. With raised eyebrows, he makes an offer she can't refuse. Flicking his lighter, the flame dances within his cupped hand and catches the little two-paper. He inhales hard, the sweet taste of dank marijuana filling his lungs. He gives it another pull and hands it to Samantha, watching the smoke roll off his tongue and unfurl into magnificent patterns before dissipating into the backdrop of stars.

Samantha overreaches her hit and violently coughs. They laugh as they chase it with wine. She smiles at The Deuce. "For real, though. If you were so good at this game everyone loves so much, why don't you play anymore?"

The Deuce eyes her suspiciously. "It's not something I really talk about... Yeah, I played some hockey growin' up. And I had some moments. Ishy used to come along with my cuz, and of course there were girls and kids askin' for autographs, the whole thing straight out of a Canadian Tire commercial."

Samantha hands him the joint. He takes another pull.

"It seems obvious now that I never had a shot. This physique doesn't exactly scream *The Show*." He stands, motioning towards himself. Not quite six feet. Not quite 180 pounds. But shredded and tan from a summer of hard labor in the hot sun.

Samantha bites her lip, a tell that does not go unnoticed.

"But back then, fuck... I had all my hopes wrapped up in it." The Deuce shakes his head again. "My mom never had any money, you know? And no one in my family ever went to college or anything. And there I was playin' hockey, and wouldn't you know it, Yale started sniffin' around. *Yale.* I mean, I knew from day one that I wasn't fuckin' Yale material, but they started askin' all the right questions and sendin' all the right letters and bringin' me down to New Haven for the weekend, and I started to believe the hype, you know?"

Samantha hangs on every word.

"And, truth be told, I was off my ass that year. The best I ever played. Top three in scoring, killin' penalties, blockin' shots, fighting everything that moved. That year when I was 17, that was as good as it was ever gonna get."

A car quietly rolls past the otherwise deserted street.

"In November, they offered me a full ride. Said my education, my room and board, my travel, all of it would be paid for. But there's always a catch, right? They said I needed to finish high school with a B-average, and that I would need to score at least 1100 on my SATs." The Deuce takes a long, deep drag. "You can probably guess how that worked out."

She looks at him with eyes that yearn for more. "Tell me."

The Deuce shakes his head in disgust. He takes another deep hit, then looks up into the stars. "I don't know when I made the leap, but at some point, I told people I was already accepted. That it was a done deal. I was going to Yale... You spend your whole life with a single mom scratchin' and clawin' just to get by... It felt so good to tell people I was going to that school. I loved the way they looked at me, as if they'd underestimated me all my life. As if getting into some Ivy League school would justify all the shitty decisions I'd made up to that point."

She watches him intently.

"The idea takes on a life of its own, you know? At some point, you've talked about something so much, it becomes part of who you are. And then, suddenly, that part no longer exists." The Deuce lets the thought hang in the night and live between them. He flicks the joint over the railing, onto the street below. "I was so fuckin' caught up in my own story and too stupid to begin with, so despite the tutor and all-night study sessions and working construction part-time to help pay some bills, *of course* I failed to hit that magic number on my SATs... and that once-in-a-lifetime golden ticket went the way of all them skippin' reels of rhyme." He slowly nods, as if he still can't believe it. "Maybe someday I'll put it all behind me and come to terms with it; file it away under 'What Has To Be, Will Be.' Maybe one day I'll laugh about how ridiculous it was to care so much, or that I thought I needed to play hockey at Yale for my life to mean something. Someday, maybe... But I can tell you that day ain't today."

Samantha gazes upon him with unfamiliar longing. "Does it still hurt?"

"Only when I'm breathing."

She reaches out to touch his hand. All is silent in the world. "I guess I shouldn't have brought it up."

The Deuce smiles. "Don't sweat it. It's not so bad, talkin' to someone with half a brain." They look into the diamond sky. After some time, The Deuce says, "It's crazy to think about how many stars are out there. How many suns, just like our sun, with all those planets dancin' around. How much exists that we don't know. How small and insignificant we are, but what an amazing fuckin' miracle it is that we're here just the same."

Samantha's longing is no less diminished.

He exhales, then giggles to himself. "I think this pot is really fucking me up." He stands and walks to the other side of the fire escape, leaning over the railing and breathing in the night air. As he does so, a car pulls into the alley, yawning as it inches along carrying the sound of asphalt and loose pebbles under tires. It comes to a stop almost directly beneath them.

The night is still and thrilling and electric, and the driver young and careless and free. He leaves the windows down and the radio playing as he exits the car. The song is "This Year's Love." He has a girl with him. She holds his hand as they walk down the alley, maybe to a friend's house, maybe to a candlelit bar, anywhere but here.

Samantha moves to where The Deuce is standing. The breeze whispers through her hair. She's tired and a little drunk and bored with the summer, wants to let herself be swept away. Between thought and deed there is not a universe, but a tiny space. She grabs his hand and pulls him close. She rests her head on his chest and pulls him closer still. She breathes him in, tasting the salty sweetness on his skin.

From the open window of an abandoned car on a powerless night, David Gray sings "This Year's Love" about how he hopes it will last as Samantha and The Deuce—Ishy's girl and Ishy's guy—sway on the rusted fire escape overlooking that midnight street, the summer disappearing into that perfect moment where everything they think they know ceases to exist, and everything else happens the way it always should and would have, forever.

Washington Heights

As Ishy comes to the top of Coogan's Bluff at 155th Street, he looks to the east. Just beyond the Polo Grounds Towers, out over the Harlem River, he makes out the shadows of the cathedral frieze and the darkened spires of Yankee Stadium. He stops for a moment to take it in: the silhouette of The House That Ruth Built under the dazzling stars. It's for everyone to see, but seems as though it stands there, majestic and unmoving, for him alone.

When Ishy reaches 163rd Street, blisters on his feet and aches in his legs, the old men from Archie's Grocery are still sitting on the corner, holding court on milk crates and an overmatched ice machine. They've been around and seen some things, but never anything like this. They take in every last drop.

Ishy offers his familiar, "*Hola.*" He's only lived in the neighborhood three months, but Archie's is the one place he's a regular. He stops in every morning for an arepa and pops down any hour of the night for milk, Combos, beef jerky, beer, anything a 21-year-old heart could desire.

Archie grins through broken teeth and congratulates Ishy on making it back. The old man hands him a beer.

"It's been a helluva day," Ishy says through a laugh that turns on him. He's so grateful for the gesture and the day that he finds himself on the verge of tears.

The beer is in a warm can and of some Latin American brand, but one of the finest things he's ever tasted. He leans against a brick wall for a long time, listening to the poetic cadence of the men's speech, wishing like hell he knew some Spanish.

Utterly exhausted but still invigorated by the city's electricity in the absence of its usable form, Ishy hangs around the men long after his beer is gone, doing his best to take it all in, hoping it'll never end. But you can't chase the night, and when your time is up, you know it. He bids the men, "*Hasta luego,*" and walks the last half-block to his fourth-floor apartment.

He looks at his watch. 3:42AM.

Along that deserted street, he hears a transistor radio from somewhere above, all treble and squawk as it carries the reggae beat of The Wailers' "Concrete Jungle." He looks up into the tangle of fire escapes and sees a man grooving on a makeshift terrace, his ladyfriend's naked silhouette barely visible in the flickering candlelight beyond the window.

The man gives Ishy a nod as he pulls on a massive joint, the embers creating a trick of the light that shrouds his face.

Ishy nods back, the exchange somehow touching in its honesty and unspoken understanding. As he walks the last few steps to his apartment, he does his best Deuce impression, saying aloud and to only himself, "That's your 'New York City Serenade,' son."

He'll never be able to explain it, but this moment will stay with him forever.

13

Ishy – Saturday: Lima, Peru

There are Jägerbombs after midnight.

Having never partaken in the ritual, Ishy finds the clanging dropped-shot of Jägermeister into Red Bull to be surprisingly thrilling. He goes back to the bar for seconds and thirds, eagerly presenting the drinks to his friends as the liquid sloshes all over his sticky hands.

The four of them cram around a rickety table, laughing their asses off as they share stories of where they've been, who they've met, and the misfortunes and fuck-ups they've had along the way. Simone busts Ishy's balls for bringing his *Lonely Planet* to the bar, and The Deuce implores Lucia to admit, all the way through "Money for Nothing," "Sultans of Swing," and "So Far Away," that Dire Straits is indisputably the biggest band in Peru.

When the waitress brings over a tray of mysterious tumbler-size shots, Ishy shakes his head at The Deuce, saying that things are getting a little dumb. The Deuce agrees and offers a toast to Lucia and Simone: "I wanna thank you both for inviting Ishy and me to this momentous occasion. We came halfway across the world to be here tonight!"

They laugh and knock back the shots. Ishy's eyes water as his glass slams the table, wondering what the fuck he's ingested.

"The drink is pisco," Lucia says sweetly. *"Bienvenidos a Perú."*

The Deuce looks his Aussie surfer girl in the eye and announces, "I'm gonna fuck you eight ways from Sunday."

With raised eyebrows, Simone says, "I hope you know more than eight ways."

The Deuce pulls the stack of ATM receipts from his wallet and makes it rain all over the table.

In the hour before closing, someone drops one sol into the jukebox and selects Foreigner's "I Want To Know What Love Is." With the video depicting people going about their lives in melancholy slo-mo, the entire bar—Peruvian, American, Argentinian, Irish, German, Canadian, and Australian alike—sings in drunken unison. The Deuce gives it his all, eyes closed and wailing into his beer-glass-microphone.

In their lives, there's been heartache and pain, but this is one moment they wouldn't trade who, what, or where they are for anything in the world.

Amidst the benevolent debauchery in that raucous bar, Ishy sits next to Lucia. His face hurts from smiling so much, and he can't help but sing in agreement with Tom Petty that, yeah, tonight does feel like Heaven. There's a charge running though his body so close to hers, the electricity indisputable and dancing between them as he aches for her in a way that defies reason. She speaks to him in broken English, asking about Canada. He tells her there is more open space than she could ever dream, with lakes and trees that go on forever. That the air tastes like mint. That when fresh snowfall blankets the city at night, the streets are so quiet, you'd swear you're the only person on earth. That when she comes, he will teach her to ice skate.

She reaches beneath the wobbly table to take his hand. Her touch shoots an impossible burst of light through his body.

Someone decides that it's time to go, and the four of them stumble away from the Calle de las Pizzas. Before they reach the park, Simone tells The Deuce she knows a great bohemian place in Barranco where they play rock 'n' roll music all night long. The Deuce agrees before she even finishes. They jump into a wrecking yard taxi as he belts out a throaty version of "Waltzing Matilda" as goodbye while they speed off into the night.

Ishy and Lucia, equal parts nervous and excited, walk through Parque Kennedy, stopping at a stand for anticuchos. Having eaten virtually nothing since Miami, Ishy's mouth waters as the skewered meat sizzles with every lick of the fire. A stray cat meanders hopefully in a figure-8 between Ishy and Lucia as they lean against the vendor's cart. Ishy devours the chunks of grilled beef so quickly that he finds himself asking for another.

It isn't until they're halfway across the park, Ishy's arm around Lucia and The Happy Llama in clear sight, that Lucia informs him he's just eaten a kilo's worth of cow heart.

The taxi swerves through late-night Limean traffic with distressing speed and audacity, but neither Simone nor The Deuce—smashed and smitten—pay it any mind. In no time, they cruise past the crumbling mansions and towering trees lining Barranco.

The surfers have long since caught the last break at Playa Barranquito, and it seems they've all come to congregate on the sand-swept streets. The intoxicating scent of sunscreen and salty breezes sprinkles magic in the night. The cab pulls alongside a rollicking old estate in a shady part of town, and The Deuce slips the driver twice the fare before stumbling onto the crowded sidewalk.

The old walls of Sargento Pimienta rattle with The Kinks' "All Day and All Of The Night." Simone and The Deuce make a beeline for the dance floor, roused by the realization that they're two of the few gringos in the bar. They share 1 liter bottles of Cristal, going sip-for-sip as they scream the lyrics to every song, jumping and spilling beer in a ritual of rediscovered youth.

"Summertime Blues," "Do Wah Diddy Diddy," "Sheena Is A Punk Rocker," "You Shook Me All Night Long." In a country where they understand little and know even less, the music speaks to Simone and The Deuce. It is in them. They're songs they've sung, songs they've shared, songs they've lived, and those songs now feel like a beacon of light taking them home.

They stop dancing only to crash the bar for Jägermeister and beer. Except for a few salsa numbers where the locals put on an impossibly sensual display, the night belongs to Simone and The Deuce, the two of them singing full throttle, feeling the electric cords pumping through their veins, thrashing and flailing as they romp.

"Baba O'Riley." "Gimme Shelter." The Deuce kisses her hard and often. "Wooly Bully." "It's My Life." Out on the dance floor. Hand down her pants. "I Fought The Law." Nobody notices. "96 Tears." Nobody cares.

They're soaked in sweat and smoking two cigarettes at a time, bouncing off bodies as they jump and wail. When the DJ spins a bristling old vinyl copy of *Please Please Me*, The Deuce climbs onto a speaker and rips off his shirt, air-guitaring with a vengeance and inciting a riot ("Come on, COME ON! Come on, COME ON!"), a gringo in all his glory, sweat splattering as he shakes his head in a crazed mop-top McCartney, going back-to-back with a Peruvian kid who joins him atop the speaker in an air guitar/single mic sequence that is pure Pan-American Bruce and Clarence.

Simone is loving every second of it. Management is not. Security asks them to leave but they're already gone.

They laugh hysterically as they run down the street, stopping only to push-start a stalled-out VW Beetle. The driver offers a ride as thanks. They hop in and he stops at a late-night Barranco mainstay with a queue stretching onto the sidewalk. All three of them stand in line to hang with the locals, sharing sips of the gigantic beer The Deuce smuggled from the bar. Once they make it inside, they order the royal with a fried egg on top, standing at the counter and watching the man who works the grill.

Food in hand, they sit on the curb and enjoy the finest burger they've ever tasted. Grease and yolk and mayonnaise on their fingers and a plate of fries resting by their side, they wash it all down with cold cans of Pilsen.

Leaning on the curb and sharing a cigarette, the driver asks, "*Dónde van?*" Simone gives the address of her hostel, winking at The Deuce and assuring him she has a single bed built for two. They climb into the car and the driver slowly weaves through the backstreets of Barranco, speaking lovingly about its poets and painters, sculptors and singers.

As Simone and The Deuce go at it in the backseat of that old VW, she unzips his pants and grabs hold of him, refusing to let go until the dawn's early light.

As morning searches for cracks in the curtains, The Deuce stumbles down the hostel hallway.

He and Simone had spent the past three hours in the throes of passion, concluding with this morning's epic *mañanero*. In post-coital bliss, The Deuce, panting and dripping with sweat, handed her a 3 liter bottle of water and suggested he might look her up if ever he finds himself down under. After a few seconds of awkward silence, they burst out laughing and she wished him luck, smacking his bare ass as he pranced around the room, surveying the floor for his belongings.

Now, he steps out into the cool air of the misty Barranco morning, the neighborhood quiet and serene and beautiful. He walks to the end of the block and speaks with a taxi driver. Ten minutes later, he is giggling to himself about last night as he climbs The Happy Llama's stairs. He pushes open the door to his room and steps inside, nearly tripping over José, who is stark naked on the floor, a handgun resting peacefully on his chest. The Deuce laughs at the sight and tiptoes to his bed. He feels around the top bunk, searching for Ishy to ensure he's made it back safely. Grabbing hold of an ankle, The Deuce smiles and nods to himself. He then collapses into the lower bunk and starts snoring almost immediately.

"Hey, Ish," The Deuce calls out from the bottom bunk. Sunlight rushes their room, their naked Colombian friend nowhere to be seen. "My dick smells like pussy."

The room is silent for a good five seconds before Lucia bursts out laughing.

The Deuce literally falls out of the bed, scrambling to look at who's in the top bunk. When he gets to his feet, last night comes back to him. Lying in the bed above him is Ishy Lords, shirtless, holding Lucia as closely as he's ever held anything. The two smile down at him.

"You dirty dawg," The Deuce scolds.

"*Buenos dias, Señor Estan.*"

"Top of the mornin', you little fuckin' lovebirds."

"So, Deuce," Ishy observes, barely able to contain his laughter, "seems like you had a pretty good night."

"Fuckin' A-1, I did. Lima-fuckin'-Peru. I think I love this place." The Deuce adjusts his aching groin, looking around the room. "Hey, Lucy, seeing as you're part of the management team, I gotta ask: What's the policy on firearms in this place? Shouldn't the Colombians check their .45s at the front desk before sharin' a room with us fuckin' gringos?"

The lovers giggle about something only they will ever understand, Lucia burying her nose in Ishy's chest.

The Deuce shakes his head and mutters about how they should get moving, then announces to everyone and no one that he needs to take a piss.

Before leaving The Happy Llama, The Deuce gives Ishy some alone time with Lucia. For the better part of an hour, he hangs around the front desk, helping himself to liberal amounts of instant coffee to keep his hangover at bay.

Standing in the otherwise empty dorm room, looking deep into her eyes, Ishy promises Lucia that he will come back for her. That he will bring her to Canada. That he will show her the earth, and everything that's in it.

She promises to teach him Spanish. She keeps repeating, "*No te vayas.*"

He gives her his favorite sweatshirt, a Blue Jays hoodie he wears every Saturday, telling her he'll be back for it soon.

She promises to wait for him.

An hour later, Ishy and The Deuce stand outside a decrepit bus terminal in the most frightening part of any town they've ever seen. Ishy puts his hands in the pockets of his shiny, new Patagonia jacket, shaking his head in disgust. "Deuce, why the hell are we taking the bus anyway?" He motions toward his *Lonely Planet.* "It says here we can fly to Iquitos in less than two hours."

The Deuce looks around nervously. "Would you put that thing away? We're gonna get shanked out here as is. We don't need you announcing to the fuckin' Shining Path that we're tourists."

Just then, a Quechua lady walks past in hand-woven attire, her brilliantly pleated skirts floating above the filthy sidewalk. She wears leather sandals and a funky red mountain sombrero. There's a baby strapped across her back.

"I'm pretty sure the cat's out of the bag on us being foreigners, Stan."

The Deuce nods. "Can't argue that one. Where the fuck are we, anyway?"

"A bus station in central Lima. Otherwise known as the Ninth Circle of Hell. Speaking of which, this whole bus thing…?"

The Deuce lights a cigarette. "Stop bein' such a fuckin' pussy, Lords. How many chances do you think you're gonna get to cross the Andes? Enjoy yourself. It's later than you think."

They walk into the terminal and purchase one-way tickets on the Económico to Yurimaguas, the port town from which they can catch the boat down the Río Huallaga to the Río Marañón, which eventually converges with the Ucayali to form the Amazon River. From this bus station, Ishy's guidebook indicates it will take five days to reach Iquitos.

With an hour to kill before departure, Ishy and The Deuce stroll around the block. The streets are squalid and teeming with stray dogs and concrete buildings stained with exhaust. The garbage is ubiquitous. Graffiti covers every wall, the letters just as likely to be revolutionary rally cries as love letters. After stepping over the legs of a beggar, The Deuce quietly asks Ishy, "How does your Capitalist ass even begin to reconcile this shit?"

There is no denying that the neighborhood is daunting, but—having promised Lucia he would sample Peru's national dish before leaving Lima—Ishy is hell-bent on tracking down the establishment she recommended. When The Deuce stops to buy a pack of Chiclets from an old lady sitting barefoot on the sidewalk, he mentions the place. She looks down the block and points to a hole-in-the-wall with "Ceviche" scrawled across a chalkboard.

They step inside and convey that they're in the market for two orders of the house specialty. To Ishy, The Deuce asks, "What the fuck is this stuff, anyway?"

Ishy laughs and shakes his head. "I have no fucking idea. But Lucia says it's the best thing to eat when you're hungover."

"Then put me down for a double, son."

Ishy peeks over the counter to see the lady fillet an entire fish, throwing cubed pieces into a metal bowl with onions and peppers. She uses a spoon to squeeze the juice from half a dozen limes, allowing the concoction to marinate. The entire process takes less than three minutes.

The lady holds up the bowl for Ishy's inspection, proclaiming, "*Ceviche de pescado.*"

As she begins filling two Styrofoam containers, Ishy says, "Whoa, whoa! Aren't you gonna *cook* that first?"

Unsure what he's saying, the lady passes the containers over the counter and says, "*Diez soles.*"

The Deuce howls with disbelief as Ishy hands her the money without uttering another word.

As they walk back to the bus terminal, The Deuce asks, "The chances of getting E. coli from that place are what, 4-to-1?"

Ishy's face is ashen. "When Lucia told me about this stuff, she didn't mention anything about raw fish."

The Deuce skeptically eyes his container. "Maybe it's good. I mean, it's possible, right?" Dysentery be damned, he psyches himself up. "Fuck it," he says, closing his eyes and ramming a giant spoonful of cold, spicy seafood into his mouth.

Ishy watches in abject horror. "Is there nothing in this world you think twice about?"

The Deuce smiles through a mouthful of soupy fish. "Ransack the universe, my man. Always." As he chews, his eyes light up. "This stuff is actually pretty fuckin' good. I'm tellin' you, the lime juice and the onions and the peppers and the fish. I can feel myself getting replenished as we speak." He motions to Ishy's container. "Get in there, bro!"

Ishy takes one more look at his food but can't get past the idea of eating raw fish from a filthy stand. Instead, he settles on a bag of Lay's potato chips from the bus station canteen.

In bewilderment, The Deuce shakes his head. "Your loss, bro." He scarfs down half of Ishy's portion before tapping out. In a gastronomic stupor, he ambles down the block for a smoke until he reaches a man sitting against a soot-stained wall. The Deuce hands him Ishy's leftovers, then crouches beside him to chitchat in broken Spanish. The Deuce gives him a few cigarettes before heading back.

The announcements squawking across the terminal's PA system are indecipherable, so Ishy and The Deuce wander around the dozen bays until they reach a bus with "Yurimaguas" scratched into the front.

They double-check their tickets, and Ishy opens his guidebook to triple-check the spelling of their destination. But there is no mistake. The rickety bus they're scheduled to inhabit for the next 26 hours is in the process of being loaded so far beyond capacity that Ishy and The Deuce can do nothing but laugh. An extended family appears to be using the bus to move all their earthly belongings from Lima to Yurimaguas. Countless suitcases and old trunks, cardboard boxes and plastic pails, mattresses, wooden chairs, a refrigerator, and two propane tanks are being tied to the roof as Ishy and The Deuce look on with horrified admiration.

Before securing all the luggage with an oversized blue tarp, the bus company's rooftop porter motions for Ishy to toss up his pack. Ishy just shakes his head and holds his rucksack tighter.

When they think they've seen it all, a granddaughter emerges from the lobby with a sickly dog, some kind of schnauzer-shepherd mix that is filthy and drooling and running wildly around the parking lot. As the porter climbs down from the roof, he goes around to the back of the bus to open the spare tire compartment, which just so happens to be right next to the diesel engine. The porter picks up the skinny dog and tosses him inside, slamming the door and dusting off his hands while the dog barks for its life.

Ishy looks at The Deuce, stunned. Then the two of them burst out laughing.

They are last to board. With no assigned seating, they're forced to the back of the bus: a fate that would spell excitement on a grade school cheese wagon, but not a 26-hour trek across the Andes. As they drag their packs through the overflowing aisle, Ishy can't help but notice that they are the only gringos onboard.

It isn't until they reach their seats in the very last row that they realize Económico means *no bathroom*.

14

Rosy – Before: Toronto, Canada

There was a time in the not-so-distant past where I spent my hours calculating density coefficients by day and championing the preservation of quasi-historic landmarks like Maple Leaf Gardens and The Matador Club by night. In those days, I never considered my job a career. The fact that I was holding down a respectable, full-time gig in something approximating my chosen field was a minor miracle, and enough in itself. But when my boss called me into his office one spring morning and informed me that I'd been assigned to the St. Clair Right-of-Way Streetcar Project— and as I embarked upon the next five years doing what I increasingly believed to be good work in the name of a greater cause—I began to take things a little more seriously.

And so, when the mayor of the City of Toronto, His Right fucking Worship, invited my team to dinner at his residence to thank us for the hard work and sacrifices we'd made to effect change in our city, I considered the gesture an important milestone in what I was beginning to recognize as my career.

I awoke early to one of those spectacular February mornings where the sun pours through the naked windowpanes, the cloudless sky a breathtaking cobalt blue. Kat was still sound asleep, so I took the gift of solitude as an opportunity to escape for a while, layering up in long johns and old sweaters, then braving the cold as I tossed my skates and stick into the backseat.

Of all the things I loved about Toronto, few were held in higher esteem than the city's outdoor rinks. The pond at Dufferin Grove was always top notch, and with temperatures having plummeted over the past few days, the ice had never been in better shape. The boards were true and the chain-link above them a fitting reminder that this was no suburban community center. The kids who played at Dufferin Grove were tough and tenacious: shit-talking, shot-blocking, and glove-dropping. When we played at night, tallboy cans crystallized on the bench. After the game, we'd warm up by the park bonfire, passing around mickeys of Canadian Club as we deduced where the finest ladies would be that evening.

But before 9AM on a Saturday, most of the beauties who ran this place were asleep, so I had the ice virtually to myself.

I laced up my skates on the bench as the Zamboni made its rounds, steam billowing as warm water washed over the ice. By the time the driver finished, a couple teenagers stepped onto that perfect sheet of glass with me, the air in our lungs so cold and fresh that we coughed on the first deep breath.

We took turns ringing shots off the iron and making crisp, rink-wide breakout passes that danced from tape-to-tape. Every now and then, I'd get the urge to skate like a madman with stops-and-starts, doing the circles, dangle-snipe-celly over the unmistakable crunch of skates.

After 45 minutes, I was breathing hard and sweating through my toque. I let the kids know I was on my way out, but not before going bardown a few times and ringing one last clapper off the crossbar, the puck bounding up and over the cage, disappearing into a snowbank halfway to Dufferin Street.

My breath was unfurling in unnamable patterns as I climbed into the car, my head still steaming. The engine groaned in agony when I turned it over, but I coaxed it to life and found an Arkells track on the radio, making my way to College Street and popping into The Common for a strong cup of coffee. The girl working the FAEMA was one I bumped into on nights we'd cram into a tiny club to catch some yet-to-be-discovered indie act, and on this morning, she was spinning a vinyl copy of Hayden's *Everything I Long For*. I did my best not to notice how good she looked in tight-fitting jeans. When she handed me the coffee, we smiled, and I told her I'd see her around.

As had become habit, I took the long way home to check in on my work-life's magnum opus: the 512 St. Clair Streetcar line. In the planning department, we had grown fond of saying we were taking St. Clair from inefficient-underutilized-stress-inducing-aggravation to fast-and-efficient-cost-effective-modern-public-transportation. By giving the streetcars dedicated lanes, we were transforming the transportation corridor from in-the-way to right-of-way.

But on this frigid Saturday morning, the semblance of progress seemed a distant dream. St. Clair Avenue resembled a war zone, with the street, track, and sidewalk torn to pieces. Small mountains of earth and massive piles of snow competed for space, the construction having ground to a winter weekend halt. The bulldozers and gargantuan excavators looked like the last dinosaurs frozen in the moment before the apocalypse.

It was only last summer when Jasmine and I—her, a rising star fresh out of grad school and newly assigned to the project, and me, the relatively tenured city planner responsible for showing her the ropes—had left City Hall and taken the University subway line up to St. Clair West. We'd climbed out of the underground and emerged into the glorious afternoon sunshine of St. Clair Avenue so we could walk the entire length of the streetcar line, from the mansions of Forest Hill to the used car lots and cash advance joints at Weston Road on the wrong, wrong side of the tracks.

The gentrifying stretch between Christie and Arlington was humming as people sipped afternoon cocktails on leafy patios, seemingly oblivious to the shredded streets. We crossed the chaos of Dufferin into the heart of Little Italy, where windowsill flowers were in full bloom, old men sat on park benches, and kids played soccer in the alleyways. We bought gelato from the best place in town and, when we crested the hill at Via Italia, Jazz stopped for a moment to take in St. Clair's grand east-west expanse. I told her that it was this view—and the endless possibilities it inspired—that made me want to become a city planner.

We crossed Harvie Avenue and I pointed up the street to the house I grew up in. We walked past the neighborhood cemetery, and I told Jazz how I used to play hide-and-seek and capture-the-flag with my friends amongst the tombstones; about how, some nights, my mom would convince us to go into the graveyard and lie down on the grass to commune with the dead.

"Even the dead can be astoundingly alive," she told us. "We're alive, always. In the grass growing and the rivers flowing. In the whisper of the trees and the soft summer breeze. In the waves crashing on the sand and the grains slipping through your hand. There's life around us, always. And we're part of it, always."

I told Jazz about how on those nights, lying there with my mom looking up at the twinkling stars, it was comforting to know I didn't ever have to be alone.

Jazz took me by the hand. We made our way under the first set of railroad tracks and came out on the other side, where the barber shops and churrasqueiras ran up against Laughton Avenue. We bought a couple Coca-Colas from a bodega and stood on the corner, dreaming about how the streetcar line would improve the lives of new immigrants and working-class people, how morale and dignity and the quality of life would be lifted, how happy everyone would someday be.

It was a beautiful thought in its irrational innocence, and we were lost in the reverie. Some kids were playing stickball down a side street, and they reminded me of how I used to be. I gave them a dollar and they ran to the tienda to buy some freezies. It felt like a glimpse of the past and a picture of the future. Jasmine looked at me softly, and there was longing in the gaze we held. Maybe in another lifetime, I thought. Maybe in another lifetime...

It was late morning when I got home, and Kat was still asleep. I drank coffee and read a few chapters of Jay McInerney's *Bright Lights, Big City*. When Kat got out of bed, we ate a quiet breakfast and half-paid attention to *Talladega Nights*, which cable TV was playing on loop at this point. It was the type of lazy Saturday we'd grown accustomed to. She smoked some weed and I scrolled through ESPN.com. As the afternoon turned from sunshine to shadows and deeper shades of gray, I began dropping hints that we should get ready, asking if she had anything special picked out for the mayor's house.

She said, somewhat disinterestedly, that I should go shower while she chose an outfit. After a steamy, invigorating shower and a hot shave, I walked into the bedroom only to find her staring into the abyss of her phone, the bed covered by dozens of outfits. When I asked if she selected a dress, she informed me—contrary to the compelling evidence in our midst—that she had nothing to wear.

I nodded and picked out my nicest pair of slacks, a freshly pressed shirt I'd purchased just for the occasion, and a tie the clerk said would have me "drippin' swag." I put some gunk in my hair and liberally applied deodorant. When I finished, I took a deep breath, walked into the bedroom, and announced that I was all set. I was doing everything in my power to convey, in a calm and caring manner, the importance of our punctuality. But Kat continued to sit on the bed in her sweatpants and T-shirt, transfixed by a video game.

I looked on in disgust for thirty seconds, then went downstairs to pour myself a drink. The whiskey was good, and it calmed me down. I put a Tom Waits record on the turntable and listened to the first side all the way through. When the needle started doing the crackle and bump, I went upstairs only to find Kat asleep on the pile of clothes.

"Kat, what the fuck?"

She groaned and rubbed sleep from her eyes.

"You can't do this to me tonight. We need to be at the mayor's house—the fucking *mayor's* house—in forty minutes. I need you to get in the shower and get dressed right fucking now. Alright? Enough."

She sat up with a wounded look. "You don't have to be such an asshole about it." She stood and began making her way to the shower, suggestively removing her clothes as she went.

I went back downstairs, flipped the record, and poured another drink. I sat with my eyes closed and listened to the entire B-Side: "Invitation to the Blues," "Pasties and a G-String," "Bad Liver and a Broken Heart," "The One That Got Away," "Small Change," and "I Can't Wait to Get Off Work."

When the album played to its flawless conclusion, I went upstairs to find Kat in her underwear, still deciding what to wear.

I went back downstairs and put my fist through the wall.

By the time we left the house, we were more than an hour late. I slammed the car door and pulled out of park too quickly, nearly sideswiping a pedestrian. I took my fury out on the engine, allowing the RPMs to tickle the red before shifting gears and flying down Symington Avenue. We hadn't said a word since getting in the car and when Kat finally did speak, I assumed I misunderstood her: "I'm sorry, could you repeat that?"

"I need you to stop at the drugstore."

I shouldn't have been surprised. I should have seen it coming. But I didn't.

"I need to get some nail polish. I ran out of the color that matches my lipstick."

I cackled like a lunatic. I gunned the engine again, putting us both in harm's way.

She had been sitting around the house all day and could have taken 10 minutes from her phone or nap or staring into oblivion to walk to the fucking drugstore, where she could have picked out 100 shades of nail polish. But she had done nothing. And now that we were 70 minutes late, she was trying to make me look even worse.

I exploded, unloading my long list of repressed but steadily mounting grievances: self-centered, late for everything, lazy, manipulative, scheming. "Are you insane? Seriously? On the most important night of my life, as you're singlehandedly destroying my reputation and career, you want me to stop to get fucking NAIL POLISH? SERIOUSLY?"

Seriously.

I turned onto Bloor Street and dipped under the Junction tracks. When we popped back up on the other side, the traffic ground to a halt, and the irony of the city planner not accounting for the newly scheduled road work struck me like a shovel in the face. I smashed my fist into the steering wheel, roaring in primal anguish. I couldn't even look at her. I was shaking my head in self-loathing and disgust. "I think you need some serious fucking help. I really do. This is all so fucked-up. How could you be so selfish? Why is it that when something's important to me, THAT's when you pull this shit? Why the fuck do you always want to sabotage me?"

She just stared out the window in silence.

As we inched toward the Dundas junction, I realized the fastest way to get across High Park would be along Humberside Avenue, so I made a move to head north. Just as I began to squeeze right, Kat spoke in a crushed, childlike voice. "I just wanted to look pretty for you."

I chortled. With 18 months of hostage episodes blasting through my head, I said with a terrifying lack of feeling, "Fuck. You."

A void in traffic appeared and I accelerated dangerously into the opening. As I ripped into a righthand turn, the hot smash of Kat's fist connected with my face. My body spun to the left, the involuntary tug on the wheel sending us swerving into the bright red path of an oncoming streetcar. I was overcome with the unmistakable taste of getting bashed in the nose.

It was unfolding in slow-motion, but it was absolutely happening: the screech of steel wheels and the blaring scream of the horn, the ironic truth of what it meant to be caught in the trolley tracks. And the inevitable impact of 25 tons of efficient public transit plowing into my VW.

A thousand thoughts run through your mind in the aftermath of a car wreck. But amidst the chaos of the scene—steam billowing from my devastated hood, the piercing and unending wail of the TTC horn, the angry faces of passengers as they tried to catch a glimpse of the crazy fuck who took a run at them, the bystanders pointing in disbelief and snapping photos with their phones, the blood streaming from my nose—amidst all the anarchy, I found myself smirking. My life was a mess, but my mind was free and clear, content in the understanding that it was finally, indisputably over.

I jumped out of the car and walked with supreme purpose toward the streetcar's folding front door. Kat was hot on my heels. To this day, I don't know if she was in pursuit to apologize or to hit me again. I came to a dead stop and put my hand up like a traffic cop, calmly advising her to get the fuck away from me.

The streetcar driver's face was purple with fury, but the deranged look in my eye must have given him pause. I flashed what was meant to be an apologetic smile, but it seemed to frighten him even more. He refused to open the door and yelled through the glass that he was calling the police. I just bit my lip and shook my head.

One of the passengers opened the sliding glass window to ask me what the fuck happened. Blood poured down my face and came out in an angry spray of spittle when I told him I wasn't sure what happened—even though I'd never been more sure of anything in my life. I asked if everyone onboard was okay, and they guy said they were.

There would be no mayor's dinner. I would probably lose my driver's license. There existed the very real possibility that I would lose my job. And yet—even as Kat was wailing in heartbreak and despair, pacing back and forth like a caged animal behind a yellow fire hydrant on the opposite side of the street, even as the traffic backed up in every direction and sirens cut the night in half as their lights swirled amongst the buildings—I could only smile.

I was a free man.

In the end, I spent two hours at the scene, showing my insurance papers and trying to explain why I'd careened into the path of an approaching streetcar. One of the officers gave me an old undershirt to clean up with, and after I wiped the blood from my face, I kept it over my shoulder like a championship belt. A city bus eventually arrived to take the remaining passengers away. I took a breathalyzer and passed, though just barely.

Three different tow trucks arrived to drag my automobile to some yard where the insurance company would take one look, write it off, and jack my rates from here to the end of time. A massive vehicle lugged the streetcar away.

When all was said and done, the ordeal ended not with a bang, but a whimper. The police slowly drove off, their sirens silenced but their lights still eerily flashing. People moved on with their lives.

And then there was Kat.

She sat on the freezing sidewalk, her arms around her knees, her head buried. I slowly approached and stood over her for a full minute. She didn't say a word.

I shook my head and snorted in disgust. In a voice I didn't recognize as my own, I said flatly, "We're done."

Then I walked down the street to Whelan's Gate and got drunk by myself.

Until Jazz arrived.

15

Rosy – Sunday: Iquitos, Peru

I stand in the kitchen, hypnotized by the steam rising from my cup of instant coffee. The past three days have been a fog of self-destructive self-preservation that saw me drinking to excess, then sleeping for long intervals at irregular hours. The pattern was easy to fall into, the familiar monotony like starched linens on a hotel bed in the early afternoon. But I understand that if I don't crawl out of it now, I'll slip away all over again.

With designs on solitude and establishing some distance from The Hideout, I shower and throw on some clean clothes. Before I make it off the porch, the sight of a lone girl stops me. She's smoking a cigarette and reading an old copy of Proust's *In Search of Lost Time*. I've seen all types in this hostel, but there's something in this girl's self-assuredness—an indifference to the outside world—that grabs my attention.

She's young and attractive, rocking that hipster librarian look. Before I can think of something to say, she puts her book down and looks me in the eye. She asks, "Where are you headed?"

"I'm not sure. Out for a walk, I guess."

"Would you mind if I join you?"

I nearly laugh, then shrug. "Whatever floats your boat."

"Splendid. Let me grab my purse." She stands, snaps shut her cigarette case, then disappears inside the hostel, leaving me to contemplate how I've let my solitude slip through my fingers.

When she returns, she smiles and announces that she's all set. I open the wrought iron gate and walk in the direction of the Plaza de Armas. Just before the city's main square, a rickety diesel bus speeds to the corner. A teenager hangs halfway out the door, yelling, "*La Marina! La Marina! La Marina!*"

I grab her hand. "This is us." With the bus barely slowing, I reach for the handle and jump aboard, pulling her with me as we stumble up the steps, nearly falling into the lap of an old lady sitting nearest the door. It takes us a moment to regain our balance as the jalopy jerks and sways through traffic, but I eventually hand the barker some coins and lead the girl to an empty seat at the back of the bus.

Safely in our seats, she laughs. "This place is crazy."

"That's one way of putting it. I'm Rosy, by the way."

"I'm Vanessa." She presents a hand.

I chuckle at the formality as we shake.

She doesn't ask where we're going, and I'm not much in the mood for talking, the two of us content to sit and watch the canvas of early morning Iquitos pass by: the concrete block houses with corrugated tin roofs, disintegrating posters clinging to peeling walls, palm trees swaying in the diesel breeze, mototaxis and Coca-Cola trucks, fruit stands and barbed wire. Iquitos in all its poverty-stricken splendor.

One-by-one, the locals empty out of the northbound bus until Vanessa and I are the last on-board. When the teenage barker announces, *"Puerto Masusa. Última parada,"* I nod to Vanessa, asking if she's up for it.

She returns a smile, and we step off the bus. Naked kids play in cracked mud while stray dogs rummage through garbage-strewn alleyways. We walk past rows of abandoned storage containers and rusty warehouses before the dock. An official with a hat pulled over his eyes sleeps in a chair at the gate.

When we reach the water, I take a seat on the ledge and suggest Vanessa should do the same. I can only imagine what's running through her head, the two of us coming all the way to the edge of town only to wind up here.

After a long pause, I say the place we're sitting in is the very spot the Río Itaya meets the Amazon. "This is the furthest inland deep-water port on the planet. 2,500 miles from the Atlantic." I pause so we can take in just how depressing this place is. "They say that Iquitos used to be one of the richest cities in the world. The crazy rubber barons built those swanky mansions up on the Malecón and imported everything. Iron. Extravagance. Corruption. Slavery. This place had it all. And every bit of it came into Iquitos through this port."

Vanessa tilts her head and asks, "How long have you been here?"

I take a deep breath. "Nine. Long. Months."

Vanessa whistles. "You must really love this place."

I emit a kind of anti-laugh. "I fucking hate it here." I have no doubt she is wondering why, but she's discerning enough to leave it alone. I take this as an invitation to continue. "The thing about these boats now," I motion toward a vessel making its way up the river, "is that they don't bring anything *in* anymore. They just take things away. Whatever they can pilfer from the jungle: lumber, oil, animals, women." I nod almost involuntarily. "They say that when it comes to imperialism, the chief weapon of the conqueror is their ability to astonish... The natives can never quite believe, until it's much too late, how heartless and greedy the conquering people really are." After a quiet moment, I admit, "I stole that from Vonnegut, by the way."

She smiles, noting that I could have passed it off as my own if I'd kept my mouth shut.

"That boat carrying all those logs down the river: I used to get so fucking angry at the sight of it."

"But not anymore?"

I pick up a small rock from the muddy ledge, the pebble dancing as it rolls through my fingers. "Not anymore."

We are quiet for a moment, until Vanessa says, "They say the great tragedy of life is not that we know less and less, but that we care less and less."

I look at her with raised eyebrows.

"I stole that from my mom."

I chuckle and admit I'm intrigued.

"What can I say? I was a pretty nihilistic teenager." She takes the small tin from her purse and offers a cigarette.

These days I don't smoke anything beyond my daily Mapacho, but I accept. The two of us smoke in silence as a giant bird lands on the weathered post. It stands on one stick leg for a long time, staring back at us, two mysterious figures on a ledge.

Vanessa finally asks, "So what changed? Why does the plundering of the rainforest not bother you anymore?"

I find myself looking at her hard, trying to decide how to explain. As if sensing the moment, the bird extends its wings and wills itself into slow-motion flight. I ask Vanessa to stand.

She gives me a less than willing look, but pulls herself from the ledge.

"I need you to take your right arm and hold it out in front of you."

She does, and I notice how good she looks standing barefoot in the dried mud in frayed jean shorts and a tight My Morning Jacket tee.

"Now, I need you to toss me your purse."

She is not amused, flashing some attitude while shaking her head.

I laugh. "Come on. Look around. Where am I gonna go? Trust me, this is all part of the show."

She smiles despite herself. "Whatever you say."

With a soft underhand toss, she throws her purse—a pretty little shoulder-strap number that she no doubt purchased at one of the Andean tourist markets in Lima. I thank her kindly, then rifle through its contents, coming across the usual items: iPhone, gum, Velcro wallet, pencil and notepad, birth control pills.

I hold up this last item with a knowing smirk as she sarcastically flips me off. I toss the pills back inside and finally come across the object of my desire. Climbing onto the ledge for dramatic effect, I say, "Alright. So, I want you to think of your arm as the entire history of the universe. As in: If you were to draw a timeline like we did back in grade school, your arm would be the entire length of that timeline. You feel me?"

"My arm is the history of the universe. I feel you."

"So, your shoulder there, let's call that the Big Bang. The gigantic, cataclysmic explosion that somehow gets this whole party started. Mass expanding at a speed and intensity we'll never fathom: gravity, photons, electrons, et cetera. There's shit flying all over the place, and that shit begins to collide."

She is smiling, and so am I. The preacher on his pulpit, sermonizing his choir.

"With all this stuff crashing into itself, enormous clusters of matter form. Maybe an inch beyond your shoulder is where the earliest stars take shape. Galaxies unfurling down your arm. Round about where your elbow is, that's where enough rubble and snowballs and metal have come together to give a name to this rock we call home."

Vanessa nods.

"From your elbow to the tip of your finger, that's the entire history of Earth. We'll go ahead and call it 4.5 billion years, give or take."

Vanessa tries not to laugh. "Go on."

I climb off the ledge and walk over to where Vanessa is standing, flashing the nail file I've removed from her purse. With some flair, I draw the file across the tip of her pointing finger. "That little smudge I just scratched off your nail is the entire history of humanity being erased from our timeline."

With a pregnant pause, I allow the weight of it all to hit home before walking back to the ledge, taking a seat next to her purse.

"I've spent a lot of time sitting in this exact spot, just watching that big river go by, day after day after day. When you do that long enough, it gets you thinking about time. About deep time. About how many full moons have looked down on that water. About the layers of mud buried beneath these banks. About how insignificant we are, despite our individuality and self-importance, our love and our loss and our memories, our hopes and our dreams. Against the weight of all that time, it's strangely comforting to know that nothing we say or do really matters... So, the imperialistic attack on the jungle? I no longer give it any thought. The poaching of species to the brink of extinction? That movie's played out a million times before. If you want to know the truth, nothing really gets to me anymore."

Vanessa smiles beautifully, slowly walking back to the ledge to sit next to me. "You strike me as the type of person who has taken many lovers."

I burst out laughing. "Lovers? What makes you say that?"

"Just a vibe I'm picking up."

"Is that so?"

"It is. I envision you as the ad hoc tour guide for free-spirited traveler types: showing them the ropes, bringing them to a few off-the-gringo-trail places around town, dancing in the sweaty Iquitos clubs until the small hours, then sweet-talking them back to The Hideout so you can get freaky while some unfortunate bystander pretends to sleep in the next bunk."

"Man, that sounds like a pretty sweet gig."

"You can't fool me, Mr. Roosevelt."

I shake my head and smile, asking for another cigarette. She hands me one, along with a book of matches, and I light one for each of us in a single swipe. I take a long, deep drag, holding her gaze. "So, what's your story? Are you one of these free-spirited traveler types you seem to know so well?"

"Ha! Not quite."

"Gap year?"

"In a manner of speaking. I'm currently taking the semester off." She inhales quickly from her cigarette.

"To find yourself, right? I'm down. What school?"

Vanessa pauses for a beat. "Columbia."

I nearly fall off the ledge: "Fuck me! Columbia?"

She takes another quick drag and turns away. "Indeed."

I whistle in admiration. "What's your major?"

"Math and environmental biology... Fractal geometrics in nature, specifically."

She says it so matter-of-fact that I roar with laughter. "A math-bio major from Columbia University. You gotta be fuckin' kidding me. I guess my Arm's Length History of the Universe bit won't be luring you back to my lair anytime soon."

She laughs and nods playfully. "Probably not. But I would definitely give you an A for effort."

I take a long drag and shake my head. "Fractal geometrics in nature... I won't even pretend to know what that is."

Vanessa is beaming. "May I?"

"Lay it on me, sister."

Vanessa rises to stand in front of me, clearing her throat in mock arrogance. "Fractals are the visual representation of the mathematics that define the physical universe."

A look of utter confusion plays across my face.

"The shape of a lightning bolt is a fractal. The pattern of crystallizing water in a snowflake, that's a fractal. The systematic way in which water erodes the landscape."

I stare blankly.

"It's a self-similar pattern within a structure where, no matter how closely you look, you always see the same pattern, the same thing. Smaller-scale versions of the total figure appearing within the figure itself. It's self-repeating. An algorithm that allows space and time to be finite, but with infinite boundaries."

I am lost.

She takes a moment to consider an analogy that might work for me. "Think of a piece of broccoli. It branches off into smaller and smaller pieces, right? But if you look closely, you'll notice that every tiny piece is essentially identical in pattern and structure to the bigger piece."

I slowly nod.

"Is it like those Russian dolls? Where you take apart the big one and there're smaller ones inside?"

Vanessa smiles. "You're on the right track. Those Russian dolls are a little bit like the fractals that collapse to zero. But what I'm more interested in are the fractals that increase toward infinity. Geometric figures with a finite area, but with an infinitely expanding perimeter."

I am lost all over again.

"If you look closely at the way a tree grows, each branch is basically a smaller version of the tree itself. And those branches—the tree's perimeter—are infinitely expanding, allowing the tree to maximize the potential of its finite footprint. That's a naturally occurring fractal."

The wheels are turning now, my leg bouncing up and down like the pumpjack on an oil well.

"If you want to take that idea one step further, the entire forest can be thought of as a fractal pattern, with the size and distribution of trees within the forest mirroring the fractal structure of that single tree."

After some long and calculated thought, I ask, "Would you say that people are fractals? And I don't mean our molecular structure and DNA, but in the sense that we're products of the places we're from, the people we've known, the struggles we've endured? The fact that we've got those experiences tattooed all over us. Does that make us fractals? Because when you talk about repeating patterns, I mean… fuck me… my life is exhibit A, B, and C." I shift my gaze to the river as the idea unfurls. "It's funny because I've always romanticized the idea of disappearing without a trace. But now you've got me thinking that no matter where I go, the traces are always there."

Vanessa eyes me with surprise. "That's a beautiful interpretation. It's something I've never considered." We are quiet for a little while, until Vanessa says, "I think the beauty of the universe is that its entire existence, and the existence of everything within it, can be unraveled and rendered down to math... That math is the language by which we can understand the complexities of nature... Even chaos, which we think of as inherently unpredictable, follows rules based on non-linear equations... The spiral of a seashell is the same as the spiral of the galaxies. You know, the Fibonacci sequence."

I look on, dumbstruck. "My flunking of grade 12 math has me feeling a little inadequate here."

"Let me show you something."

Vanessa goes into her purse and produces the tiny notepad and pencil. She jots something and hands me the following:

$$3 \cdot s \cdot \left(\frac{4}{3}\right) n$$

I concede that there's zero chance I'll ever understand that formula.

"Exactly. This equation represents the perimeter of the Koch snowflake and when written numerically it is virtually meaningless to everyone. But when translated into a visual concept..." Vanessa draws an equilateral triangle and—like a magician demonstrating she has nothing up her sleeve—presents it to me:

She then creates a smaller triangle in the center of each of the original triangle's sides, so that her figure resembles the Star of David. She erases the base of the three triangles, then presents it:

She gives me some time to consider what she's doing, the schematic a dangling modifier awaiting meaning. When I indicate that I'm ready to see what comes next, Vanessa repeats the triangles on every available line, drawing 12 more baseless triangles. By this point, the inadequacy of the pencil-top eraser becomes apparent, but she presents her figure nonetheless:

This third figure triggers something within me. I begin to understand. With my leg going like a jackrabbit, I run through some rudimentary multiplication in my head, jumping to my feet as I see the future, pointing to her notepad and shouting, "FORTY-EIGHT MORE TRIANGLES!"

Vanessa's face lights with a smile. The image running through both of our minds looks like this:

Followed immediately thereafter by:

Holy fuck.

My mind races as I consider the possibilities, the consequences, the implications, and the meaning.

Sometimes a switch gets flicked, and the world is never the same. I don't know how much of this I'm able to express to Vanessa in my manic rambling, but it's enough to convey that I "get it" on some molecular level. That I am *with* her. That now we are playing for keeps.

I sit back on the ledge, my heart pounding and my soul momentarily content. I take a deep breath and laugh in something like post-coital satisfaction. "I think I'm gonna need another one of those cigarettes."

She laughs and hands me her pack.

I inhale deeply, surveying the slow-moving water on the river. "I have to say, that's some pretty mind-bending stuff. And you're telling me that these patterns just *happen* in nature?"

She nods as if to show the fact continues to astound her.

I shake my head in awe. "That's extremely fucked-up, in all the right ways."

I pick up the notepad and examine this geometric figure with a finite area and an infinitely expanding perimeter. But there is something missing, something I can't quite wrap my mind around. "So... When this sort of fractal thing happens in nature, what's in the center of that first triangle? What is this finite thing that sets the infinite patterns into motion?"

"I'm not sure we've figured that out yet. The truth, maybe?"

"Because the truth will set us free, right?"

Vanessa smiles. "It will indeed... But not until it's finished with you."

It is early afternoon by the time we make it back to the dusty road and the rickety bus that will deliver us to the Plaza. We take a seat amidst the locals, many with small children on their laps. The transistor radio at the front of the bus squawks cumbia music and the sun shines brightly through the open windows as we make our way back through town. Under virtually any other circumstance, a ride on one of Peru's ramshackle micros is about as unpleasant an experience as possible: noisy, cramped, and unabashedly dangerous. But with Vanessa pressed up against me and the suddenly endless possibilities of life unfolding, I feel relaxed. At one point, the loop of cumbia is broken by Bobby McFerrin's "Don't Worry, Be Happy," the non sequitur song so perfectly haphazard that we can't help but smile, bopping along to the beat.

As we approach the city, Vanessa leans over to rest her head on my shoulder. Without a second thought, I put my arm around her and feel the warmth of her body against mine, the smell of her hair enveloping me in a way that comforts beyond description. I want to gently kiss her forehead, and to tell her that the past four hours have been the closest I've come to happiness in a long time.

But I do neither.

Instead, I let her fall asleep on my chest, hoping like hell that our stop will never come.

16

Ishy & The Deuce – Monday: Peru

A 26-hour bus ride across the Andes is grueling at the best of times, but if the passengers happen to be two wholly unprepared, utterly hungover gringos sitting at the back of an Económico, the journey is Hell on Earth.

The first few hours, Ishy and The Deuce talk themselves into the merits of the ride's authenticity. The seats are torn and devoid of legroom, the windows are grimy single-pane sliders, but the view of the barren desert as the bus climbs out of Lima and into the foothills of the Andes is otherworldly.

Passengers routinely hang out of the windows to buy bananas and Inca Kola from derelict roadside entrepreneurs, while the more persistent peddlers board the bus, travelling a few kilometers down the road to hawk everything from beer nuts and plantain chips to juice of a suspect origin they serve in strawed plastic bags. The Deuce buys one of everything, including a pair of scissors capable of

Yurimaguas

Tarapoto

Juanjui

Tocache

Tingo Maria

Huápuco

Cerro de Pasco

Lima

cutting through a compact disc, as gratuitously demonstrated by the salesman wandering the aisle.

Instrumental pipe music blares from crackling speakers as overhead TVs show stout Andean women in colorful, pleated skirts parading the streets of nameless chola towns, endlessly turning and twirling, back-and-forth, side-to-side, the festival footage interrupted only by fleeting pastoral mountain scenes: Cusco, Huancayo, Titicaca, Ayacucho. To the untrained ear, the music sounds like the same song on loop, and what seemed a mildly interesting cultural quirk soon devolves into something irrationally infuriating, the absurdity of it all ultimately breaking Ishy and The Deuce as they laugh maniacally at the onset of every new song, masochistically hoping the music will never stop. The two of them are like hostages with Stockholm syndrome, but merely sit at the back of a bus without a bathroom.

Three hours into the trip, the Económico stops in a tiny village, where the driver disappears into what appears to be the house of a relative. Most of the riders slip into the town's only restaurant to order from the *almuerzo* menu. As the sun sets beyond the gray mist of the mountains, Ishy and The Deuce find a seat at a plastic table on the sidewalk, eating a French-fry-hotdog-ketchup-coleslaw concoction while watching the dog from the spare tire compartment play with local kids in the street.

By the time the group boards the bus again, darkness falls, and the novelty of economy-class trans-Andean transportation is gone. As the diesel engine sputters and groans up every pass, there's constant whipping from the overhead tarp and a hiss from the frigid mountain air as it whistles through the creaky windows that refuse to shut. The tortured barking of the reconfined dog goes on for hours; the yelping is relentless, desperate until it suddenly stops altogether.

Acknowledging that he'll most certainly go to hell for saying so, The Deuce thanks God for the engine fumes that appear to have finally gotten the best of the little bastard. But when the bus stops for a bathroom break three hours later, the mutt jumps out of the spare tire compartment, running around with its drooling tongue hanging out and trying to hump everything in sight.

Searching for distraction on the next leg of the passage, Ishy dives back into his guidebook. Using his pocket flashlight to skim the pages, he comes across a section explaining that hundreds of people die every year in Peruvian bus accidents. Looking out the window, he notices clusters of little roadside crosses. Ishy typically understands his life in terms of equations and probability, but now he avoids the numbers racing through his head as the jalopy coughs around switchbacks and hairpin turns. He knows too well that the sheer cliff faces and bottomless abyss lurk in the blackness just beyond the window.

At some point in the night, the onboard entertainment changes from pipe music to a Steven Seagal movie about a hero waking from a coma to take revenge on his wrongdoers. The volume is cranked to a staggering decibel, and Ishy cringes, thinking that people around the world hate America precisely because of movies like this. He is on the verge of sharing his theories of geopolitical propaganda, but The Deuce is too busy re-enacting the fight scenes and reciting the dialogue to pay attention.

When the movie ends, the Andean bedtime instrumentals begin: a lullaby of pan flutes and slow drumbeats as the lights dim and most of the Peruvians fall asleep in their seats. Ishy finds himself wondering when there'll be another bathroom break, but the stop seems more elusive with each passing hour. When The Deuce begins snoring like a chainsaw, it occurs to Ishy that he is the last passenger awake.

The temperature steadily drops as the bus climbs to higher and higher altitudes. By midnight, there is ice on the inside of the windows. With the violent jarring of every bathtub-sized pothole, Ishy grows more convinced their vessel is going to skid over the edge and plummet hundreds of feet below. It is the first time since being trapped in the NYC elevator that he is confronting the very real possibility of his own death. His heart and mind are racing. He's shivering and exhausted. Uncomfortable and afraid. He swears he feels something crawling up his ankle and, after swatting it, he shines his watch light on the floor and sees a cockroach scurrying away. He feels utterly alone in the darkness and on the verge of tears.

Ishy's body no longer able to withstand the exertion of worry, he mercifully dozes off, but it isn't long before he awakes to the sputtering stop of the diesel engine and brightening interior lights. People wearily shuffle and Ishy realizes the bus is pulled onto the side of the road. It's just after 4AM.

He tries to shake The Deuce into consciousness but there's no waking him. Cursing as he climbs over his comatose companion, Ishy files into the freezing night. There, he spends the next 45 minutes huddled in mountain darkness, praying for the salvation of the driver and porter attempting to fix the flat as transport trucks roar around the dead man's curve.

By the time everyone is allowed back on the bus, dawn is bleeding through the ice-laden windows. Ishy falls into a deep sleep, slumbering well into the morning. When he awakes, the pipe music is whistling again, and the temperature rises considerably as the Económico slides down the backside of the Andes.

A landslide detour, a traffic jam that allows for tree removal, a 35-minute construction delay for pothole repairs, three bathroom breaks and before they know it, they're soaking in the stifling heat of Yurimaguas.

It is 6PM. The Económico is right on schedule.

Utterly exhausted, Ishy and The Deuce stumble away from the bus station to find a dilapidated *hospedaje* with crumbling walls and unlaundered sheets. They're too defeated to look for lodging elsewhere. The room is bathed in the dusk's diminishing light and appears to have been vacated only minutes ago. They're unconscious the moment their heads hit the pillows, sleeping straight through until morning.

Later, Ishy awakes to a frantic pounding on the door. Disoriented, he stumbles towards the knocking, groggily opening the door to a wide-eyed local who can't be older than fourteen. The kid grabs Ishy by the arm and pulls him out of the room, saying, "We are going now, yes? Boat for leaving early today! Boat for leaving *ahora*!"

Ishy wipes sleep from his eyes. "Wait, what?"

"Going for Iquitos, *sí*?"

"Yeah, but—"

"Desk man says you go en boat for Iquitos, *sí*? *Cómo se dice*, you esleep LATE! Boat for leaving *AHORA*!"

As the message sinks in, Ishy determines what missing the boat would do to their itinerary. He breaks out in a cold sweat. "Fuck! Deuce?"

The Deuce groans.

"Deuce, we need to get moving."

The kid shouts, "*Ahora! Ahora! Nos vamos AHORITA!*"

"Lordsy," the Deuce's voice is haggard, "what the fuck is goin' on out there?"

Ishy isn't entirely sure. "I think this kid is saying the boat is leaving early today."

"*Sí, sí!* Early! Boat for leaving *AHORA!*"

Ishy nods. "I think he's saying we need to go now if we want to catch the boat to Iquitos."

"*Sí, Iquitos!* Boat for leaving *AHORITA!*"

The Deuce opens his eyes. "I thought you said the boat leaves at four."

"I know what I said, but this kid's saying something else."

There's a moment of honest deliberation as The Deuce weighs his options. Then the sound of sheets being ripped from the bed. "FUCK me! What the FUCK?"

Ishy turns to see The Deuce struggling with a pair of shorts. He exhales in disbelief and asks the kid to give them a minute.

"*Sí, claro. Pero rápido!*"

Ishy and The Deuce furiously pack, brush their teeth, and use the bathroom while the kid stands in the doorway, tapping his watch. Before they can process what's happening, they're blinded by the hot morning sun as they toss their packs into the kid's mototaxi. They sit on top of their gear and jolt into traffic.

After a couple minutes, the kid asks, "You have hammocks, *sí*? For to sleeping?"

Ishy and The Deuce look at each other and groan.

"Do not be worry. I get for you. *Vamos al Mercado.*" The rickshaw pulls alongside a busy market and the kid turns around. "*100 soles por uno. 200 soles por dos.* I go for to buy."

Ishy and The Deuce look at one another warily. Ishy asks, "Are you sure? Maybe we should just go with you."

The kid wags his finger. "No good for to leaving *las mochilas en la moto aqui en Yurimaguas. Están locos?* People stealing from gringos *todos los dias.*"

Ishy squeezes his pack a little tighter.

"200 soles, yes? I go now. Boat for leaving *ahora*!"

Cursing the kid up and down, The Deuce pulls a crisp 100 from his wallet. Ishy does the same.

"*Ya regreso en un momentito.*"

When the kid disappears into the crowd, The Deuce shakes his head. "This little bastard is robbing us blind. Fuckin' 40 bucks for a cocksucking hammock. That's some bullshit right there. What's your fuckin' guidebook say about how much a goddamn hammock should cost?"

Ishy reaches for his pack, then looks at The Deuce with panic in his eyes. He pats himself down and checks his backpack before smacking himself in the forehead. He leans back and emits a long, defeated, "Fuuuuuck! I forgot the book at the hotel."

The Deuce shakes his head. "Fuckin' Lordsy. You'd forget your nutsack if it weren't sewn to your scrote."

Ishy is disconsolate. "Our whole itinerary was in that book! I had it all figured out: where we're supposed to go, how to get there, schedules, maps... What the hell are we gonna do?"

The Deuce lights a cigarette and takes a long, satisfying drag. "Don't sweat it, bro. If you ain't makin' mistakes, you ain't tryin'." He takes another pull off his cigarette and taps Ishy twice on the leg. "We'll be golden."

The kid emerges a few minutes later with two hammocks folded over his arm, chomping on a Snickers bar as he leisurely walks to their moto. He tosses the hammocks to them as he climbs onto his seat, announcing, "I get for you special deal. Beautiful hammocks. *Dulces sueños.*" He takes the last bite of his chocolate bar and fires up the engine, tossing the wrapper into the street.

Once they reach the port, the kid rushes them out, tossing their packs and hammocks from the backseat and pointing them toward the ticket booth. "20 soles," he announces.

"20 fuckin' soles for a 10-minute ride to the river?" The Deuce is irate. "Fuck this little prick."

Ishy smiles in embarrassment, handing the kid a 20.

"And a tip, *señor*? I get for you beautiful hammocks, *sí?*"

The Deuce is howling. "The fuckin' balls on this kid."

Ishy begrudgingly slips their driver a five spot.

The kid snatches the money and peels out, squealing with delight.

Two minutes later, there's some frenzied confusion at the ticket booth as Ishy and The Deuce try to convey that they need two tickets for the boat leaving *ahora* for Iquitos. The clerk gives them a sideways look and glances at the chalkboard schedule behind him before shrugging and handing them each a ticket for the 100 sol fare. He then points to the Eduardo V, the only boat on the wharf. Soaked in sweat, Ishy and The Deuce frantically run down the muddy embankment to the dock, waving their arms and imploring the captain to "WAIT!"

The Deuce secretly hopes they'll have to throw their packs over the rail and jump for it, *Indiana Jones*-style, but they run through the gate without stopping, crossing over the bridge and bursting into gigantic riverboat bound for Iquitos.

Hunched over and out of breath, it takes them a confused moment to realize what's happened.

"That little cocksucker motherfucker..."

Ishy is still trying to piece it together as The Deuce shakes his head in masochistic reverence.

"Gotta hand it to the little son-of-a-whore. That asshole at the hostel musta been in on it too. Fuck me, they saw us gringos comin' from a mile away."

Save for an old man pushing a broom across the empty deck, the Eduardo V is completely deserted.

It isn't until early-afternoon that the next passengers arrive: a trio of Scotsmen in their early 20s, along with the 19-year-old Irish girl they met in Ecuador. Ishy and The Deuce welcome them aboard and help them sling their hammocks near their own, creating a little gringo sleeping collective. As the afternoon wears on, they are joined by a well-travelled German wearing a T-shirt that reads, "SAME SAME BUT DIFFERENT," an American in his mid-30s who was a rookie firefighter in New Orleans when the levees broke, a Swedish girl with an expensive camera who speaks impeccable English, and a quiet Israeli couple fresh off their mandatory three-year military stint.

Large Peruvian groups begin boarding after 4PM, bringing picnic baskets and young children who run excitedly around the boat, peeking over the railing into the river below. What had been an empty space hours before is now a happily chaotic cluster of music and laughter amongst crisscrossing hammocks.

Beneath the passenger deck, the boat crew begins the arduous task of loading cargo. Strong men in filthy shirts carry colossal plantain bunches on their backs, trudging back and forth from the muddy shore along a bouncing wooden plank. Others carry immense bags of rice and beans on their shoulders, cigarettes dangling from their lips. Ishy and The Deuce lean against the rail, watching it all unfold.

After all the dry goods are aboard, the crew loads the livestock: squawking chickens and bleating goats, followed by docile cattle who seem resigned to their overcrowded pens. It is only after the last cow has been locked in that Ishy and The Deuce hear the first scream. It is the guttural murder-wail of a man as a handsaw's cold steel bites into the back of his neck, a pillowcase over his head in a foreign place, these horrifying last seconds of life as he cries for his dad to save him.

The crew drag pigs by their ears, their tails, their snouts, prodding them with hot irons as they buck and squirm and run, every instinct telling them that this boat signifies slaughter. One of the pigs jumps off the makeshift bridge and into the water, taking two men with him.

If the voice is the organ of the soul, the pigs' souls are in incomprehensible anguish. The screams are blood-curdling and demonic, human but beyond what any human should have to endure. Ishy closes his eyes and covers his ears, but it's no use.

It is only when the sun dips beyond the trees that the boat is finally untethered and set adrift. Having been rushed to the docks early this morning half-asleep, the notion of purchasing provisions hadn't occurred to Ishy or The Deuce. And now, as darkness sets in, it dawns on them that they don't have any food. Thankfully, their new friends in the gringo hammock collective are more prepared. The Swedish girl offers Pringles. The American slices off a hunk of cheese. The Irish lass gives them an avocado. The Israelis share bread and olives. A nearby Peruvian family takes note of the charity and hands Ishy and The Deuce a hunk of something tied in a banana leaf. Upon unwrapping the offering, they discover a softball-size mound of rice. It's sprinkled with garlic, herbs, spices, vegetables, half a boiled egg, and a little piece of chicken for good measure. "Juane," the German informs them. "A jungle delicacy."

Considering the circumstances, it is the most delicious meal they've eaten in a long time.

Less than an hour downriver, the boat picks up more passengers. The upper deck is already a little cramped and if the boat continues taking on riders, things are going to get *tight*. The Scots determine that there is only one way to cope with this encroachment: two bottles of pisco. The backpackers smile knowingly, and it isn't long before they're taking long swigs and soothing fiery throats with Inca Kola chasers. The combination tastes like grappa-soaked cotton candy bubblegum. They're so enamored with the concoction that they baptize it Gringo Thunder. They laugh through every drop, regaling one another with backpacking misadventures and running the gamut of cultural differences that define and delineate them: soccer and smoking, Quentin Tarantino and real maple syrup, losing your virginity and learning to surf.

The German kid pulls a small guitar from his pack, admitting he recently purchased it in the hopes of learning a few chords. He offers it to anyone who knows how to play and when there's hesitation all around, The Deuce mutters, "Aw, fuck it," and reaches for the axe.

Ishy looks at him in disbelief.

"What can I say, Lordsy? I'm a fuckin' Renaissance man." As the group giddily awaits, he tunes up and says, "Alright, so this is the first thing I learned to play on the guitar. It was one of those songs that just came into my life at the right time." He strums a couple times, then begins picking with surgical precision. The song is "Round Here" by Counting Crows.

Ishy's mouth makes a perfect O. Although he knows The Deuce to be a man of some very specific talents—the best hockey player Ishy has ever known, the life of every party, a world-class swordsman with a knack for getting into the pants of the most attractive female in any given setting—this particular display is one that Ishy did not see coming.

The Deuce's voice is soft, sincere, and pitch-perfect, sounding every bit as good as Adam Duritz in his dreadlocked heyday of dating the two hottest girls from *Friends*. He sings with his eyes closed, feeling every ounce of pain, and when he closes in on that gut-wrenching, insomniac crescendo, there are tears in the eyes of everyone in their circle.

At the song's conclusion, there is a moment of stunned silence, then a rousing, cathartic roar that echoes across the river and leaves the Peruvians onboard wondering whether they'll ever get some sleep.

The Deuce smiles big, nodding his approval at the scene he's played a role in creating. He reaches for the pisco and takes a swig, then gives a hell of an encore, including a smile-until-your-face-hurts sing-along rendition of "American Pie," a timely take on Chuck Berry's "Havana Moon," and a version of the Foo Fighters' "Everlong" that has the group stomping the floorboards and pounding the metal beams by way of percussion that feels so damn good and reminds them of what exactly it means to be alive.

When he finishes this last track, The Deuce offers the guitar to any takers, but he might as well be Jerry Lee Lewis torching the piano. Nobody follows The Killer.

The pisco ensures that hammock sleep will come easy and, by 11:30, it feels as though Ishy and The Deuce are the last two humans awake. They drunkenly giggle about the people in proximity, the symphony of full-throated snoring in full swing. Ishy fails to be discreet when he leans over and whispers, "Deuce, I gotta tell ya, I can't believe how fucking poor this place is. It's crazy here."

"Fuck, Lords. The places you travel for work? This shit should be old news."

Ishy shakes his head. "Dirty little secret: I never see anything real. It's just boardrooms and hotel bars... But this?" Ishy takes a deep breath and tries not to think of how his fast-cash, consumerist culture contributes to the poverty in his midst. "This is some intense shit."

They are quiet for a moment. The Deuce smiles in the darkness. "Hey, I ever tell you about my first business meeting?"

Ishy laughs. "Nah, I don't think I heard that one."

The Deuce lights a cigarette. "It's the kinda story that could get me jailed or killed, but seein' as it's just us girls and we're gettin' to know one another all over again..."

Ishy leans in a little closer.

"The construction world is a shady fuckin' place, as I'm sure you've heard. Backdoor deals, offshore accounts, stacks in brown envelopes straight outta *The Sopranos*. I'd heard about it here and there, but it's all just rumor when you're a nothin' fuckin' laborer. But when I turned 25, the big boss started movin' me up the food chain and before I knew it I was in a position I probably had no business bein' in." The Deuce takes a long drag on his cigarette. "About two weeks into the new gig, this other contractor, a competitor of ours, shows up at the jobsite and says he wants to buy me a drink. Keep your friends close and your enemies closer, right? It's close to quittin' time, so fuck it, I meet the guy at this classy little churrasqueira in Little Portugal. There's a couple guys from this other outfit already there, and we dive into some truly epic chicken, and the smokeshow waitress keeps bringin' jug after jug of Super Bock, and there's a lot of back-slappin' and shots of Macieira...

Ishy nods, eyes coaxing The Deuce on.

"I shoulda got the fuck outta there while I was ahead, but I was feelin' pretty good and it was Friday afternoon, so I just kept it rollin'. More beer. More shots. The waitress sittin' on my lap. I don't even know what the fuck time it was when we piled into the back of somebody's pickup, but we were headin' to the titty joint come hell or high water. The place wasn't exactly The Brass Rail, but what it lacked in class, it absolutely made up for in access, because these guys literally owned the fuckin' club. Like I said, serious *Sopranos* shit."

Ishy stares, mesmerized.

"So, we're back in the champagne room, and we're snorting coke off the ass of some chick. Things are a little fuzzy by this point, but I remember clear as day the big boss from this other company— the guy who owned the jobs and trucks and the titty joint too— sittin' across from me." The Deuce takes another haul from his cigarette for dramatic effect. "Fuckin' guy. As he asks me if I'm havin' a good time, the naked chick we're takin' bumps off gets under the table and unzips my pants."

Ishy's mouth hangs open.

"I can barely string two words together by this point, but I tell this big ol' fucker that ,'Yes, indeed, I am having a GREAT fuckin' time.' Then his smile disappears and he looks me square in the eye, and says, 'This is how it works around here. We get jobs A, B, and C at price point X, Y, and Z. You play ball, you keep your mouth shut, and we all make a little money.'"

Ishy squeals in disbelief.

The Deuce is smiling now, drinking it in.

"He musta read the look on my face, 'cause he started laughing and said, 'Come on now. Don't sweat it, kid. The guy before you and all the guys before him felt that same sting of integrity, but they all came around.'"

Ishy shakes his head in wonderment.

"By then the chick under the table is gagging on my cock, and I don't know what to believe. I'm drunk and high and pretty sure I'm committing a felony, and I definitely know I'm about to splooge in front of all these fuckin' roofers. And just as these truths are all converging, that big boss man drops a gigantic stack on the table. 'Ten thousand dollars,' he says. 'Say yes, shoot your load, and shut the fuck up.'"

Ishy practically yells, "Holy shit!"

"Indeed."

"Did you take it?"

"Well, that chick under the table certainly did, but..."

Ishy howls with delight as The Deuce takes another puff.

"I remember Rosy's dad sayin' to me, 'I know how it is working that contractor game. If you're thinking about taking a bribe, make sure it's a good one. Cause chances are it'll be the last one you ever take.'"

Ishy is incredulous. "I don't have much experience when it comes to kickbacks, but that sounds like pretty good advice."

The Deuce laughs to himself, nodding.

"So? Did you take the money?"

The Deuce pauses just long enough to leave Ishy hanging.

"Well?"

"You know that piece of shit car I drive... That and a blowjob from a crackhead stripper is what ya get for an honest livin' these days."

Ishy cheers so enthusiastically that he's shushed by multiple unseen Peruvians. He lowers his voice. "Fuck me! Deuce, that's killer. Truly killer."

The Deuce smiles, crushing his cigarette out on the floor as they agree to make a conscious effort to shut the fuck up.

It isn't long after that each is smiling to himself, trying to piece together exactly what in their lives has led them to this place at this time, lazily swinging in these hammocks as the Amazon night hangs electric and alive in the panorama just beyond.

17

Rosy – Tuesday: Iquitos, Peru

The Hideout is awash in the grainy light of dawn as Vanessa opens the door to my room. I am mostly asleep but can sense that she's there, standing in the doorway like a dream. She whispers my name. Then she whispers it again. I feel her walking slowly and silently to my mattress on the floor. She kneels by my side, gently running the palm of her hand across my forehead. She takes a deep breath and says, "I have to go now."

I find the strength to open my eyes and give her a confused look.

"I'll be back in nine days. I know you're not planning on going anywhere, but just in case." She slips a small, folded note into my hand.

I sit up and try to clear the cobwebs. Vanessa's eyes are puffy. "Wait, where are you going?"

She forces a smile. "To see The Shaman... Remember?"

Fuck me. Two nights earlier, while sharing a beer on the porch, Vanessa asked if I knew anything about The Gringo Shaman. I told her what little I knew: I'd seen him around town; he apprenticed under some badass natives deep in the Amazon; he's supposed to be a legit healer and his ayahuasca is rumored to be the most powerful in Iquitos... The conversation is like a forgotten dream that comes flooding back all at once. I take a deep breath and feel it in the pit of my stomach. "And, again, why're you going to see him?"

It's her turn to breathe. She looks away for a moment, searching. "I'm not entirely sure yet... I think I just want to take a peek behind the curtain."

Over the past two days, Vanessa and I have grown close in a way I can't explain. Our conversations went late into the night, profound and heartfelt and easy. It feels as if I've known her forever. "And what exactly are you hoping to find?"

She doesn't hesitate for a second. "The truth."

While Ishy and The Deuce enjoy an uninterrupted, pisco-induced slumber, The Eduardo V stops at countless jungle ports. So, when they open their eyes, hammocks are slung so close together that they can practically feel the breath of their neighbors. Ishy reaches for his pack, profoundly relieved to find it where he left it.

Moderately hungover and aching from a night of contorted torpor, Ishy and The Deuce fall out of their hammocks to make their way to the railing. They stand in the glittering sunshine, barefoot on the metal floor, content to get the kinks out as they stretch. The distant riverbank is a tangled mess of vegetation, deep and lush with shades of green Ishy and The Deuce have never seen. When they look closely, they can make out monkeys swinging from vines with staggering artistry. The sky is a blue that leaves them searching for words.

"Hey, Deuce... I think this might be the most glorious morning I've ever experienced."

The Deuce takes a deep breath and exhales satisfaction. "I gotta go take a shit."

With The Deuce off in search of a suitable commode, Ishy walks across the deck to marvel at the number of passengers the boat picked up during the night. Traversing the web of hammocks, hanging limbs, and scattered bags, Ishy reaches the far railing. There, the churning pulse of the majestic river and the sparkling rain forest vista is as awe-inspiring as the other side. He stands there for a long time, unable to believe he's floating down the Amazon, or that he spent his first night south of the equator in the arms of a Peruvian girl. It was only four nights ago, but it feels like weeks. He whispers her name to the river, its beautiful sound filling him with a warmth rivaling the morning sun.

When The Deuce returns to their hammocks, he's pale and unsteady on his feet.

"Dude, I don't know what the fuck I ate, but I just spent the past hour pissing out my ass on a toilet with no seat. Stay away from that shitter, by the way. It's an old factory nightmare."

One of the Scots next to them chews on a stale bun slathered with peanut butter. "Welcome ta Peru. Havin' the fookin' shites is as much the experience as the fookin' llamas, yeh?"

The Swedish girl inhales grimly. "Yes. My poo has been a little runny these days as well."

Ishy makes a face.

The American chimes in, "Just keep drinkin' that pisco, pal. The alcohol will kill every parasite in your system."

It sounds like good advice to The Deuce, but the thought of drinking anything makes his stomach churn. He needs to get horizontal, quick. He thanks them for their sympathy and crawls into his hammock, doing whatever he can to keep from shitting his pants. He spends the morning moaning and shivering in a cold sweat, periodically making his way to the toilet to purge all over again. On one of his return trips, Ishy notices The Deuce looking extra shaky and dehydrated. The gringos try giving him whatever liquid they have, but The Deuce isn't feeling it, insisting he just needs to catch some Zs.

But daytime hammock sleep doesn't come easy. With the excitement of their first full day on the river, kids run around the deck, the hollow clang of their feet pounding a chisel into The Deuce's searing temples. A toddler screams all morning because her sister won't share a doll, and some little boys kick a soccer ball through the tangle of humanity. A baby two hammocks down vomits breastmilk all over the floor, its warm splatter tickling the Deuce's outstretched hand while the rest of the mess is left to bake in the jungle heat. When kids start playing smash-up derby with their Hot Wheels near The Deuce's hammock, he lifts his head to look at Ishy and say, "Stop me before I commit a hate crime."

As The Deuce once again makes a bee-line for the bathroom, the Eduardo V pulls into another port. Noticing a few vendors down on the dock, Ishy steps off to acquire some provisions for his ailing friend. Heat radiates off the dock, meaning meat dishes and fish soup are out of the question. But Ishy gets his hands on some bananas, soda crackers, a hunk of sweet cake, and a big bottle of water. He also purchases a couple beers from a metal cooler, the big bottles clanging beautifully as they bob in the ice water.

Before climbing back aboard, Ishy eyes the waterline on the side of the boat, noting that it is well below the crest of the river. He only shakes his head and laughs at the absurdity of it all, crossing the bridge to rejoin the mass of humanity.

With the boat precariously overcapacity, the captain seemingly decides to forego additional stops. Amazingly, this does nothing to deter the deluge of Iquitos-bound patrons, who, upon realizing the Eduardo V has no intention of stopping, pile into motorboats and speed out into the middle of the river. Ishy and The Deuce watch in disbelief as they pull alongside the barge, throwing their gear onboard and daring to leap over the guardrail, tumbling into the cargo deck below.

After watching this same stunt play out over and over, The Deuce turns to Ishy and says, "This voyage is getting a little too biblical for me, bro."

Ishy nods, smiling. "Be loyal to the nightmare of your choice, Stan."

The rest of the afternoon drifts by slow and sweet. Their world is a womb-like cocoon of lazy hammock swinging as they admire the sloping, labyrinthine vegetation. The Deuce feels better as the day wears on, the crackers and bananas working wonders. The river pushes them forward and invites long, meandering conversation. They speak about their lives, their dreams, and their heartache. Things they've let slip away. What they want from this world and what they know they'll never get.

They open their beer in the late afternoon and whistle that David Wilcox tune. The Deuce observes how the afternoon feels like that scene in *Stand By Me* where the guys sit around a campfire, talking about the things that seem important before discovering girls. "It's funny," he says, "how two guys can know each other their entire lives, but it takes being trapped on an Amazon River barge for them to actually talk to one another."

With the beer gone and the sun getting low, Ishy gets around to asking The Deuce about his daughter. It's something he's wondered about a long time but knows The Deuce doesn't talk about her much.

The Deuce shoots him a cautious look. "Clara? I don't know. Five years old? Likes *Dora the Explorer*. I got a picture here." He reaches into his wallet to produce a bent photograph.

Ishy smiles at the cute kid with dark brown pigtails and a wide, squinting-eyed smile.

The Deuce slips it back into his pocket. "As you probably know, I'm a fuckin' dirtbag of a dad. I barely ever see her."

Ishy nods slowly, as if understanding.

"I wish it coulda been different. But me and her mom, we couldn't make it work. Couldn't keep it together, you know?" The Deuce lights a cigarette, inhales deeply. "Not sure if you caught on yet, but compromise ain't my strong suit." He allows the words to fade, but Ishy isn't about to let him off the hook. The Deuce continues, "My life's always been all about me, you know? And Clara's mom, Josie, we used to fight about it all the time. About changes I need to make. About how I need to grow up. How I need to spend less time with my friends and more with her and Clara. I knew she was right, but I refused to settle." The Deuce takes a long drag. "That's what I kept telling her, too. 'I don't settle.' As if that somehow fuckin' justified it all."

Ishy nods, coaxing it out of him.

"The more she kept on about it, the worse things got. I was bitter and vindictive, throwing the smallest bullshit back in her face even though she was the good one, even though she was doing all the sacrificing... I couldn't accept that she knew better, or that I was wrong, or that our misery was my fault." The Deuce ashes his cigarette on the floor. "Consequences of being an only child, right? My mom always telling me how wonderful I am, sacrificing all her dreams for me. That's the world I grew up in. I was the star of the movie of my life." The Deuce takes a moment to pull out another cigarette. "Josie started spending a lot of time at her parents' place. She'd take Clara there for days at a time. Guess I thought she just needed space, that she'd come around." The Deuce laughs at himself. "She asked why I never told her to come home, and I couldn't give her a reason."

Ishy says nothing.

"One day, after another big blowout, she gave me an ultimatum. *An ultimatum.* That's the fuckin' red cape for me. And she knew it, too. She said, 'I'm sorry, but some things have to happen right now.' I blew up and read the laundry list of every fuckin' thing she ever did wrong, as if that would convince her to stay... She walked out without another word, and she took Clara with her." The Deuce stares off into the riverbank, smoking in contemplation for a long time. "I was a different guy back then, you know? You wouldn't have liked me much in those days."

"I can barely stand you now, Deuce."

They smile as The Deuce shakes his head. "I don't know what to tell you, man. Forgiveness is sort of in the rear-view on this one. We said vicious things we can't un-say. I wish I could see Clara more, I really do. But it's too hard bein' civil with her mom. Things are too far gone. Time waits for no one, right?" The Deuce quietly crushes out his cigarette. "I guess it's a little like life, right? It comes together. It's magic. And then it falls apart... One day you look back and realize it's a fucking miracle it happened at all."

The river silently churns as Ishy ponders what to say. "Far be it from my place to empathize with what it's like being a father, or to have created life, or to be responsible for it. But just let me say this: The things that are most difficult to overcome, they're the most rewarding. Almost without exception. The hard stuff is the good stuff. And I don't know. I can't help but think if you work through some issues with Josie, those problems that seem like too much work and impossible to overcome... If you could somehow swallow your pride and begin putting the pieces back together, for *your daughter*... If you did that and were able to come out on the other side, you'd look back at where you're standing right now and wonder how the fuck you ever considered giving up."

The Deuce nods absently. "You're probably right, my man. You're probably right." He props himself up and looks Ishy in the eye, as if on the verge of conceding something profound about himself and the inherently flawed nature of humanity. "Fuck me, you got anything I can read? I gotta hit the jacks again and I don't think I can face those walls alone."

Ishy smiles and goes into his pack, producing a copy of Gladwell's *Outliers*. "Keep it, my man. That's the kind of journey my books don't need to come back from."

Knowing The Deuce will be out of commission a while, Ishy takes another walk around the boat. The late afternoon light is like two glasses of good scotch, washing the deck in warmth as the sun drops below the distant riverbank. Ishy comes across a group of Peruvian kids making a game of throwing Coke bottles and plastic bags over the side, laughing as the trash bobs and swirls in the river. It's on the tip of Ishy's tongue to say that it's bad for everyone to lob garbage in the river, to convey that this river is integral to the survival of the region and the whole planet, to convince them to appreciate what they have... But he doesn't have the stomach to initiate confrontation, not even with little kids who don't know any better.

Instead, Ishy walks to the back of the boat alone. He leans against the railing for a long time, losing himself in the beauty of light dancing on the water. Just as he's about to head back, he notices a pink dolphin surfacing near the stern. He's read about these rare, mystical mammals in his guidebook, not fully understanding how dolphins could survive in freshwater, let alone a river 4,000 kilometers from the sea. He stands and watches in awe as the dolphin toys with the barge, its skin almost translucent as it spouts from its blowhole, eventually leaping clean into the air like something in a *National Geographic* video. It is serene and somehow spiritual for Ishy, one of those Wordsworthian spots of time he knows will be with him for the remainder of his days.

When the dolphin breaks off and dissolves into the murky depths, Ishy continues to stand by the rail, hoping in vain to catch one more glimpse. By the time he turns to make his way back to the hammocks, the sun is gone, too.

The Deuce waits for Ishy at their post with a dinner of soda crackers slathered in peanut butter and slices of banana. They wash the feast down with Inca Kola. After the long day lazing around the deck, most of the backpackers turn in early. Even the lively Peruvian children are sound asleep. As if to commemorate this tranquility, a warm breeze carries the soft, verdant scent of the jungle across the deck.

Ishy takes a deep breath and considers the question that's been weighing on him since before they left Toronto. Through the hum of the diesel engine, he turns to his accomplice and asks, "Hey, Deuce... How are we gonna tell him?"

The Deuce sighs. "That's one thing I can't tell you. I honestly have no idea. I mean, is there any decent way to ruin a guy's life?"

They're quiet for a long time, lost in what they might do or say when the moment arrives.

"This place we're going to, Iquitos... You ever think about the significance of it?"

"It weighs heavy on me, Ish. It really does."

"I know, but I don't mean the significance of what we're doing, I'm talking about the significance of the place itself."

"I don't follow."

Ishy takes a deep breath. "Let's say you want to be completely anonymous. You move to a big city, right?"

"Always."

"And if you want to be left the hell alone, you're gonna hide out in some place that's halfway around the world and borderline impossible to get to."

The Deuce is nodding.

"I'm just thinking, if you're a white guy from Toronto and you've decided to hole up in the biggest city in the world that can't be accessed by road, you probably don't want to be found."

The Deuce considers this then reaches into his pack. He pulls out a Ziplock of weed. Ishy has no idea how or when he acquired the contraband. As if sensing his befuddlement, The Deuce offers, "José."

Of course, The Deuce would hit up the sketchy Colombian at The Happy Llama within the first hour of their arrival. Ishy looks on with curiosity as The Deuce falls into a near-meditative state swinging in his hammock, breaking out the pot on his stomach. Though Ishy would never admit it, this is the first time he's seen someone roll a joint. "Hey, Deuce... You ever think about dying?"

The Deuce chuckles. "No easy ones tonight, eh, Lordsy?"

Ishy returns a sheepish smile.

The Deuce swats a mosquito away from his arm and says, "I used to tell myself that when you're dead, the only thing they put on your tombstone is two dates and a dash, and the only thing that matters is that dash. So, live every day like your last, carpe diem and all that shit. But once you have a kid, fuck, it changes things. Even though I've been a total fuckwad of a dad, knowing that someone's gonna be around after I'm long gone, it gets you thinkin'. Makes you realize we're all on the clock, you know? That time is tickin', and the more track you leave behind, the faster this fuckin' train rolls on." He shakes his head. "It's a fucked-up thing, but I remember sittin' around the kitchen table with my grandmother late one night. Poor old doll's heart had been broken so many times, you wondered how she ever got out of bed in the morning. But she had these little rituals that got her through the day, you know? These meager indulgences that kept life worth living. She used to love havin' a cuppa tea in the evenings. Her beautiful reward for making it through another day." The Deuce takes a deep breath. "One night we got to talkin' about all the people she'd known who had come and gone. The ones who died or drifted away. Friends. Parents. Her husband. My dad. People she'd been young with. People she'd shared life with... She got real quiet, then looked up at me with these sad eyes and said she couldn't believe her life was almost over. That it seemed like just yesterday she was a little girl."

The pain of it dangles in the night.

After a long time, Ishy says, "The day before we came down here, I transferred all the photos from my phone onto my laptop. I was sitting at my computer, watching these images flicker past, each picture appearing on the screen for a split second—just long enough to register in my mind. Just long enough for me to smile or get sentimental before it disappeared and was replaced by the next one. I was literally watching the last two years of my life flash before my eyes." Ishy exhales. "I can't help but think that's what it must be like the moment before you die."

The Deuce smiles. "That ain't the last moment of your life, son. That's life. Period."

They're quiet a long time before Ishy asks, "Does it scare you? The thought of dying?"

The Deuce licks the paper to seal the joint, neatly tucking the masterpiece behind his ear. "A little bit. But that's the deal, right? You're gonna die. I'm gonna die. It's the great equalizer. We're all gonna die, and some sooner than fuckin' later. Does that make it any easier to stare down? Maybe for some... All I can say is for me, the closer it gets, the more terrifying it all becomes."

Ishy never considered The Deuce being afraid of anything.

"What about you, Ish? You scared of dying?"

Ishy takes an unsteady breath. "Honestly? I can't stop thinking about those pigs screaming."

The Deuce laughs, taking the joint from his ear and snapping his Zippo. Shadows momentarily dance between them.

"I'm serious," Ishy protests. "It's like they know what's coming. They know they're rinds. And that screaming... I feel like that's what we should all be doing, all the fucking time! We go about our lives pretending the all-consuming imminence of death isn't hanging over everything, but—when you get right down to it—our life isn't any different from the lives of those pigs. Because we'll all be in the ground someday, and then the only thing we've ever had or known will be extinguished forever." Ishy shakes his head in disgust. "When I think about that, about how short and precarious and temporary life is, about how there are no do-overs, about how every minute is one we'll never get back... I just wanna fucking scream like those God-forsaken pigs."

Without saying a word, The Deuce passes him the joint. Ishy doesn't think twice, taking a long, deep hit. He coughs a couple times, pounding his chest before handing it back to The Deuce. "First time for everything, eh, Lordsy?"

They smile in the darkness.

The night is velvet, the air thick with the earthy, citrus bouquet of good weed, the sweetness lingering and softening the edges. When Ishy closes his eyes, he swears he's somewhere in the summer of his youth, the perfect evening that exists only in the memory of a feeling.

"Hey, Ish, you're a stock market guy. What do you make of the idea of buying time?"

Ishy's gaze is locked on the beam from which his hammock is slung. "What do you mean?"

The Deuce takes a long haul off the joint. "Imagine you could buy fifteen minutes here and there. To read. To jerk off. An extra hour or so to sleep in the morning. What do you figure that would be worth?"

Ishy nods definitively. "I know some who would pay a substantial sum for that commodity."

"Or, better yet, what would you give to be 18 again? To go back, knowing everything you know now about how the world works. Knowing you can do whatever you want in life. That you can be whatever the fuck you want. That you can travel the world for years at a time and everything'll work out in the end. What would you give up to go back and relive the past 10 years?"

Ishy takes a while to consider this. He thinks about the success he's achieved: how much money he has in the bank, the people he knows, his swanky King Street condo, all the childhood dreams that somehow seem to have faded away. "Everything," Ishy finally says. "Send me back, naked as the day I was born. I'd give it all up to have that time back."

The Deuce nods with conviction. "Indeed."

Conversation waxes and wanes from there. Sentiment takes the night. Movie scenes they love and why. Girls they wanted to love but hadn't. Joe Carter and Wendel Clark. Places they'd like to see someday. They are gloriously high, soaking it all in. Their voices trail off and their words are slow. It isn't long before The Deuce notes Ishy's deep, steady breathing. Dragging himself from his hammock, The Deuce navigates through throngs of sleeping people, searching for equilibrium and the toilet one last time.

In the light of a dangling bulb, The Deuce studies his reflection in the rusted bathroom mirror, incredulous as he observes the small creases around his eyes and the gray hairs scattered about his head, wondering when and how the fuck he'd gotten so old. The bulb flickers, then burns out completely. He thinks about something he heard someone once saying, maybe Lester from *The Wire*, that life is the shit that happens when you're waiting for moments that never come.

He laughs and laughs and laughs, loud and for the entire world to hear, sitting alone in the dark on a river barge shitter, somewhere in the middle of the Amazon.

And then he weeps in silence.

Before climbing back into his hammock—smiling now, but with his eyes drinking tears—The Deuce gently puts his hand on Ishy's shoulder and whispers, "You're a good man to go down the river with."

18

Vanessa – Tuesday: Peru

Nov. 15th, 2011
Three hours downriver of Iquitos

I'm not sure where to start.

I met a great guy at The Hideout. He is a beautiful person and wounded soul, and I have mixed feelings about leaving him behind in Iquitos. A big part of me—most of me, in fact—wanted to stay with him. I have no idea what I hoped would come of it. Perhaps that I could somehow help him, or that he could reveal something within me. I don't even know if I can properly formulate thoughts or feelings; I just know it felt right being near him. I don't know what comes next.

I said goodbye to Rosy in the early morning, living an Otis Redding song as I choked back tears and walked from the hostel. I met our small group of truth-seekers and spiritual wanderers at the Plaza de Armas. Iquitos at dawn—before chaos sets in—was magnificent. When you find peace in a place where peace was once unfathomable, it is a stunning experience. The group of us quietly boarded a little *colectivo* that took us to the docks, where we climbed into a small, open-air boat.

We set off down the Amazon River, and it was spectacular, everything I dreamed it would be. But—and I hesitate to write this because of how awful I will come off sounding—it's amazing how quickly you can grow bored of your surroundings, no matter how breathtaking. I swear, after a very short time looking out at the riverbank—a view I'd been dreaming of since I was a little girl—I found myself growing weary of it all... Have I become completely desensitized to the beauty of the natural world? Is it because the internet has made me crave incessant instant gratification? Is this what it means to be a millennial?

We arrived at the camp three hours later, and I must tell you: This place is VERY rustic and VERY isolated. It is little more than a small jungle clearing with a few thatch-roof huts. There is no power. No phone reception. No air conditioning. No hot water. The beds consist of mosquito nets hanging over futon-style cotton floor slabs. But the place is gorgeous, and perfectly suited for reconciliation with the natural world.

I am sharing my hut with three other women (we are the only females at the camp), one of whom is an older woman from Jersey City: Linda, who seems to be one of the nicest people I've ever met. There's also a sweet girl from Oregon in her late twenties and a Russian who is almost certainly a retired supermodel or movie star. Any reservations about sharing a room with three strangers were immediately dispelled. These are wonderful people with big hearts who have a knack for knowing when you need someone to talk to, and when you need space.

One more thing I don't quite know how to explain: Everyone here seems somehow familiar. I remember having that feeling during my first few weeks at school, since everyone kind of looked like someone I knew, or they'd say something just like one of my high school friends would say... I get the same sense here. It is striking, and it is undeniable.

After getting settled into our cabins, we all met in the main lodge for a lunch of grilled dorado fish, hearts of palm salad, and soda crackers. The food here is delicious and is the very definition of farm-to-table. All of which is wonderful, but I'll be honest, I've been craving a cheeseburger since I got here!

After lunch, we got the chance to meet The Gringo Shaman. Some people have a presence about them, and The Gringo Shaman is one such person. I swear that the hair on my arms stood on end when he walked into the room.

The Shaman conducted a little icebreaker/orientation with the group. One of the themes he emphasized is that ayahuasca is not a drug, but a medicine. The Shaman couldn't stress enough that this wasn't going to be a psychedelic party scene. This is a place of healing, a place for spiritual discovery. The truth of this concept is reflected in the rules:

No drugs permitted at camp (carrying spells expulsion)
No alcohol
No sugars, sweets, or fruits

No pork
No music
No sexual contact, including kissing or holding hands
No masturbating
No caffeine
Fasting is mandatory after 2 PM on ceremony days.

The Shaman said he could make no guarantees on anything except that—if we strictly adhere to these rules—we will live. Anything beyond that, we're on our own.

After hammering home that this is gravely serious business, The Shaman lightened things up by taking us for a walk through the jungle. He introduced us to some of the plants we'll be using to make ayahuasca.

First impressions of the Amazon rainforest: This place is slightly terrifying. It is magnificent and its secrets and possibilities are seemingly infinite... but there are so many things that can kill you! Spiders and snakes and poisonous plants, even frogs whose mere touch can leave you dead before hitting the ground.

And then there are the birds! In the Amazon, the birds DO NOT sing sweetly. They screech and wail and shrill. It's abrupt and alarming and piercing and violent, and it sounds more like a cackling warning than anything else; nature's way of telling us we have no business being here!

But we are most definitely, absolutely, undeniably here. And in experiencing the power of this place, it's impossible not to recognize that something truly awesome created and sustains this perfectly balanced system.

Throughout our jungle walk, The Shaman encouraged us to speak to the plants. I'm not totally positive where I fit on the spirituality scale, but this is generally where I draw the line. But The Shaman kept at it, telling us to ask the plants what we want of them, reiterating that the spirits are willing to give you everything.

As crazy as it sounds, the deeper we went into the jungle, the more I was drawn to some of the plants. I was trying to ignore the feeling and play it cool, but when one of the older, more experienced guys implored me to let go and give one of those big, old trees a hug, I did... And it felt great! Before I knew it, I had joined the others in whispering my intentions to the plants. By the end of the walk, I found myself rapping my knuckles against the trunks of giant kapok trees, quietly asking them to go easy on me in the first ceremony.

Beyond talking to the plants (*did I just write that?*), we did some hunting and gathering. Some of the medicinal plants we handpicked for our ayahuasca brew included:

> Ayahuasca vine (vine of the soul)
> Chacruna leaves (to give you visions)
> Capirona bark (for cleansing)
> Ayahuma bark (protects the soul from spiritual trauma)
> Remo Caspi bark (to move dark energies)
> Nicotiana rustica (Mapacho, or jungle tobacco that the shamans smoke during sacred ceremonies)

One of the other native shamans, Don Alberto, came from a village two days up the river. As far as I can tell, he is the master shaman under whom The Gringo Shaman apprenticed, and—even though he speaks no English—you somehow understand everything he means. He brought with him a number of plants from his part of the jungle that we'll be using for tomorrow's ayahuasca brew.

After the hike through the humid jungle, we spent the remainder of the afternoon focusing on inner reflection. I did some reading and took a long, cold shower that felt like an open fire hydrant in a heatwave. When darkness fell, we made our way to the ceremony house for the Sacred Plant Ceremony.

There is a kid here from California who is the only person younger than me. He lovingly referred to the concoction we would be consuming tonight as "The Dream Juice."

Dream Juice is a mixture of tree bark and camphor that tastes like Vicks VapoRub and 151 proof rum. Drinking Dream Juice in this setting, on the night before our first ayahuasca ceremony, is supposed to give us vivid dreams of learning and healing as a dress rehearsal for tomorrow. An older guy from Martha's Vineyard said tonight is like riding a bike with training wheels on a quiet cul-de-sac, whereas tomorrow the training wheels will be ripped off, and the bike will be doused in gasoline and set on fire as we ride off the side of a cliff!

Regardless of what tomorrow brings, the training wheels and cul-de-sac on this night were just fine by me. It was pouring rain and we sat around the ceremony house, listening to The Shaman and his apprentices singing and whistling ícaros: shamanic songs used to commune with spirits in the natural world to heal, to protect, and to give visions. We sat on the floor and tried to take it all in: the smell of the jungle in a nighttime downpour, the air thick with humidity, Mapacho smoke, and bodies in close proximity. When it came time to drink the Dream Juice, I was a little nervous, but willing to take the leap.

The drink felt good going down. When I sat back on the floor, I felt like I had crossed the first threshold. A small accomplishment, yes, but I was proud of myself.

After that Sacred Plant Ceremony, a group of us went back to the main hut, where we drank green tea and talked the night away. I quickly learned that there are many repeat visitors here. My roommate from Jersey City is here for her seventh tour. The man from Martha's Vineyard is on his fourth visit. He admitted he broke the no-sex-for-30-days-after-leaving rule and has been trying to get right ever since.

It's amazing to listen to these people and all the challenges they're trying to overcome. These stories make me stop and wonder: What is the human condition? Is it truly a shared experience that we all grow old, that we all break down, that we all lie in bed at night, afraid...? Shouldn't we acknowledge this solidarity? Shouldn't we try to embrace this one-ness? Aren't we all just the same person living different lives? Why the façade and veneer? How do we resist the compulsion to stick our heads out the window and scream, "I'M ALIVE FOR NOW BUT WILL BE DEAD ONE DAY SOON! I HURT AND I FEEL AND I'M ALONE AND I'M TERRIFIED!"

(Deep breath... Okay.)

Of all the conversations tonight, the most memorable was with an older man from New Mexico. This man, Hamish, was explaining his understanding of the nature of time and the universe. It was a little mind-blowing, but I will attempt to navigate the concepts here:

We think of time as existing in a straight, continuous line. But just because we understand it that way doesn't mean it *exists* that way. Maybe time isn't so much linear as it is spatial. As in: instead of functioning like and containing all the properties of a straight line, where one thing follows another in sequential order, maybe time functions like and contains all the properties of *place*.

For example, my dad is in Harlem while I am in the Amazon. We wouldn't dispute that he's still my dad and still exists in the same plane of reality, even though he's in a different location than me. And just because I can't physically see him or hug him or talk to him doesn't mean he doesn't currently exist.

Is it possible to understand time in the same way? My entire relationship with my dad is with me in my consciousness, just as my entire relationship with, say, Otis Redding, is here with me now. Now, I can't physically see or hug or talk to my dad just as much as I can't physically see or hug or talk to Otis Redding. One is separated by the physical limitations of place, while the other is separated by the physical limitations of time... Maybe the two are more closely related than we understand.

I know I'm struggling here, but maybe the best analogy is the one provided by New Mexico Hamish himself. He implored us to think of our existence, and the existence of the universe, as being like a vinyl record. When it comes to a record, all the music is always present. Everything exists simultaneously, even if we can only experience it one song or one note at a time. When and how we wind up listening to the music depends on where the needle happens to be dropped. But that doesn't change the fact that the music is always there.

Is this akin to time and reality?

Is it always the present moment, for everybody?

Are we all always here together, just in different places?

Is reality simply a continuum of perpetually present moments that are all equally real right now, where the moment I'm writing this (NOW!) happens to be *my* present, even though it appears to be the future for my grandmother in *her* perpetual present, and the past for my yet-to-be conceived children?

I think my head is going to explode.

A couple final thoughts on the vinyl record analogy: What would happen if we ever figured out how to move the needle ourselves?

And also: What happens when the entity that controls those vinyl records puts our little LP back into the sleeve, then leaves it on the shelf to collect dust for 9 months, or 9 lifetimes, or 9 billion years?

19

Ishy & The Deuce – Wednesday: Peru

Ishy and The Deuce awake in the cool mist of dawn to people shuffling and gathering their belongings. Shanties and tin-roofed storage facilities hug the riverbank, giving way to a jagged skyline of concrete low-rises and telecommunication antennas, the horizon shrouded in woodsmoke and fog. The gringos rub sleep from their eyes and grab their packs, leaving behind a pile of trash and their empty hammocks swinging in place as the boat pulls into the docks.

Unlike the frenzy of Jorge Chávez airport, early morning Puerto Masusa is eerily subdued, with families embracing as mototaxi drivers, too tired to hustle, lean against their motorcycles, sipping coffee from Styrofoam cups. After dragging themselves through the mud, Ishy and The Deuce approach one such driver. The man looks up from his steaming cup with bloodshot eyes and asks, "Taxi, *amigos?*"

The Deuce nods.

"Where we are to going?"

Ishy and The Deuce look at one another as if the question had never occurred to them.

The driver grins Cheshire. "*Desayuno, sí?* Brake-fast?"

It seems as logical a destination as any. They peel away from the port, tearing through an endless array of cinder block shacks with makeshift metal roofs, faded paint on concrete walls and tropical trees lining sand-swept streets. The air smells of moist earth and burning wood. The Deuce tugs on Ishy's arm, pointing out a gas station where female attendants are decked out in crop tops and Daisy Dukes, the sight reminding them just how long they've been confined to that riverboat.

When the taxi reaches the Plaza de Armas, the driver points toward a sheet metal monstrosity and announces, "*Los Testículos de Perro. Desayuno para los gringos!*"

Packs slung across their backs, Ishy and The Deuce step out and are immediately brushed back by a throng of mototaxis.

"Note to self," Ishy grimaces, "pedestrians do not have the right of way."

"This place is fuckin' mayhem," The Deuce says. "I think I kinda dig it."

As they cross the street, Ishy spots an ATM. "Hold up, Deuce. I need to take out some cash."

Always leery of using an ATM in a foreign place, Ishy struggles with the unfamiliar touch-screen, constantly checking his back for lurkers. The Deuce rifles through a pile of scattered receipts. Ishy stuffs the fresh soles into his wallet and grabs The Deuce to head towards The Iron House.

Having subsisted almost exclusively on bananas and crackers on the Eduardo V, the Ulster fry breakfast is a Godsend: bacon and eggs, sausage and soda farls, baked beans and black pudding, fried potatoes and cups of strong tea. The Dog's Bollocks is on the second floor of The Iron House, where they can watch the world unfold from a balcony. Understanding that ahead lay the monumental task of tracking down their friend amidst the chaos of Iquitos, The Deuce concedes he is going to need a few minutes to gather his thoughts. He orders a beer and leans back, loosening his belt and lighting a cigarette. It's 7:30 in the morning.

Looking down into the bustling plaza, Ishy asks, "Where do we even begin?"

The Deuce picks something from his teeth as the waitress pours Iquiteña into two glasses. Ishy can't hide his revulsion. The Deuce shrugs, sliding both glasses to his side of the table and downing the first in a long, refreshing swig. "Guess we just have to blanket the town like a couple Magnum P.I.s, ask the locals about a gringo named Rosy. You got a photo of him?"

Ish shakes his head.

"Me neither. Fuck me."

The waitress comes back to ask if they want anything else.

"*Solamente la cuenta, por favor.*"

She leaves the bill on the table as Ishy and The Deuce weigh their options. They need to get their hands on a map. Their best bet is to employ a circular search pattern. They should try to stick together... It isn't until Ishy reaches for his wallet that he realizes what he's done.

"FUUUUUUUUUUCK!" He smashes his fist into the table, spilling The Deuce's beer. The clang of silverware still echoes through the restaurant as he hits the stairs.

The horrifying scene plays out in his mind as he sprints to the corner: the ATM's next customer walking up to find the screen blinking, 'WOULD YOU LIKE ANOTHER TRANSACTION?', the customer quickly glancing over his shoulder to ensure no one's watching...

When Ishy reaches the ATM, his card is nowhere to be seen. The sickening feeling of his checking account being drained 500 soles at a time brings him to his knees. He sweats profusely and shakes his head, repeating, "FuckfuckfuckfuckFUUUUUCK!" as the locals look on in confusion.

When The Deuce reaches the corner and sees Ishmael Lords losing his shit in the middle of the street, he doubles over with laughter.

"How the FUCK can you possibly find this amusing?"

"I wish you could see yourself right now. Fuckin' classic."

"My BANK CARD is gone. My fucking BANK CARD! What am I gonna do?"

The Deuce is still laughing. "Dude, you *work* for the bank! Give 'em a call and cancel your shit. You think you're the first asshole to lose his card down here? Don't sweat it. It's all part of the ride!"

"Part of the ride, my ass. This is FUCKED."

This elicits another roar from The Deuce, who playfully puts his arm around Ishy's neck and drags him to an internet café advertising *cabinas telefónicas*.

Ishy spends the better part of an hour trying to get through to someone capable of canceling his card. The Deuce passes the time at a table on the sidewalk, smoking cigarettes and watching the girls walk by. When Ishy finally emerges from the café, he is soaked with perspiration, but looking moderately relieved.

"All good in the hood?"

"Fuck me, that was hell. But yeah. Card is cancelled. All funds intact and accounted for."

"See? Sweat off a donkey's balls. Like they say, 'It ain't an adventure 'til everything goes wrong.'"

"Yeah, something like that. Listen, it'll take a few days to UPS a card here, so it looks like I'm gonna need to live off your dime for a while."

The Deuce's grin is beyond shit-eating. "Is THAT fuckin' so? In a million fuckin' years, who woulda ever guessed that the Golden Boy, Ishmael Lords, would have to suck off the ample teat of ol' Stanley Doucette?"

Ishy looks as though he's just stepped into a steaming pile of dog shit. "You know what? Forget it. I'd rather starve."

The Deuce howls with delight as Ishy turns to walk away.

They spend the morning walking Iquitos in a wayward attempt to hunt down Rosy. Packs across their sweaty backs, they traverse filthy sidewalks, doing their best to avoid the warm runoff dripping from window A/C units. They can't believe the noise of the place: TVs blaring from every window, music booming from storefronts, ramshackle busses speeding past with teenagers dangling from the doors and screaming indecipherable destinations.

Amidst the bedlam, Ishy and The Deuce ask every gringo whether they know of a Canadian named Rosy. They pop into hostels and rifle through guestbooks. They even stop into a restaurant where waitresses wear Texas Longhorn cheerleader outfits, but the American owner can't say whether or not he knows the kid. With nowhere else to turn, they head back to The Dog's Bollocks to cool off and consider their next move. Crossing the Plaza de Armas, Ishy freezes in his tracks. The Deuce turns to see what's keeping him, and as he follows his gaze, he mutters, "Walkin', talkin' Jesus..."

Shuffling through the ragtag mob of roustabouts as he makes his way across the sunny square, is Roosevelt Robinson.

Ishy is paralyzed, possessing no point of reference for the protocol on this type of encounter. But it doesn't matter, because The Deuce is shedding his pack in a full-on sprint, closing in on Rosy like a strong safety. He leaps onto Rosy's back and howls with adolescent rapture as they crash to the ground amidst the gawking hustlers leaning against the fountain.

My first instinct is self-defense. Gringos get ripped off, pickpocketed, and just plain embarrassed in this square daily. So, if I'm getting jumped, I'm coming up swinging. A vicious elbow and some sweet chin music, and let's see if this bastard ever wants to fuck with me again.

"What the FUCK, cuz? Where's the fuckin' love?"

I'm lying face-down in the grass but recognize the voice. I must be hallucinating. The heat, the sleep deprivation, the binge drinking, all of it must finally be getting the best of me. But when I roll over, sure enough, it's The Deuce, all bloody-lipped and smiling satisfaction, relief, and sheer jungle exhaustion.

I gasp in utter disbelief. "What the FUCK?"

"Greetings and fuckin' salutations, cuz." The Deuce spits blood and climbs to his feet. "What the fuck was that, anyway? This how you welcome all your fuckin' guests?"

"How the fuck...?"

He's laughing now, extending a hand to help. "Me'n' Lordsy are like the Mounties, son. Always get our fuckin' man."

"Wait... You and *Lordsy?*"

The Deuce gives me a quizzical look. "What'd you think, I'm makin' this trek all by my lonesome? This place is a motherfucker to get to." He nods in the direction of my customary internet café, and I catch Ishy Lords trudging towards us from across the plaza, schlepping two gigantic backpacks.

"Ishy? What the...? How the fuck did you guys...?" It's too much to process: Ishy and The Deuce standing here in the sunlight, a stinking, sweaty mess, smiling like a couple kids who just stumbled upon their dad's stash of *Playboy*s.

"What can I say? We fuckin' missed you, cuz."

They're two relics from home, living reminders of a life I was convinced I wanted to forget. And now they're here, 7,200 kilometers from the last place I'd seen them, in this place I never *dreamed* I'd even be—let alone them.

The Deuce finally says, "So, I'm not usually one to impose, but I think it's high time you take us back to wherever the fuck it is you're stayin'. We're fuckin dyin' out here, bro."

I find myself nodding, unable to speak. I make a move to pick up one of the packs on the sidewalk, but I stop midway, overcome with emotion. I grab Ishy and The Deuce in an awkward man-hug that guys never know how to pull off. There is back-slapping and head-shaking, "Aww fuck"s and choking on words until we eventually turn to make our way up Putumayo.

When we reach The Hideout, Ishy and The Deuce can't believe they hadn't stumbled across it during their search. I open the wrought iron door and we pass through the breezy porch, making our way to the little desk that passes for reception. I greet the proprietor's wife with a sheepish "*Hola*" and introduce her to my friends from home.

"You hear that, Lordsy? She's married to the owner, so hands off, Casablanca." The Deuce gives me a wink as he hands Maria Luisa his passport.

She scribbles some information in her ledger and clicks her tongue, giving us a helpless look. "*Solo tengo dormitorio. Lo siento, amigos.*"

"Dorm room is fine. *Gracias.*"

Ishy makes a face like he'd prefer a private room, but The Deuce is quick to comment he can upgrade their accommodations the day he picks up the tab. Ishy can only shake his head, muttering, "Fuck me."

Eyeing the dead animals on the walls, The Deuce says, "Nice fuckin' digs you got here, cuz."

Maria Luisa pretends she doesn't hear, returning their passports with a feigned smile. She places sheets and pillows in each of their arms, then motions us to follow her to the second floor. Climbing the rickety stairs, we're confronted with the fact that each step brings a more intense wallop of jungle heat. The air is soup and this floor's brand of body odor is overwhelming. A naked lightbulb dangles from above as she leads us down a hallway, pointing to an open door.

"*El dormitorio. Disfruten, señores.*"

We step inside a barren room with peeling paint on cracked concrete. The only furniture is five exposed mattresses on metal bed frames. An industrial fan oscillates in the corner, pushing hot air in our direction as it rumbles with exertion. Ishy and The Deuce toss their packs on the floor and haphazardly spread their sheets on the beds.

I stand in the doorway, observing that it doesn't look like either of them have made a bed in their entire lives.

Ishy laughs through the sweat dripping off his face, asking, "Where's your room in this place, anyway?"

I take a deep breath and lead them back downstairs, through the small kitchen, eventually stopping at the concrete hovel I've been calling home. Somewhere along the way, the room I'd chosen became acceptable, regardless of how deplorable it felt in the beginning, or how fucked-up it surely seemed to the objective observers standing in my doorway now. Over these past nine months, it hadn't occurred to me that my living quarters were bleak or depressing, or that I might consider moving to a room with a window or some paint on the walls. I never conceded that my living situation was something I should be ashamed of. But the true nature of my existence in Iquitos hits me all at once as I stand alone in my den of self-loathing, looking back at Ishy and The Deuce as they maintain the kind of stunned silence that forces you to take stock of your life.

I can't look them in the eye.

After far too long, The Deuce settles it: "This won't fuckin' do... You're stayin' in the barracks with us, son."

Ishy and The Deuce carry all my worldly possessions to their dorm in one sweaty trip. After placing the items next to their packs and shaking their heads in sympathetic disgust, my two oldest friends stretch out on their beds and groan luxuriously, insisting they're just going to close their eyes a minute.

I smile and assure them I've seen this movie before, understanding what three days on the slow boat to Iquitos can do to a couple of gringos. I run downstairs to grab some water from the communal refrigerator and by the time I get back to the room Ishy and The Deuce are sound asleep. I stand in the doorway for a long time, listening to them breathe peacefully in the afternoon heat, shaking my head and laughing under my breath, unable to believe they're here. I place the bottles beside their beds, then sneak out of the room.

The streets of Iquitos are abstract chaos and legitimately dangerous for tenderfoot pedestrians, but the alleyways are perfect for clearing your head and truly locking yourself in the moment. As frantic asphalt gives way to dusty dirt roads and the garbage-strewn pathways near the riverbank, I do my best to make invisible the white elephant fact of Ishy and The Deuce's arrival, what compelled them to traverse the equator, the Andes, and the Amazon, only to arrive unannounced at my doorstep. Part of me already knows. But I'm unwilling and unprepared to dig up that long-buried piece of me, let alone look it dead in the eye.

I've been gone close to two hours by the time I get back to The Hideout's front porch. There, Ishy and The Deuce drink cervezas in front of a mound of crushed-out cigarettes. I smile at the familiar sight and pull up a seat, helping myself to Ishy's bottle. The beer is cold and hits the fucking spot.

"You had us worried, cuz. Thought you mighta jumped ship on us again. Where you been?"

"Out for a little stroll. You know how it is."

The Deuce smiles and shakes his head as a soft breeze rolls through the front porch, whispering its intentions. "Ish and I spent half the day walkin' this town and we still can't tell our ass from our elbow. Any chance of you takin' us on a tour?"

I nod. "I know a few places that might be of interest."

Just then, a girl who can't be more than 13 walks by with a baby in her arms. We stop mid-conversation. Ishy's face is nothing but confused revulsion.

I laugh. "Sometimes it's hard to tell if it's the mother or sister."

"This fuckin' place," The Deuce says, not altogether under his breath.

We're quiet for a long time, content to take in the opera of the street. The air is thick with sweet humidity and charged with an indescribable, electric thrill. I wonder whether they can feel it the way I do, but I don't ask. We should be talking about a thousand different things. We should be bursting with tales of debaucherous misadventure, filling in the blanks of the past nine months. I want to ask them about who they've been dating, what the boys back home are up to, how the Leafs are looking... But I don't. And I don't ask because, if I do, I know they'll ask the same of me. I am somehow incapable of interacting with the people I've known my entire life.

The Deuce eventually breaks the silence. "I'm gettin' a mad case of the munchies here, and I'm outta sticks. Which way to the nearest Kwik-E-Mart, cuz?"

I point up Jirón Putumayo. "There's a tienda on the corner that'll have everything you need, but I'm pretty sure it's gonna piss rain in about three minutes, so you might wanna hold off."

"The fuck you think I am? Afraid of a couple fuckin' raindrops?"

Before I can say another word, the wrought iron door slams shut behind him.

"You ladies need any tampons?" he calls as he breaks into an easy trot.

Ishy and I laugh in wonder. "He's gonna get fucking soaked out there."

Ishy nods. He takes a long swig of beer, looking me up and down in disbelief. "How do you even EXIST here?"

I return a confused look. "Do you mean *philosophically?*"

"I mean literally. This place is fucking ridiculous."

I nod, taking the beer from Ish. "It takes some time, my friend. And a drinking problem helps. As does a total lack of ambition. Stick with that regimen long enough, and you too can fall into this way of life."

Ishy takes a moment to consider. "This way of life, I just don't get it. Let me ask you something about the bathrooms here: What's with the toilet paper going into the garbage cans instead of the john? That's the most fucked-up thing I've seen."

I shake my head. "Lordsy, if you think that's the most fucked-up thing about this place, you're in for a hell of a ride."

Ishy takes the beer from me and smiles.

I find myself looking at him long and hard. "I still can't believe you guys are here."

He nods, as if he's having a hard time himself.

"Tell me something: How did you survive traveling all this way with The Deuce?"

Ishy shakes his head and begins to laugh. "This whole thing has been a Molotov cocktail of absurdity. That guy is a fucking maniac! I'm telling you, this past week has been the most harrowing experience of my life. And I wrote the CFAs! That guy is gonna die out here, mark my words."

I smile, knowing full well how insane spending time with The Deuce can be. "He still collecting those ATM slips?"

Ishy's face lights up. "Yeah. What the hell is up with that? Every time we pass an ATM, he stops to rifle through the trash."

I grab the bottle from Ishy. "That's his thing. He finds these bank receipts with huge balances and stashes them in his wallet to use as 'scrap paper' for when he meets a lady. He writes his phone number on the back, figuring the girl won't be able to resist checking the balance on the flip side. His theory is, after she sees that giant bankroll, there's no way she's not calling him!"

Ishy shakes his head in admiration. "What a sick fuck."

I nod, handing back the big bottle. Ishy takes a sip and continues, "Half the time I think he's got an intellectual disability, and then he'll drop some tiny nugget of wisdom, and I'm just like, 'Where the hell did THAT come from? And it's not just that rope-a-dope intellect either. I'm flabbergasted by what a douchebag he can be. Womanizer. Compulsive liar. I mean, the guy never even mentions the fact he has a daughter... But then he sprinkles in these moments of incredible kindness. It makes you wonder if you're hallucinating. The man is an enigma wrapped in a riddle."

I take the bottle from Ish.

"Snap judgments are easy, right? Black and white will always be the default setting. I don't want to get all philosophical or anything but seeing The Deuce in action these past few days has me thinking maybe we're not supposed to read people like binary code. Maybe the things we believe to be mutually exclusive can exist simultaneously... Maybe it's possible for truth to exist in the black and the white."

I take one last swig as Ishy homes in on the right stuff.

"I'm thinking maybe light doesn't eradicate darkness. It illuminates it."

While The Deuce's friends contemplate his idiosyncrasies, he browses the aisles of the tienda, comparing South American chocolate bars and bags of chips to those back home. At the rear of the store, a lady stands behind a small counter, overseeing a dozen barrels of olives. There are flies buzzing about, but The Deuce is a few beers deep and undeterred. Having no idea what it might buy him, he asks for three soles' worth of pristine black jungle olives. The lady is a true artisan with the ladle, fishing a variety of tiny globular fruits from various buckets. The Deuce's mouth waters as she places them on a medieval-looking balance scale, with the plastic bag of olives on one platform and a rock—presumably weighing three soles' worth—on the other.

The lady drums the counter as the scale steadies, and The Deuce can't help but notice the dirt caked under her fingernails. He smiles weakly, and she beams back, revealing a lifetime of dental neglect. When the scale finally settles, the lady reaches into the bag so she can use her broken, grimy fingernails to poke and stab every last olive until she retrieves enough to balance the scale. The Deuce only laughs, wondering why she ever bothered with the ladle in the first place.

Olives in tow, The Deuce flips through some Latin teen magazines before loading half a dozen bottles of Cusqueña into his arms. While he does, he catches the eye of the pretty cashier. His grasp of Iquiteños culture is limited, but he can recognize a seductress vibing him in any corner of the world. When she returns his smile, he calls in one of his favorite plays. Casually perusing the aisle where they keep shaving cream and deodorant, The Deuce puts his remedial Spanish to work, picking out a colorful box with the words "*ultra largos y anchos*" front and center. When he gets to the pretty girl at the register, he tosses the extra-large condoms on the counter, winking as she blushes. He reaches into his wallet for a trusty bank statement as thunder rumbles overhead, rattling the windows and the street.

Sipping from a second beer, the unease between Ishy and I begins to dissolve, and we get around to the things that matter.

"No doubt The Deuce has been wheeling ladies every step of the way, but how have the *señoritas* been treating you?"

It's impossible for Ishy to suppress his smile. The look on his face is a rare thing, but it's unmistakable.

"Holy FUCK! Seriously?"

"It's nothing, really. I mean, I don't know if it's more than what it was, but I met a girl at the hostel in Lima."

"Of course you did! What? A backpacker?"

Ishy's laugh is involuntary. "No, not a backpacker. Actually, she's from Lima. She works the—"

"A *Peruana*! Holy shit! How the fuck did that happen?"

Ishy giggles like a schoolgirl. "What can I say? Serendipity and coincidence. It's the photosynthesis of romance."

"ISHY! For real? *Te amo, Perú*, you sly little pimp!"

Ishy takes a long swig of beer, momentarily lost in a world where the fierce Latin love he's been envisioning can actually exist. After a moment, he quietly asks, "Hey, Rosy, what do you miss most about Toronto?"

I take a deep breath and whistle through my teeth. "That's a hell of a question." I borrow the bottle and take a sip. "The usual stuff, you know? Playing hockey. Bumping into people I know. Driving a car. And the smells, too. Things you wouldn't think. Fresh-cut grass. Lilacs. The way you can taste winter coming. Grabbing coffee at The Common."

"Yeah," Ishy says, nodding. "Coffee here really sucks."

"Bet you thought the coffee would be awesome, right? I did. Just because they grow some of the best beans in the world here doesn't mean these tiny, tucked-away places get any. It's nothing but Nescafé and hot garbage water here."

Ishy nods. "Remember that time we drove down to Mississippi to find some blues bar you heard about in a song?"

"'Went down to Rosedale, rider by my side.'"

Ishy shakes his head. "That place was such a shit hole."

"Nothin' but boarded storefronts and menacing stares." We're quiet for a moment before I add, "Ain't that just like life sometimes."

It's at that moment that the clouds burst open and rain pelts the asphalt, silver dollars bouncing on the sidewalk. The downpour is torrential, cooling the air in an instant, the smell of wet pavement enveloping the porch. Ishy stands at the door, marveling at the miracle of Amazon rainfall, the splatter tickling his feet as tarped mototaxis part tiny rivers in the street.

A few minutes later, The Deuce comes bounding down the sidewalk, his plastic bag swinging wildly in the deluge. Ishy and I take a few extra moments to unlock the door just to fuck with him, water pouring off the roof as he screams like a little girl.

His hair is dripping, and his clothes are soaked through, but he has a huge smile on his face. "Rainforest rain, that's the real fuckin' deal, bro!"

As if the statement is reason enough, Ishy and The Deuce run into the street, dancing and giggling like children as water rushes over their feet and the locals look on in bemused wonderment. I eventually grab a couple of towels so they can dry off on the porch. We laugh our asses off as The Deuce regales us with his account of sweet-talking the corner store *chica*, proudly displaying his prophylactics. We sit on that porch well after the rain stops, content to let the afternoon slip away, snacking on olives and sipping beers as The Deuce blows smoke rings.

When darkness arrives, we drag ourselves off the porch and take turns using The Hideout's outdoor showers, the fresh air and cool water rejuvenating our weary bodies. We put on whatever passes for our best clothes, then set off into the night, winding up at a little restaurant off the gringo trail called El Zorrito, where they grill meat over rainforest charcoal in an old, metal drum right there on the street. Inside, the place is all fluorescent light and plastic tablecloths, so we grab a rickety table on the sidewalk, watching the *parrillero* work his magic. When the food arrives, we gorge on cecina pork and grilled piranha with the head intact, tacacho and chorizo and anticuchos, dipping everything in the fiery ají sauces, cutting the pica pica with yucca and rice and hearts of palm salad, and washing it all down with jugo camu camu and ice-cold Pilsen.

When the bill arrives, The Deuce makes a big production of being the breadwinner, throwing his wallet on the table and counting the money three times. Through gritted teeth, Ishy thanks him for picking up the tab.

"Don't kid yourself, son. The vig is running."

We walk the twelve blocks back to the hostel with the saccharine night air filling our lungs. The streets are lined with people looking to escape the oppressive heat: Young families sit on the steps of their homes, glasses of gaseosa in hand; elderly couples rest on kitchen chairs set on the sidewalk; teenagers perch on railings and ledges, playing cards and whistling at passing girls. There's an old-school feel to the place that leaves me briefly nostalgic for a lemonade-and-swinging-screen-door childhood that now seems like it happened in another lifetime.

There is a tiny bar around the corner from the hostel called El Musmuqui, and I suggest we pop in for a nightcap.

We sit at a wooden table and order bottles of Iquiteña as an acoustic guitar duo bangs out American pop with mangled lyrics, each song inexplicably sung to the tune of CCR's "Lodi." One of the musicians sits on a box and occasionally plays it like a drum. The simplicity mesmerizes The Deuce. During a break, the guy who plays the *cajón* asks where we—the only gringos in the bar—are from. When Ishy proudly responds, the man comes back with, "Canada? Justin Bieber, yes?"

The Deuce finds this endlessly amusing.

As we finish another beer, I tell the guys this place is famous for a drink called the Rompe Calzón, a panty-breaker of a concoction made with Peruvian moonshine, honey, lime, and rainforest bark. Despite Ishy's protests and my better judgement, I order a round as I make my way to the bathroom.

With the table to themselves, Ishy gives The Deuce a look that goes beyond concern. The conversation to that point has been a tiptoe through the tulips, only ball-busting and easy laughs.

The Deuce kills the last of his beer, slowly nodding. "Don't worry. I got this."

I get back to the table just as the waitress delivers the 4 oz. glasses. The liquid is sludgy and smells like musty tree bark and brandy in the back of a liquor cabinet. We suspiciously eye it and balk at the consistency, ultimately toasting our friendship and slamming back the medley. Ishy chokes and coughs through it, but The Deuce suggests it isn't half bad. We wash it down with more

Iquiteñas and find ourselves growing fonder of the music, singing along to every track, jumbled lyrics and all.

By midnight, we are spent.

We step out of the bar and into the stillness of the night, the evening damp and surprisingly cool, the puddles reflecting lampposts in the street. We're quiet as we walk toward the hostel, and there is an irrefutable tension between us. With The Hideout in sight, and just when it seems as though everything will go unspoken, there is a voice.

"Why'd you stay with her, cuz?"

I can't breathe. The only sound is our footsteps on the wet sidewalk.

"The two of you were a fuckin' disaster together. I knew it. Ish fuckin' knew it. Christ, everyone knew you needed to get out."

Ishy raises his voice like I've never heard. "STAN. DROP IT."

"Fuck you, Ishmael. You don't get a vote when it comes to the tough questions. I mean, FUCK, all these years, all this time we've been down here together, and you still can't ask the ONE question you're dyin' to ask me."

I look over at Ishy. He's trembling with dread and rage and shame, but before he can formulate how to ask if the man looking him square in the eye fucked his girlfriend on that powerless night in Toronto, The Deuce turns his attention back to me.

"So, fuck it. I wanna know. We came a long fuckin' way to see you, cuz. I think it's the least you can do. Tell us: Why couldn't you just fuckin' walk away?"

It's something I could never explain. I was always so envious of people who could just duck and run at the first hint of trouble. How did they fall asleep at night without having ridden things to their bitter, bankrupt, inevitable end? Didn't the arc of a relationship include that excruciating terminus where you hang on beyond the point of hope, then hang on some more, until everything's been broken and scattered? For some reason, I always believed giving up on a relationship was like breaking a promise.

I look to the sky, but the stars are buried in the evening fog. "I don't know... I just... I didn't want to hurt her."

We are no longer walking. The Deuce is shaking his head. "You shouldn't of fuckin' gone down with the ship. It shouldn't of happened."

We walk the rest of the way to The Hideout in silence. Once we arrive, it is understood that we will all sit together on the front porch for one last drink. I pull out my Mapacho cigars and hand them out, slow and deliberate. We light the cigars and let the embers glow, tasting the tobacco in contentment. The streets are deserted; the night air is soft. We sip from bottles of Cusqueña.

As if he's been working up to it all night, The Deuce starts, "There are these islands off the coast of PEI with deserted beaches that go on for miles. You can pitch a tent in the sand and not see anyone for days. The Magdalen Islands." He takes a long haul on his cigar. "Josie and I spent a month livin' on a beach out there, back before Clara was born. Fuck, those were good times. Every morning, I used to step outside buck ass naked."

Ishy and I can't help but chuckle.

"On maybe our third day out there, this mangy dog came limpin' up the beach. I'm no fuckin' doctor, but it sure as hell seemed like it wasn't long for this world. Skinny, hair all fuckin' raggedy, cut up and fleas jumpin' all over. I'm not sure why, but we decided to give him some food and water, the occasional scratch behind the ears." The Deuce laughs to himself. "After that, there was no getting' rid of the little bastard. Every day he'd come and every day we'd make a little extra food for him... It's amazing what a little love can do. We noticed the dog getting better and by the time we were ready to leave we'd pretty much nursed him back to health. Truth be told, I wanted to bring that old mutt back home, but there was just no way... The morning we left, we packed up and said goodbye, leavin' that pooch just sittin' there to disappear in the rearview."

We frown and nod.

The Deuce takes a long drink, looking into the street. "Fast forward two years. Josie's already had the baby and fuck, you know how it is. I decide in my fucked-up head that I can't handle the responsibility and commitment, the work and the sacrifice... I was fucked-up all the time and I eventually decided to get out... Or maybe Josie just finally came to her senses and kicked me out. I'm not sure it matters anymore." The Deuce is nodding, slowly. "For some reason, I thought it would do me some good to go back to that beach on Magdalen. As if I could find some perspective there or figure out what the fuck I was doin' with my life. So, I drove all the way out to PEI in one shot, then took the ferry over to the islands by myself."

A lone mototaxi cuts through the night.

"My first day on the island, I swear to God, that same fuckin' dog comes walkin' along the beach. I have no idea how to explain it, but somehow he just fuckin' found me. He had no way of knowing I'd ever come back, or that I would be there on that day, but somehow, he just found me."

Ishy and I exchange a look.

"I was so happy, you know? My life was crumbling all around me, and I was so alone, and then to have this dog show up... My old friend. I loved that fuckin' dog."

We are perfectly still.

"For the next few days, he didn't leave my side. I gave him whatever food I could spare. He slept at the end of my sleeping bag, keeping me warm while that crazy wind was blowing." The Deuce shakes his head. "I was pretty fucked-up in those days... Chemicals and things I knew would hurt me. I can't even explain it..." Tears well in his eyes as he looks for the words. "One night, when the dog was sleeping in my tent, I woke up and went out onto the beach. I found this big rock and took it back to the tent... And I smashed his head in... I just..."

Everything stops.

"I don't know why I did it. I loved this dog... And I killed it."

There is nothing but absolute silence.

The Deuce does everything he can to keep it together. "Sometimes at night, this dog, he finds me again. He visits me in my dreams... And he always asks me why I did it." The Deuce wipes his nose, then takes a deep breath. He looks me in the eye. "Fuck, Rosy, you know we didn't come all this way to eat piranha and talk about the old times."

I feel the world collapse in the pit of my stomach. It all happens so fast. The life we once had is gone in the blink of an eye. Like waking from a dream.

"Your mom's sick, cuz."

A heartbeat.

"She's really sick. You're comin' home with us."

20

Vanessa – Wednesday: Amazon, Peru

Nov. 16th, 2011

There was a torrential downpour for 10 hours last night. The hypnotic hammering of Amazon rain on our thatched hut, along with the effects of the dream juice, ensured that my dreams were vivid and indescribably sweet.

We awoke before seven this morning to get to work brewing the ayahuasca. There is something amazing and poetic and comforting in the fact that we are brewing it ourselves. Ayahuasca is essentially a tea made from plants, vines, and tree bark. We used 17 in total, including the ayahuasca vine, chacruna leaves, and Capirona bark. The tea is boiled to a highly concentrated mixture—think of the very best part of a Chinese hot pot, but with medicinal/healing/hallucinogenic properties!

The brewing ritual began by washing the ayahuasca vine and pounding it into tiny, fragmented tendrils. The importance of handling the sacred vine was not lost on us. As a biology nerd, let me say that the double helix/DNA qualities of the vine were completely mind-blowing. Holding it in my hands, inspecting it up close, and breathing in its earthy essence was a powerful experience. Pounding the vine into thin strands was incredibly hard work but watching the sacred plant break into fractals literally took my breath away... Vine of the soul, indeed.

We threw the ayahuasca vine, as well as the other plants we gathered yesterday, into three giant, iron cauldrons that sat atop a roaring jungle fire. We also threw in some Uchu Sanango, which we would later learn is the basis for another medicine that renders you BLIND for three days... Good times!

The ayahuasca was left to boil and reduce for eight hours, with The Shaman and his apprentices tending to the fire and blowing Mapacho smoke into the cauldrons to bless the spirits inside. We were encouraged to write a list of things we wished to purge, and to burn our lists in the fire. Someone had a list that was six pages long. Getting a sense of the trauma some of the people here have gone through, it makes me so grateful to come from a loving family and to have experienced a happy upbringing.

I walked over to the fire a few times throughout the morning, stirring the brew with a big stick. Watching the ayahuasca bubble and roil, I thought about the odds of discovering the combination of these 17 plants from different parts of the jungle, and somehow crafting this amazing, life-altering medicine.

There are more than 40,000 plant species in the Amazon— an overwhelming percentage of which would kill you upon ingestion... What are the chances of selecting the correct 17? Are we talking one in a billion? One in a trillion?

This big math got me thinking about the universe, and just how improbable our very existence is. The thought of it continues to baffle me. Because what are the chances of taking a bunch of non-living materials flying around at dizzying speeds in every direction, smashing them all together, and somehow creating life?

How do we mix these unrelated, inanimate bits of earth to achieve body and mind and cells and consciousness? How does carbon + minerals + electric pulses = memories? Or self-awareness? How do dirt and metal and rocks wind up creating imagination? How is it possible that this stardust gets stirred together and we somehow come away with the unmistakable feeling of love?

We filtered into the main lodge around noon for a light lunch (pasta, salad, herbal tea), then gathered for an informal shamanic Q&A.

Much of yesterday's session was spent discussing what to expect in tonight's ceremony, so today's session meandered into the philosophical. The Shaman spoke about how the universe is ONE, with every particle dependent upon and connected to every other particle. In the same way that the human body is made up of billions of tiny, interconnected parts that exist as one body, so too does the universe exist as one.

We also spent some time discussing dimethyltryptamine (DMT). By no means am I an expert in the field of psychotropic medicines, but I was able to glean the following:

DMT has been called the spirit molecule, and The Shaman maintains that it allows us to fully comprehend *everything*. DMT is produced by the human body and The Shaman believes this is purposeful; DMT exists to show us the architecture of reality and the fabric of space-time.

When orally ingested, DMT gets broken down by the enzymes in the stomach, rendering it ineffectual. One could eat a fistful of Psychotria viridis leaves, which are literally dripping with DMT, and it would have no effect whatsoever.

The only way to realize the effects of orally ingested dimethyltryptamine is to combine it with a monoamine oxidase inhibitor. If this sounds incredibly complex, that's because it is. Yet somehow the shamans—thousands of years ago and without the ability to read, write, or conduct scientific experiments—figured out how to neutralize the body's breakdown of DMT. They combine those DMT-laced chacruna leaves with the monoamine oxidase-inhibiting ayahuasca vine—even though those plants don't grow anywhere near each other!

When one of the guests asked how this was possible, The Shaman deferred to Don Alberto, who just shrugged and said that the plants told them how.

Of course they did.

The Shaman described the DMT molecule as being like the light switch that allows you to see the entirety of your consciousness, as well as the contents and makeup of the universe.

One way to get a hit of DMT is by snorting it—think of the Yanomamo and YOPO snuff. This method of ingestion provides a quick burst of mind-annihilating consciousness, blasting you to the center of the universe. By all accounts, the visit is short-lived, disorienting, and virtually impossible to navigate or comprehend.

But when you combine the DMT-laden plants with the neutralizing effects of the ayahuasca vine, DMT can be absorbed by the bloodstream in an active form (unlike when it gets broken down by stomach enzymes), so we can experience the medicinal properties of the DMT in its richest form over a prolonged period. It's that relatively slow and gentle slope of the ayahuasca voyage that allows us to navigate our consciousness and learn about ourselves, our life, and the nature of the universe. It is this spiritual teaching component of the medicine that differentiates ayahuasca from simply freebasing DMT.

At the conclusion of the Q&A, I went back to the hut and slept on and off for a couple hours, waking up late and jumping in the cold shower (indescribably refreshing in the stifling heat). Darkness has since begun to creep in. I find myself writing by candlelight as the jungle makes its nighttime noises.

Someone once told me that tectonic plates move at the speed fingernails grow. Never has this felt truer than tonight.

30 minutes later

We're down to the wire now. It's time for some honesty: I'm afraid.

On some cellular level, I've always believed we have a finite number of hours on this earth and when your body tells you it's time to rest, that's what you're supposed to do. All of those waking hours accumulate and when you reach your limit, the lights go out.

I've seen it in close friends who do the kinds of drugs that keep them awake for unnatural durations of time. The chemicals allow them to cheat the system in the short-term. They stay awake for three days running, feeling great and prescient and alive, so long as they keep consuming more. But I can't help but think the odometer keeps spinning, and they continue to squander those fixed hours. I believe that we are allotted a finite amount of time within the infinite construct of the universe. And I believe that time needs to be treated with the utmost reverence and respect.

I have no idea what will happen to me tonight.

I'm terrified of what I'm going to experience.

I'm terrified of the scars that may be ripped open.

I'm terrified that this experience might change me.

I'm terrified that I might shit myself right there on the floor in front of everyone.

I'm terrified of the way time will expand and contract, and what that experience might do to those finite hours I have allotted.

But most of all, I'm terrified of the unknown. And I know life is supposed to be about encountering the unknown and experiencing as much as possible, learning from the mountains of adversity that we should strive to summit, but still...

I'm terrified of what awaits on the other side.

21

Vanessa – Thursday: Amazon, Peru

Nov. 17th, 2011
Sometime after 3 AM

The universe is a screaming blast of light and energy all at once and for eternity.

Every moment endures, always.

We are all everything, always.

22

Rosy – Thursday: Iquitos, Peru

I awake before dawn with my heart pounding and impossible thoughts racing through my mind, uncertain of everything but the need to get the fuck out. I dress in the dark, sneaking away from Ishy, The Deuce, and The Hideout.

Even the mototaxis are still at this hour.

Choking back tears, I make my way across town. Lost. Confused. Past the shuttered storefronts. Shaken. Numb. Through the deserted Plaza. Denial. Denial. Denial. Past the dogs sleeping in the street. Trembling. Broken. Until I finally reach the Malecón.

I have no idea why I'm here.

I lean against the concrete wall for a long time, gray mist on the river and woodsmoke in the air. In all my days in Iquitos, this is the only time I can recall birdsong. I take a deep breath. The Malecón is deserted but for an old man sweeping the sidewalk. I look out onto the riverbank as a woman emerges from a shack below, quietly stoking her fire as a rooster begins to crow. I take another breath and shake my head. I feel it coming on. The dull ache in my throat persists and intensifies until it consumes me, and it is impossible to stop the tears. I collapse against the wall, burying my head in my hands, weeping uncontrollably.

I remain there, crumpled and catatonic, for a long time. A stray dog wanders over to clumsily sit at my feet, happily panting and pawing at my arm. I laugh through a stream of snot at his beautiful oblivion, eventually picking myself off the ground to watch the Amazon give birth to a fiery sun.

It isn't long before an old lady arrives on the Malecón with a pushcart full of snacks and cigarettes. I trudge over to greet her as best I can. I hand her some money then return to where the dog sits. I open the bag of yuquitas and eat a few, tossing some to the devoted mutt before emptying the rest onto the sidewalk. I scratch him behind the ears then turn to walk away.

I wander the streets, searching for conviction in my next move. When it feels like I've sufficiently gotten my shit together, I pop into a hole-in-the-wall called Café Alicia to procure some provisions for the guys.

It's just before seven when I return to The Hideout. I drag myself up the rickety stairs to the dorm room, then place the warm paper bag on the edge of a bed. Ishy and The Deuce snore majestically but as the smell of fried pork belly, sweet potatoes, lime-soaked onions, and fresh bread fills the room, they slowly open their eyes.

The Deuce recognizes a good hangover cure when it's in his midst. "Dude, what is that righteous smell?"

The bag crinkles as I reach inside. "Chicharrón. Breakfast of champions." I take a bite of the softball-size sandwich and exhale, satisfied. I nod and take another big bite. "Rise and shine, kids. We got a big day ahead of us."

The Gringo Shaman spends most of his time at the healing lodge three hours downriver, but I've seen him around Iquitos every now and then. Living in a hostel for the past nine months, I've heard the stories about his mythic capacity for healing, but I've never considered his help.

Things change. Often suddenly and almost always irrevocably. And now I have the overwhelming urge to seek the Gringo Shaman. Ishy and The Deuce don't even try talking me out of it. When they show me the boarding passes for a flight back to Toronto, I know that the fix has been in from the beginning. We aren't scheduled to fly home for another three days, and—after last night's emotional gutting—we're all eager to leave The Hideout's graveyard walls behind. We figure that our best chance of finding someone to take us to the Gringo Shaman will be to split up and hit as many sketchy travel agencies as possible. Knowing full well that the most ruthless operators work the Plaza, I volunteer to scour the immediate area while Ishy ventures up Calle Fitzcarrald, and The Deuce heads toward the Belen market.

Ishy isn't sold on going deeper into the jungle, and he finds the prospect of visiting a shaman flat-out terrifying, but he's willing to go along with the plan if it means getting Rosy back home. After stumbling into three tour operators of varying legitimacy, he comes to a conclusion that is well understood in Iquitos: The Gringo Shaman doesn't do trade with the local agencies. With the few coins jangling in his pocket, Ishy steps into a tienda to buy an Inca Kola. The old man behind the counter snaps off the cap with an opener in the shape of a naked lady.

Ishy sits on the front step of that nameless tienda, the taste of bubblegum cream soda bringing a smile to his face as he watches the morning street scene play out in operatic splendor.

Some say travel is little more than nuisance and delay, but it is often the loitering moments of misfortune that stay with us the longest. For reasons unknown to Ishy, this moment feels as though it will stay with him forever, and it fills him with a happiness he has not felt since he was last with Lucia.

I have no luck with the scoundrels working the Plaza, nor the agencies in the surrounding blocks, so I sit on the ledge of a monument, waiting on Ishy and The Deuce. The morning sun beats down on me, and it is impossible not to feel the weight of the moment. I have long convinced myself that I hate this place, that I came here only to escape and be left the fuck alone. But the truth is, if you spend enough time somewhere, no matter how depressing and decrepit, it seeps into who you are. It dawns on me that I will be leaving Iquitos soon, and these moments alone in the square are beset by the sense of an ending.

Ishy returns to the Plaza at the agreed upon hour, but The Deuce is nowhere to be found. With little choice but to lean against the fountain and wait, we do so for a duration that drags in correlation to the heat's escalation. Just as we begin to worry, we hear The Deuce calling out from the bed of a loaded plantain truck. He leaps from the pile of green bananas and knocks twice on the side of the truck as thanks.

Ishy and I only laugh.

"Well? You cock-knockers find anything?"

"Nah, man. Same story all over."

The Deuce shakes his head. "Like tits on a fuckin' bull, you two. Lucky for you pussies, I was able to sort us out. Boat leaves in *dos horas*. That's two hours, Ish."

"Get the fuck outta here! Really? You found someone to take us?"

"Was there ever a fuckin' doubt?"

"There still is. To the Gringo Shaman, right? No bullshit?"

"No bullshit. Let's just say I got a friend in Jesus."

We bounce over to the tienda for a big bottle of Pilsen to toast our good fortune, slugging it back in the midday heat to seal the deal. Then we crisscross town in the general direction of the Belen market, stopping at a breezy, bustling cantina called Pollos Locos for lunch. The Loco is a local mainstay where pretty waitresses carry plates heaped with fire-roasted chicken and perfectly crisp, hand-cut fries. The place is known for their array of hot ají sauces, and we take full advantage of the table options, ordering a side of yucca fries for mop-up duty. The beer is cold and the vibes are good, with Ishy and The Deuce lovingly christening the place "The Peruvian Swiss Chalet."

After basking in the glory of gastronomic stupor, we check the time and realize we need to get moving. We follow The Deuce, walking at a slightly nervous pace through a dangerous part of town, until we reach a shuttered storefront with a black and yellow sign that reads: VAYA CON DIAZ: Tours + Aventure

I laugh, but Ishy finds no humor in the scene. "You have to be kidding me, right? *Vaya con Diaz?* This guy is gonna slit our throats and leave us for dead!"

"*Tranquillo, amigo.* Trust me on this one. I know people, and this Jesus motherfucker is a good cat."

"Deuce, I'm pretty sure it's pronounced Hay-Zeus."

"Not where I come from, son."

As if on cue, the President and CEO of VAYA CON DIAZ: Tours + Aventure comes sauntering around the corner. "Eh-Stan! *Hombre! Cómo estás, amigo?* And these ees your friends, *sí? Buenas tardes, chicos. Soy Jesus Diaz. Bienvenidos a VAYA CON DIAZ: Tours + Aventure. Pasen por aqui.* Please, eh, come inside." Jesus removes the padlock from the door without a key, hoisting the metal roll-up the way one might open a storage locker. The windowless room is dark, but we can make out a desk with scattered papers. The metal walls are bare except for a beer poster that doubles as a calendar, featuring bikini-clad Amazonian women. The year reads 2004. "If I has a seat, I ask you to seat, but as you see..."

Ishy shakes his head in disgust, but knows he has no say in the matter. He would give his right testicle for access to his bank card, understanding now more than ever that people never appreciate money until they are utterly devoid of it.

"Jesus, tell these guys: You work with the Gringo Shaman. *Sí?*"

"*Claro. Gringo Shaman? Sí, sí, por supuesto. Jesus and Gringo Shaman son hermanos.* How you can say in United States? Brothers from another mothers?"

This butchered turn of phrase actually brings a smile to Ishy's face.

"See? I fuckin' love this guy. You're my homeboy, Jesus!"

"*Claro que sí.* Jesus ees your motherfucker!"

Ishy now laughs aloud. "Holy shit. We're gonna die."

I know everything about this scene is wrong, but I am desperate and willing to be taken for a ride.

"Okay, okay. Ees time to make the business, yes? *Para tres personas,* for to go visit the Gringo Shaman we are saying... 900 soles each?"

Ishy snorts. The Deuce whistles and shakes his head.

I like to think that nine months in town has bestowed a smattering of local savvy, but when it comes to ad hoc journeys downriver to visit a shaman, I am a little out of my depth.

"Jesus, for this 900 soles, what exactly are we getting?"

"*Sí, sí.* That is for the everything package. Transportation, foods, for sleeping, ayahuasca. *Todo, amigos.* Like I say to Eh-Stan, VAYA CON DIAZ Tours is all-exclusive!"

After a pregnant pause, The Deuce says, "I don't know, Jesus. 900 a pop sounds pretty steep. You think you can do us a solid on this one?"

Jesus considers his options. "*Estoy entre sí y no.*"

Ishy gives a confused look. "What does that mean?"

"He's between yes and no."

Jesus smiles. "Okay, okay. For you, I make a special price. 2,000 soles for every bodies. But ees best Jesus price."

"DONE!" The Deuce sticks out his hand and Jesus heartily shakes it, an irrepressible smile on his face as Ishy and I look on in something between reverence and horror.

"Cash only, *sí*?"

"On the dash, bro." The Deuce reaches for his wallet and turns to Ishy and me. "See? What did I tell you? Jesus is my motherfuckin' *homeboy!*"

Fifteen minutes later, we throw our gear into a dented boat tethered to a post on the Río Itaya. Once inside, Jesus yanks the starter chain on the suspect outboard motor, but it violently shakes then dies. This scene repeats for several minutes. Just as it seems like we'll need to make use of the paddles, the engine sputters to life in a cloud of smoke. We nervously congratulate one another as Jesus guides the boat away from the riverbank. As he does, he tosses The Deuce a bucket and winks. "Just in case, *amigo*."

As Jesus weaves through the huts of Belen, Ishy and The Deuce are awestruck. Although they've seen poverty in parts of Lima and Iquitos, nothing has prepared them for this.

Noting their faces, Jesus pipes up, "Like Venice, no?"

Not even The Deuce can muster a reply.

We're soon beyond the floating shantytown and onto open water, where we're afforded a panorama of rickety cell towers and church steeples. The soot-stained brick and block buildings with spray-painted political messages will never grace any postcards, but they signify a kind of home, and—like the Plaza's chorus line of con men—I know I'll come to miss them.

At the spot where the Río Itaya spills into the Amazon, the water changes from black to a silty mud-brown. Recognizing the significance of this transformation, the three of us nod, acknowledging that, if nothing else, we have achieved this. It is at this moment that water begins to spout from a hole in the bottom of the boat.

The look on Ishy's face is utter disbelief, but the calamity appears to be standard operating procedure, given Jesus' "*Bienvenidos a Perú, amigos!*"

We have no choice but to spend the next three hours bailing muddy water from our aluminum vessel, dismally failing to keep our clothes and gear dry. The Deuce insists on singing, "*There's a hole in my bucket, dear Lye-za, dear Lye-za / There's a hole in my bucket, dear Lye-za, a hole...*"

It takes everything in Ishy not to brain him with an oar.

It is hotter than Hades and stickier than a peep show floor, but it is impossible to find a moment's respite without risking the boat sinking. On the river for hours, it seems obvious our guide has no idea where the fuck he's going. We're pissed off and exhausted and stinking of exertion, and Ishy is on the verge of coming undone. Just as we're realizing that we've been bested by this punk, Jesus slows the boat and points to a rickety dock, announcing, "*El campo del Gringo.*"

I can't fucking believe it.

Jesus pulls the boat alongside the makeshift pier and before even tying off, he heaves our packs onto the dock with a saturated thud. We exit the boat, steadying ourselves on the dilapidated jetty, which, based on the precarious journey to reach it, feels like the greatest engineering feat in the world.

As The Deuce stretches his weary muscles, Jesus says, "Gringo Shaman, he lives there, *en la Selva ahí. Vamos*... He knows you ees coming, homeboys."

Before Ishy can ask if Jesus will be accompanying us to explain the details of our arrangement, the President and CEO of our esteemed tour company uses his foot to push off the dock. At a safe enough distance, he jams the motor into drive. Through a gigantic shit-eating grin, he shouts, "*VAYA CON DIAZ, MUCHACHOS,*" howling with laughter as the boat races away.

We stand dumbstruck for at least thirty seconds.

There's murder in Ishy's eyes. "Are you fucking happy, Deuce? What the hell are we gonna do now?"

The Deuce removes the cigarette from behind his ear and fixes it between his lips. He pulls the Zippo from his pocket and lights it, taking a long, deep drag.

"Are we even sure this is the Gringo Shaman's place? That asshole might have just left us for dead."

Ishy shakes his head. "'Jesus is my homeboy.' You're such a fucking idiot, Deuce."

The Deuce quickly inhales. "What can I say, boys? It's a big fuck-up. Let's just move on."

"Move on? Where the hell are we gonna move on to?"

The Deuce uses his cigarette to point up the riverbank.

With no other choice, we pick up our sopping backpacks and climb the slippery riverbank, a fog of mosquitoes ominously descending upon us with a screaming hum that makes my skin crawl. The jungle is thick with humidity; the smell of lush vegetation is almost overwhelming. We follow a path carved out of tangled undergrowth, half-joking that we're heading into some ritual sacrifice. About a half-kilometer down the path, dripping with sweat, we come to a clearing that houses a large jungle hut, as well as some smaller structures off to the side. We stand motionless a moment, unsure of our next move.

As if in a movie, a shirtless man in Wellington boots walks by with a machete, paying us absolutely no mind.

After a few moments of startled silence, The Deuce pipes up. *"Perdón, señor?* Ahhh..." He can't even speak without laughing. *"El Gringo Shaman?"*

The man turns, looking at us with mild annoyance. *"Sí, Sí. Están ahí."* He points his machete towards the large hut in the center of the commune, then continues about his business as if it's the most natural thing in the world for three white dudes to emerge from the jungle and inquire as to the whereabouts of a shaman. As the man with the machete disappears into the jungle, we carefully walk towards the hut, stopping at the door. We hear hushed voices inside.

"Alright, cuz. This is your show. Lead us onward."

I nod slowly. Then I open the door.

A group of nine people sit in a circle and every one of them turns to see who's walking in, unannounced.

Vanessa is first to speak. "Rosy? What? How did you—"

"Hey, V. Ahhh, sorry for interrupting."

The Shaman, sitting on a rickety chair, is taken aback. "Hi, guys. Is there something we can help you with?"

"Yeah, ahhh. Not quite sure where to begin, but this guy, Jesus Diaz, from VAYA CON DIAZ—"

"'Tours + Aventure,' incorrect spelling," Ishy adds.

"Yeah, we paid Jesus a bunch of money to bring us out here. He said he has some business arrangement with you?"

The Shaman knowingly shakes his head. "I have absolutely no affiliation with Jesus Diaz. What did he sell you?"

We should have known. I think deep down we probably did. Fuck me. I laugh sheepishly. "I think he signed us up for the deluxe package. Transportation, accommodation, ayahuasca ceremony, you name it."

The Shaman exhales. "And what did he charge you?"

I bite my lip, but our eyes remain locked. "2,000 soles."

The entire circle groans as The Deuce shakes his head, quietly cursing himself.

The Shaman chuckles. "That guy's pretty good, isn't he? Rest assured; you aren't the first he's swindled... Yet you're the first he's brought all the way out here, mind you." The Shaman thinks for a moment. "I'll have a word with Jesus when I get back into town next month. We don't have a boat going back to Iquitos for another couple days. In the meantime, you guys are welcome to stay. I think there are a few beds available in one of the cabins. Did you happen to see Gustavo on your way in?"

"The dude with the machete?"

"The one and only. We'll have him show you to your cabin." The Shaman calls out in Spanish, and the shirtless man walks through the door. "Today is an off day for us, so there won't be a ceremony until tomorrow night. Drop your stuff off in your cabin and then come back to the circle. We'll get you guys oriented and tell you everything you need to know."

The three of us look at one another, unable to believe things could be this simple, or that this man could be so understanding. We thank him profusely as we shake hands and fail at explaining all we've been through. In the middle of it all, Vanessa gets up and gives me a long, beautiful hug. We both get a little emotional, her touch bestowing a transcendent sense of warmth and home.

The cabin is a small, barebones structure perched four feet off the ground. We climb the steps and open the screen door, stepping into a room with three mattresses on the floor. Mosquito nets hang over each like a wedding veil, giving the place a sense of foreboding. There is a tiny bathroom in the corner. We set our gear beside our chosen mattress and make our way back to the main hut, where the Gringo Shaman is hosting an open forum, discussing the intricacies of ayahuasca. Our instinct is to stand on the periphery, but The Shaman invites us to take a closer seat.

It takes some time to wrap my head around the dizzying concepts. Even though I've heard backpackers speak abstractly about ayahuasca, I have no idea what it's all about. I find myself nodding as The Shaman speaks about the tangible world and our role within it. Even Ishy, as cold-blooded a rationalist as there is, recognizes some truth and virtue in what he's hearing.

But The Deuce is a tough sell. When the conversation turns to the existence of spirits within the plants themselves, he shakes his head derisively. When The Shaman encourages us to not only spend time amongst the plants but *talk* to them, The Deuce shoots me a look that asks, *Can you believe this shit?*

The scoffing is not lost on The Shaman. "I completely understand how some of you may have doubts. Trust me when I say that there wasn't a greater skeptic than me. But then something brought me here, in the same way that something has brought you here. And I found out, in the way you will find out: Ayahuasca isn't about believing. It's about experiencing."

There are plenty of knowing smiles around the circle.

"Often, people are afraid when they come here. And that's natural. It's to be expected. But I'm here to tell you that if you follow the rules, which—"

"ARE IN PLACE FOR OUR SAFETY AND WELL-BEING," the group responds.

The Shaman smiles. "If you follow the rules, there is nothing to be afraid of." He sits back with an ease that invites dialogue.

One of the attendees speaks up, "You know, my friends and family, they're afraid I'll have some kind of transformative, drug-induced experience that could change me. As if I'll go home in a couple weeks and they won't know me anymore."

The Shaman nods in understanding. "A totally natural anxiety. The best way I can describe how the medicine will affect you is to say that, after working with ayahuasca, you become more yourself. It's an alembic. It helps purge all the negative things that have been keeping you down. It helps you eliminate all the excuses that prevent you from fully living life, leaving you with a truer version of yourself."

The dialogue is informed and inspiring, but The Deuce isn't buying. At one point, he looks to the ceiling for an extended period of time. I follow his gaze and notice the crisscrossing beams and intricate columns holding the palm leaf roof in place. I allow my gaze to return to The Deuce's face and see that he's concentrating on something, as if calculating the spans and the load capacity, or running through the logistics on how to actually build a structure in this godforsaken place.

Before I can dial back in on The Shaman, The Deuce pipes up.

"Sorry for interrupting, Doc, but I gotta ask: This building... I work construction. And I've never seen anything like it. Who designed this place? And how the fuck did you get it built way the fuck out here?"

The Shaman doesn't flinch. "It was easy. I asked the spirits and they told me."

There are five seconds of silence.

"You're shitting me, right?"

The room erupts in laughter. The Shaman smiles and gives the Michael Jordan shrug, somehow signaling the end of the Q&A.

Before leaving the main hut, Vanessa grabs me and asks how I'm doing, wanting to make sure I'm okay. She says she has so many questions she wants to ask, so many things she wants to say. She confides that she's shattered from the previous night's ceremony, and that she isn't entirely sure what's real anymore. She gives me a hug and says she needs to lie down for a while, making me promise to track her down later so we can talk.

Having never been big on inner reflection, Ishy, The Deuce, and I walk back to our hut, figuring we'll do our best to escape the sweltering heat. In the intervals between cold showers, we splay ourselves across the mattresses, our mosquito nets ominously tied overhead. Ishy and I lounge in our boxers, while The Deuce prances around naked and proud as a peacock, giving us his increasingly indelicate takes on mysticism.

"Careful, Deuce," warns Ishy, "you may want to treat those spirits with respect."

"You know what? The spirit of sexual gratification can lick my sweaty, jungle nutsack for all I care."

We double over in our beds.

"Hey, Deuce, remind me again: Which plant does the spirit of sexual gratification live in?"

"That's a fuckin' no-brainer. The spirit of sack-slurping lives in a *kum*quat!"

As the sun goes down, somebody rings a bell for dinner, and we head for the main hut. The food is boiled chicken, boiled plantains, and hard-boiled eggs we wash down with sweaty glasses of water. The food is probably bland and tasteless, but after the ridiculous expedition to get here, it tastes extraordinary.

After dinner, The Shaman and his staff retire to their cabins, leaving us in the main hut. Outside, the jungle rhythmically pulses: a symphony alive with the noise and chaos of life at its most primal. But inside, the setting is peaceful and serene. The room is cast in the soft glow of a kerosene lantern, and we huddle around it like a crackling fire. In the absence of alcohol and electricity, meaningful conversation comes easy, the words spoken in hushed tones as we sip from steaming cups of green tea.

With the Shaman out of earshot, everyone is eager to know how the three of us appeared out of the blue. Almost without exception, they undertook months of fastidious planning to make their way here. They're astonished we simply paid some kid in Iquitos to ferry us out here. The Deuce is happy to take center stage, filling them in on everything from their night in Lima to our misadventure with VAYA CON DIAZ: Tours + Aventure, romanticizing the tale as only he can.

After laughing at our misfortune, the conversation drifts into the metaphysical. The group is curious why we would risk our lives to see The Shaman.

Ishy and The Deuce turn my way. I shrug and borrow Vanessa's line about wanting to peek behind the curtain, though we all know there's more to it than that.

One of the people in the group, an aging musician from Spain, asks about our impression of The Shaman.

"I have to say," Ishy pipes up, "The Shaman isn't anything like what I expected."

"What do you mean?"

"I don't know, I guess I was expecting more pretension. More narcissism. Maybe a God complex? But this guy seems so... normal. I mean, I could see him joining my fantasy baseball league back home."

This sentiment gets a big laugh from the group.

"And he's so much younger than I thought he'd be."

"And whiter," The Deuce adds, getting another laugh.

We all take a moment to sip our tea.

There is something I've been trying to ask, seemingly since the moment I arrived in Iquitos. "So, what have the ceremonies been like?"

The group looks to one another, unsure how to answer.

Finally, Vanessa offers, "Pretty intense."

The room is quiet but for the kerosene hiss.

An older lady from Jersey City, Linda, speaks: "This stuff gets in you, and it never leaves. The spirits. The plants. The earth. It stays with you forever."

There is a ragged hippie from New Mexico, Hamish, with a voice like an old soccer ball that's been dragged from a drainage ditch. "You know how drugs give you an escape from reality? Ayahuasca is the exact opposite. It brings you face-to-face with reality. It locks you into a staring contest with your life. Your past, your future, the mistakes you've made, the pain you've inflicted... It forces you to confront reality in a way you've have never had the guts to otherwise. It's Jacob Marley in the jungle." The rest of the group agrees, and Hamish continues through his cigarette, "And you don't just see your problems. You see the *reasons* behind them. Believe me as a guy who's been there, if you've done hurtful things, hold on to your hats, boys, 'cause this shit will destroy you. It'll open doors you've kept locked for a long, long time. Just be careful tomorrow."

I take a deep breath and steal a glance at Ishy and The Deuce. Like me, they're taking inventory of their existence.

The Deuce lights a cigarette and asks, "Yeah, but aside from all that, you're trippin' balls. Right?"

This gets a quiet laugh from the group.

There's a skinny kid from California with sun-soaked hair and a surfer's tan. He looks The Deuce square in the eye. "For parts of it. Parts of it are a serious fucking trip. Like mushrooms times a thousand. But parts of it are the most terrifying experience you'll ever encounter. Things you can't begin to fathom."

The room grows quiet again, and Jersey City Linda speaks softly, "I've been here a few times before. What I've learned is that ayahuasca won't give you the answers you think you're looking for. It might not give you any answers at all. Not right now, anyway. But over time, almost imperceptibly, the knowledge and awareness will seep into your soul, answering questions you didn't even know how to ask."

New Mexico Hamish nods with conviction. "It'll help simplify your life. It'll strip away all the bullshit and let you see things more clearly, and for what they truly are. You'll be able to better understand yourself and the world you live in. Shit that used to bother you—traffic, ignorance, airport security—you begin to understand that it's not worth gettin' worked up over. That it's all part of the ride. The truth is, when you're in the thick of it, life seems like chaos and anarchy: random, fucked experiences spilling into one another and overwhelming your sense of control, crushing your dreams and destroying the things you think your life should be. But then you get older and look back, and it all seems like a finely crafted novel."

It's a beautiful thought, and we all sit back in contemplation.

A bald Irish kid sits in the shadows, just beyond the light. I hadn't noticed him until he began. "The Shaman saved my life. I can tell you unequivocally that I would be dead if it weren't for this man, for this place." He pulls out a bag of Mapacho cigars and offers them around the table.

We all light up in silence, savoring the sweet jungle tobacco. They call him Donegal, and he leans in closer. In the faltering light, I can barely make out his blotched complexion.

"I had this... skin disorder. It started on my foot and then spread to my ankle and up my leg. At first, it looked like eczema, this red, scabby kind of rash. But it got worse and worse as it spread... I was eventually covered head-to-toe." He takes a moment to show us his skin. His movements are deliberate, revealing a tale of agony. "I looked like Freddy Kruger. It was the most painful thing I've ever felt. I couldn't even move. I was living with my parents at the time, and I would scream all night long because I couldn't take the pain and I didn't know what to do." Donegal takes a quick hit from his Mapacho. "After a while, my skin started flaking off. That's when I became frightened. I could literally peel my skin like a banana, and when I did, it would leak this black ooze."

The Deuce and I exchange a concerned look.

"Months passed, and my parents didn't know what to do. They brought me to every specialist in Ireland. Not a single doctor had an explanation for what was wrong with me. They all said they'd never seen anything like it... They wouldn't speak it aloud, and nobody would tell me to my face, but I knew I was dying." He nods. "I have no idea who did it, or why they wanted to remain anonymous, but one day someone slipped a *National Geographic* magazine under my parents' door. There was an article about the Gringo Shaman, and how ayahuasca was curing all these addictions and diseases... I knew my parents would never go for it. They were too conservative. Too Westernized. Too *Irish*. But I was out of options." He quietly laughs. "I took 5,000 quid from my dad's account without telling him."

He looks at us with tears in his eyes.

"Desperate times, right? I wrote a long letter to my parents, and I cried all over the pages, telling them how sorry I was, about how this was the only chance I had. I didn't even tell them where I was going, because I didn't want them to find me. I put the letter on the kitchen table and left in the middle of the night. Taxi to airport, Dublin to Lima, Lima to Iquitos."

We are transfixed.

"My first ayahuasca ceremony with The Shaman, I was completely freaking out. It was intense, maniacal shit. The Shaman knew something was wrong. He could sense there was something evil in me. In the middle of the ceremony, he grabbed my foot, my rotting, oozing, decaying foot. He began biting and tearing away at it like a wild dog... I didn't know what the hell was going on, didn't know if it was real or I was hallucinating or dying. But he kept at it, viciously. I was screaming like a desperate child... And then he found what he was after."

No one dares breathe.

"There was this black talisman lodged in my foot. I had no idea it was there. None of the doctors who looked at me had ever found it. None of the X-rays had revealed it. But as sure as I'm sitting here now, The Shaman sucked this sharp, occult object out of my foot and spit it on the floor."

The silence is a physical entity.

The Deuce whispers, "What the fuck?"

"I think I must have stepped on it years ago, when I was on LSD at this rave in Africa. I was barefoot and knackered in this awful place." Donegal shakes his head. "After that first ayahuasca ceremony, my skin started getting better. Very slowly, but noticeably over time. I've been purging with The Shaman ever since. Once a week, until all the bad is out. I still have a long way to go, but I'm getting there."

Nobody moves.

I finally ask, "When did you last see your parents?"

Donegal nods in resignation. "They still have no idea where I am. I send them an email every now and then when I go back into Iquitos, but I keep it vague. I let them know I'm getting better, but the only way I'm going to stay better is by seeing this thing through... I haven't seen them in eighteen months."

There's another long silence as we try to wrap our minds around it.

"For the three of you staring down your first ayahuasca experience tomorrow night, there's no way to describe what to expect. It's completely different for everyone, and it's completely different every time. But what I *can* tell you is this: I learned more in my first night drinking ayahuasca than I had my entire life."

23

Rosy – Friday: Amazon, Peru

As is often the case when darkness descends in an unfamiliar place, I sleep like shit the first night in the jungle. The unbearable humidity and the mosquito nets play tricks with my equilibrium. Unspoken fears race through my mind while lying in suffocating blackness. The screaming is terrifying and unending: monkeys and birds and giant bugs and frogs unleashing wails of the tortured and damned. The Deuce convinces himself that an anaconda could slither into our dwelling, so he sporadically patrols the floor with a pocketknife like a young Vern Tessio. And if that isn't enough, a bat perches in the rafters to spend the night shitting through Ishy's mosquito net. The invisible swoosh of its wings makes our skin crawl with each sonar-directed dart.

At the first hint of dawn, the three of us drag our carcasses into the cool morning air. Gustavo kneels next to a fire, working something in a pot. He gives us a nod as we zombie into the main lodge for green tea and bread with maracuyá jam. We are bleary-eyed and crippled with fatigue. By the time the other guests filter in for breakfast, we know we are in desperate need of our beds.

Rest comes easy in the daylight, so the world outside soon ceases to exist. We sleep like the dead, devoid of movement, snoring, or dreams. Even the heat can't wrestle us from our stupor.

In the relative quiet of late morning, Ishy is first to wake. He sneaks away from the cabin to the main hut, where Vanessa sits alone by the screen window, reading from a hostel exchange copy of *Slaughterhouse-Five*. Ishy pours a cup of hot tea and inquires where everyone is.

"I was just going to ask you the same thing."

"Yeah, we had a rough time last night. Those guys will probably sleep all day."

"It certainly does take some getting used to out here. The nights especially."

Ishy looks around the room, taking in the long communal tables, the bean bag chairs for lounging, and the circular carpet that, like a kindergarten class, is used for important conversations. Ishy motions to the emptiness. "So where exactly do people disappear to around here?"

Vanessa smiles. "Most people spend the mornings alone, focusing on themselves. Meditation, yoga, writing in their journal. I like to read when I can. I was actually considering a little rainforest hike if you're up for it."

Ishy gives her a suspicious look. "Is it *safe?*"

Vanessa laughs, then leads him to the back of the room where she opens an old trunk full of jungle gear. She takes out thick cargo pants, some Wellington boots, and a "Buffalo Bills, 1991 Super Bowl Champions!" long-sleeve tee. They clumsily pull the ill-fitting items over their clothes, then douse themselves in industrial grade mosquito repellent.

Sufficiently lathered in DEET, Ishy and Vanessa walk across the camp to the clearing's perimeter, disappearing into the thick jungle brush like ghosts in an Iowa cornfield. Although invisible to the untrained eye, Vanessa assures Ishy that there's a trail underfoot that loops around the camp. Ishy has his doubts, but she advises deep breaths and to enjoy the moment.

They walk in silence for quite some time. The heat is like a kick in the groin, and it isn't long before their layers darken with sweat. But they continue, spellbound. Everything they encounter is gargantuan and wet and growing; the smells of verdant earth are almost too much to process. The overgrown plants are every shade of green, and they seem to move in rhythmic slow-motion as rays of light poke holes through the canopy. Vines form disorienting angles in unexpected places. The shimmering, feathered patterns of birds are breathtaking; the insects are otherworldly. Every now and then, they happen upon the shadows of monkeys jumping tree to tree.

After traversing the trail for half an hour, Ishy notices Vanessa periodically crouching to pick up something from the jungle floor. After the third time, he asks what she's gathering.

Vanessa opens the palm of her hand, revealing a collection of seeds patterned with brilliant red and black. They look like tiny marbles painted with an artist's rendition of yin and yang. "They're called *wayruro* seeds. I've been told they symbolize universal duality. They remind us that there are always two sides to every story, that things are never cut-and-dry, good or bad... that truth is complex."

Ishy is taken aback by their stark, dual-quality beauty. He holds one between his thumb and forefinger, inspecting it.

Vanessa continues, "The indigenous people of the Amazon wear the seeds for good luck and protection. The red symbolizes masculinity and life. The black symbolizes femininity and eternity."

Ishy is enchanted. He nods, thinking on the fly. "Hypothetically speaking, do you think someone might like to have a set of earrings made from these?"

Vanessa smiles beautifully. "She'll love them."

By the time Ishy and Vanessa return to camp, a lunch of fried dorado fish, rice, and hearts of palm salad is being served in the main hut. The Deuce sits at a table with a few guests, so Ishy and Vanessa join them. The river fish is fresh and meaty, unlike anything Ishy has ever tasted, and The Deuce admits he has no idea what the heart of a palm is, but he's all in on them. Vanessa tells them to eat up since this will be the last meal of the day.

Everyone sits around the tables long after the food is gone, drinking water. They talk a little about home and where they've been, but the night's ceremony weighs heavy on their minds, so it isn't long before they drift away, leaving Ishy and The Deuce alone.

The Deuce lights a cigarette. Ishy watches him smoke, feeling something slowly and deliberately washing over him. He feels undaunted, unfaltering. He looks The Deuce dead in the eye, understanding that this thing needs to happen. Right. Now.

"Did you do it?"

The Deuce sits stone-like, ice in his veins as he returns the gaze, long and hard. He's back in Samantha's apartment all over again, the power gone yet the night electric and still.

Ishy's heart races. It's like he's stepping off the ledge and falling. It is the juncture where everything hangs in the balance, and nothing will ever be the same.

The Deuce exhales slowly. "Nah, man." He shakes his head and flicks the ashes from his cigarette. "Couldn't bring myself to do it. I mean, I wanted to. Fuck, did I *ever*."

Ishy doesn't blink.

"I don't need to tell you that she was a smoldering, little rocket. A demon in the sack, I bet... But no, not in this lifetime."

Ishy exhales.

"I've done some bad things in my day. Things I'll take with me to the grave. But I didn't go there. Everybody's got a line they don't cross. And I don't fuck my boys' girls. End of story." The Deuce crushes out his cigarette and steps away without another word, leaving Ishy alone with nothing but the truth, and the faded traces of the way things used to be.

I awake in the stillness of the sweltering afternoon to find myself sitting at the end of the bed, my body glistening with sweat. I am transfixed by the moment, unsure how to reconcile the fact that I am in the Amazon while my mom is back in Canada, in a hospital bed, dying. I am half asleep but more sentient than I can remember. The moment and the feeling and my thoughts and my memories are nothing, but they are also everything. I am infinite and I am already gone.

Ishy creeps into the cabin, hoping not to disturb me. His look of concern reflects my existential crisis. He speaks quietly. "How are you feeling?"

"Hotter than a motherfucker."

"It's quite something out here, isn't it?"

I am lost, shaking my head. "Everything's so fucked-up."

Ishy nods slowly. Then he leaves me alone.

I don't know how long it takes to pull myself together, but I drag myself into the bathroom to take a long, cold shower. I let the cool water rush over me, my body and brain gradually finding a temperature they can tolerate. The clatter of the shower swallows external noise, leaving me alone to face the truth. I feel the lump in my throat. I try to stop myself from breaking down, but it's no use.

Still soaking wet, I slip on a pair of cargo shorts and a T-shirt, then venture over to the main cabin. A few guests gather around a table, but human interaction is an impossibility for me, so I set off on an unmarked trail, hoping it will provide something approximating respite, or answers, or anesthesia.

I run along an overgrown trail with no idea where I'm going, oblivious to the chacruna leaves tickling my ankles. I climb beneath the ayahuasca vines and over hanging bitterwood, crushing the fruit of the cannonball tree as the chuchuhuasi and palo santo whisper in the breeze. The mosquitos form walls in my path. In the early afternoon, the air is so fragrant, it tastes like it's born of flowers and trees and leaves and soil in that very moment. I slow my pace and take a few deep breaths, coming to a massive tree with prehistoric roots taller than I can reach. I disappear between the walls of roots and marvel at the colossus, making my way in and out and around the circumference before knocking with my knuckles. The ancient wood answers with a hollow *tock* that echoes all around. I follow the trail for another kilometer, until it opens into a bright clearing where a palm-leaf gazebo overlooks a rainforest pond. The water is warm glass, the entire scene a vision of tranquility. It feels too beautiful to be true.

A solitary figure sits in the gazebo.

Newton's law of universal gravitation states that every body attracts every other body with a force proportional to the mass of each. I am gutted and hollowed, and even though I want nothing more than peaceful detachment, I make my way to The Shaman, drawn by an energy beyond my comprehension.

He expresses an unspoken welcome.

I smile meekly, taking a seat next to him. I am almost certainly interrupting some ritual of spiritual introspection, but he doesn't seem to mind.

We sit in unmoving silence for a very long time.

"Roosevelt, I sense that you've been through a lot. That you have endured considerable hardships."

I nod slowly.

"Even though it can't possibly feel like it, you should know that everything that's ever happened to you has been a gift." The Shaman looks me in the eye, unflinching. Under virtually any other circumstance, another man speaking while looking into my soul would be insufferable. But in this moment, profound connection feels like the most natural thing in the world. "Life is the only teacher. Experience is the only lesson. Just know that whatever you've done, and whatever you do, it's what you were always meant to do." The way he looks at me, it seems as though he understands things he can't possibly know. "There's a reason life has brought you to this place, at this moment. The reason may not reveal itself for months, maybe even years. But one day you will understand. The spirits have been calling you here."

I don't know what to believe. We sit in silence as the turmoil of my mind struggles to weather the storm. After many minutes, I ask, "How do you explain everything that goes on in there? In the ceremony house, with the spirits and the visions and the foretelling of the future."

The Shaman smiles. "I can't explain it. I don't even try to understand it. I only know that it exists."

Skepticism bleeds all over my face.

The Shaman continues, "A caterpillar is a living entity, just as we humans are living entities. We are both biologically limited animals, existing here in this world. But the way you and the caterpillar perceive the world is very different. A butterfly doesn't understand the concept of a lawyer, and it certainly could never fathom the intricate workings of a federal courtroom, but those things exist nonetheless... Presumably, there are things as much beyond our cognizance as the United States Constitution is beyond the understanding of a butterfly."

I take some time to digest this, the possibilities unraveling in my mind's eye. How much exists within us, amongst us, beyond us, the significance and meaning of which we can never begin to comprehend? It is dizzying to contemplate. As if preordained, a blue morpho flutters across the pond, landing with an inaudible click on the ledge of the gazebo.

The Shaman nods, looking to a place in the jungle I can't see. "It will not be easy. You'll be in the fire tonight. Just know that you've made it here. Whenever you feel like you don't have the strength to go on, understand that the journey to the present will have taught you everything you need to know. The universe gives you everything you need, in every single moment, to be you. Look within yourself."

The Shaman stands to leave, understanding that I will need more time, always.

I watch him make his way down the path. He is a young man, but he moves with the labored canter of someone burdened by the responsibility of wisdom. Watching him disappear, I am almost overcome by the realization that I can't remember the last time I have felt so loved.

It is close to four when I make it back to camp's main building. All the guests keep one another company in the nervous, crawling hours that prelude the night's ceremony. They greet me warmly as I amble through the room, their kindness a reminder of just how welcoming they've been to a trio of ragtag stowaways. I sit at a table with Vanessa, Ishy, and The Deuce.

"Where you been, cuz?"

I smile sheepishly. "What do they call it here? Inner reflection?"

"Do you use your left hand or your right hand for that?"

Everyone cracks up as The Deuce congratulates himself on another successful *Stand By Me* reference. Vanessa flashes me a concerned look. I subtly nod to assure her I'm okay.

"Hey, cuz, we've been debating something since you been gone. In all your time down here, you ever swim in the Amazon?"

"No, man. Never got around to it."

The Deuce is smiling. "Grab your trunks, son. Today is your lucky fuckin' day."

Fifteen minutes later, we're standing on the banks of the Amazon, staring into the billowing swell of river-sea. Vanessa, Ishy, and The Deuce talk a big game, but, looking into the brown surge, everyone is having second thoughts. We each wait for someone else to make a move. I look at Vanessa, hoping she'll call the whole thing of.

She only shrugs and giggles. "You know, a few years ago, scientists discovered a new species of predatory worm in the Amazon. They call it the tyrant king leech. The Tyrannosaurus rex of leeches. These suckers are three inches long with teeth you can *see*. They've been known to slither inside various human orifices to make a nice little home for themselves, feeding off their host for weeks at a time."

We all look incredulously at Vanessa, then burst out laughing. The fact that we're even considering this feels insane. Just when it seems we're going to back out, The Deuce strips down to his boxers. He charges down the riverbank, launching off the dock for a world-class belly-flop. The painful slap of skin on water reverberates all the way back to the trees.

We're still laughing in disbelief when he surfaces 30 feet downstream, joking the current will drag him halfway to Brazil.

"Better watch out, Deuce," Ishy calls. "Piranhas gonna get yer pecker!"

The Deuce laughs his ass off as he fights the current back to shore, failing miserably in his attempt to splash us. Vanessa bites her lip, smiling. She begins to undress, revealing the type of heartbreaking bikini nobody would expect to see at a shaman's camp. Ishy and I walk with her down to the dock, and after she slips into the river, Ishy kneels to test the water with his hand. As he does so, The Deuce grapples onto him, squealing with delight as he pulls Ishy ass-over-teakettle into the muddy swill.

Vanessa looks at me, smiling conspiratorially. If my life were a movie, this would be the part where Japandroids' "Younger Us" plays loud and distorted as I take my shot, running and leaping off the end of the dock in a clumsy cannonball, the group of us splashing wildly with fleeting exuberance.

Some moments are infused with such significance that you know, even while living them, that the thrill of the memory will stay with you forever. I know as we're splashing like children in El Río Amazonas—hours before the dread and the shit and the torment that will surely stare us down in the ayahuasca ceremony—that this is one moment I'll always come back to.

With a kind of serene acceptance, I paddle away from the group and float on my back, letting the current carry me as I look up into the perfect blue sky, the treetops dusting the field of my vision. In that moment, for all it's worth, I understand that I have found some happiness.

After a while, Vanessa and I stretch out on the sandy riverbank. The sun is warm on our bodies, the golden light an entity unto itself, sparkling across the water. I take a deep breath and say that it really is beautiful when you stop to take it all in. She agrees, citing Henry James' belief that there are no two words more evocative than *summer afternoon*.

She motions toward Ishy and The Deuce. "Your friends really care about you to come all this way. They strike me as beautiful souls."

I smile at this description. "They're alright, aren't they? I can't speak for the condition of their souls, but..."

I mean it to be funny, but Vanessa isn't smiling. We're quiet for a moment, and it gets me thinking.

"The soul, I can't even remember what that is anymore."

Vanessa looks out at the river. "It's the one thing that subsists after everything else is gone."

I nod, recollecting something from home. "I used to walk past this graffiti alley back in Toronto, and there was one mural that always struck me. It said, 'IN THE INFINITE MOMENTS THAT IT TAKES TO READ THIS, YOU'LL HAVE LIVED FOREVER.' I feel like it's getting harder to remember what it's like to be wild and young. Sometimes I can't believe my life could've ever been anything except what it is now... Those days seem like they happened to someone else, in another life."

Vanessa looks somewhere beyond the water. We sit in silence for a long time.

"So, V, there's something I've been meaning to ask."

She looks at me now.

"From what I see, everyone here is trying to work through something: addiction, disease, abuse... Back at The Hideout, you said you just wanted to peek behind the curtain... Why are you *really* here?"

Vanessa smiles. "I guess you missed that first day when The Shaman advised us never to ask that question."

I grin, knowing I probably would have asked anyway.

She takes a deep breath. "I can't say for sure. Maybe for a lot of the same reasons you are." She lets this idea hang between us. "I think maybe I need to learn how to love again."

Now it's my turn to look across the river, wondering how I can possibly explain. Like so many other times when confronted with tough questions, I defer to someone else. In not so many words,

I tell her the only thing I learned from love was how to let someone else make the tough decisions.

Vanessa waits a beat before calling me on it. "Leonard Cohen or Jeff Buckley?"

"I was thinking k.d. lang, but, gun to the head, I'll take the Buckley version."

She smiles. "Is that really how you feel about love?"

"Sometimes."

"And now?"

Shadows grow long across the water. "I don't feel much of anything these days."

Vanessa waits for more.

After a long silence, I continue, "Do you believe there's some kind of mirror universe out there? A place that looks and feels just like this one, with all the same forces at work? A world almost identical, except maybe things work out a little better for us?"

Vanessa nods. The wheels are turning. She asks, "What do you know about entangled particles?"

I can't help but laugh. "I know precisely nothing about entangled particles."

She smiles with a vitality that shines through her eyes, the light of it warming the darkest parts of me. "There's a theory that suggests when two particles are created in the same instant, they become... connected. But connected isn't a strong enough word. The coupling is an kinship that confounded even Einstein, who referred to it as 'spooky action at a distance.' It's as if the particles are so deeply linked, they essentially share the same *existence*."

I am more than a little lost.

"Quantum physicists have done countless experiments where they shoot these entangled particles through a splitter, which sends them in opposite directions. They measure the behavior of those particles after they have been separated."

From below, Ishy and The Deuce splash like maniacs.

"Time and time again, those entangled particles, even after they have been separated and sent spiraling to opposite ends of the universe, somehow remain connected and will continue to share the same experience *forever*."

I nod but am unsure why.

"Those particles will act the same as their entangled partner for eternity. It could be thousands of years later and the particles trillions of miles away, but if Particle A is turned 90 degrees, Particle B would instantaneously turn 90 degrees as well."

The ramifications begin washing over me. It all unfurls through the smoke rings of my mind.

She gives me another moment, her smile like a sunrise. "Understanding that these entangled particles exist in the manner we believe them to, wouldn't it be reasonable, or even *probable*, to expect that the Big Bang split trillions of entangled, universe-forming particles, sending them screaming to the furthest reaches of whatever it is that inhabited the void before existence?"

The hair on my arms stands on end, receptors tuned to the inner workings of life.

"And knowing what we know, with those trillions of entangled particles sharing the exact same existence, wouldn't it be logical, or even probable, that an entangled, mirrored universe exists somewhere out there?"

It feels like warm déjà vu. There's something in my soul that understands this to be true. It takes me a long time to find the words. "So, if this mirrored universe is out there, where do you think it exists? Is it in the great beyond, outside the margins of our own universe, expanding and somehow racing toward us in the same way our existence is expanding and racing towards...?" My words fail me.

Vanessa smiles beautifully, putting her finger to her temple as she looks to the sky. "I can't decide if it's in here... or out there."

We try wrapping our minds around what we're trying to wrap our minds around: the impossible and possible existing simultaneously, the ultimate tautology defining our existence.

Once it becomes clear that Ishy and The Deuce are getting ready to climb back onto the bank, I take a deep breath. A soft breeze swaddles us in summer essence, giving me the courage to look her in the eye and quietly ask, "Hey, V... What do you know about leukemia?"

I see it in her eyes, her heart dissolving as things fall into place. As her eyes fill with tears, I feel the overwhelming urge to console her. "It's not me... It's just— I just want you to lay it on me. As cold and clinical as you can. When we're talking about those patterns in nature: How self-repeating and reproducing is the stuff in leukemia? I mean, is it the kind of stuff that just spreads and takes over and there's no going back?"

The dull ache in my throat consumes me.

Vanessa takes a deep breath and reaches for my hand. She can't even look me in the eye.

Nightfall comes early in the jungle. By six, it's difficult to see in the shadows, the grainy light giving way to darkness. I sit at the makeshift desk in our tiny cabin, unable to move. It feels as though I've slipped outside of time, as if what measures our existence ceases to exist. Gustavo lights the kerosene lantern on my desk, but I don't register his presence until after he's gone. During these long, indistinguishable intervals, I am by myself but at peace. Loneliness has not yet set in: the loneliness that wraps itself around you, the suffocating kind that's impossible to shake, the loneliness you can taste, desolation so complete it becomes fact.

Ishy and The Deuce are in the main lodge with a few others, doing their best to prepare. With a nervous pit set deep in their stomachs, they sip chamomile tea as conversation meanders like the river, gradual but always leading to *that* place: life, and what it means. How they've gotten here. The burden of their sins. Unforgivable mistakes that haunt them every day.

Jersey City Linda, who's done more living than anyone, tries to put us at ease. "Remember when you were in high school, and every little event seemed to carry the weight of the world? How every teenage crush was the love of your life, and every social misstep, if not the death of you, was the death of your ego?"

Ishy knows it all too well.

"I often think about that time in my life. How I used to look at my parents and wonder how they let their lives slip away. How I could never understand or forgive them for the compromises they made, even though those compromises were the reason their shithead teenage daughter even existed!"

Everyone chuckles.

"Did you know there's a scientific explanation for the disconnect between adolescence and the reality of adulthood?"

They dangle at the end of her line.

"When we're teenagers, we have more dopamine pumping through our brains than at any other time in our lives." Linda takes a moment to let this sink in. "That's the reason we feel so intensely. It's the reason our teenage selves can never understand our parents, and the reason we believe they will never understand us. It's the reason the songs on the radio in high school feel like prayers whispered through your soul." Linda quietly laughs, half embarrassed. "It's the reason I still can't get through 'You Don't Have To Say You Love Me' without breaking down. The things we love when we're 16, they stay with us forever. They're the things we think about late at night, the things we don't dare speak to anyone. It's sad and beautiful to know we'll never love anything as much as we did when we were wild and young."

After a beat, The Deuce asks, "So that's it? It doesn't get any better for us?"

Linda gently smiles. "I'm saying we eventually have a reckoning with the adult world. It doesn't happen in a single shot, not even with ayahuasca facilitating the brain's dopamine receptors... But you live long enough in the real world, and you accept that life is no longer wide open. You lose some illusions about what life is going to be. You figure out how to accept limitations while staying true to yourself. You decide how to make compromises and believe in the blessings those compromises bring. That's what this journey is all about. That's what growing up is. That's what life is." She takes a deep breath. "I think you'll find that as you get older, life gets less ecstatic, but more meaningful... You'll feel it all in that ceremony house tonight. Just make sure you leave your heart open. Tonight and always."

I sit alone in the table's lamplight, writing with purpose. My eyes remain fixed as Ishy and The Deuce enter the cabin. I know they're standing behind me, and they know that I know. The quiet is forced and uncomfortable, the kerosene hiss somehow rendering the silence absolute.

Eventually, Ishy and The Deuce retire to their beds, their mosquito nets hanging grotesquely to the floor. They brace themselves for the onslaught, whispering about the ceremony. After much deliberation, Ishy decides to leave his wallet and watch behind. The Deuce opts for a weathered Monte Alban Mezcal T-shirt, emblazoned with a smiling cartoon larva and the words: **Eat the Worm!** The sounds of people making their way along the jungle path are barely audible. Ishy picks up the watch on his bed: 7:43.

At some point in life, you decide where you're going to stand, and who you're going to stand with. Ishy and The Deuce stand by the door, patiently waiting on me. I understand by the sounds they *aren't* making that their concern for me is real. When I'm finally ready, I fold what I've written and carefully place it inside an envelope. I stand and quietly walk to the door. I hand Ishy the envelope and look him square in the eye.

"Just in case."

Ishy feels his stomach fall away. "That's not even funny, man."

24

Friday: Hurtling Through the Universe at 2,160,000 km/h

We silently step into the ceremony house where the soft glow of candles plays tricks with the shadows. The darkness beyond the screened windows is an ocean of black so vast and consuming, it feels as though it will swallow our space entirely. The room is sweltering but hushed, the sweet smell of burning palo santo wood in the air. The guests are settled on the floor with familiar disorganization, and The Shaman sits near the front, flanked by Don Alberto and Gustavo. Ishy, The Deuce, and I are last to arrive. The Shaman welcomes us with a nod.

We anxiously smile and make our way through the room, staking our claim to a small space on the floor close to Vanessa. Butterflies do backflips in my stomach, the unknown like a living entity stalking us from the other side. The same dread is in Ishy's eyes. We turn to The Deuce, whose inability to empathize with or even identify the terror suffocating the room is strangely comforting. The man is a narcissist and likely a sociopath, but he is also our rock. And in these terrifying moments before *the* moment, rather than concerning himself with fate or dimensions beyond his comprehension, The Deuce asks The Shaman, "Hey, Doc? If you were a professional wrestler, what would your entrance music be for tonight's ceremony?"

After a beat of disbelief, the room erupts in laughter. Including The Shaman. "I'll be honest, Stan. I didn't see that one coming."

The California Kid looks around, desperate to chime in. He offers, "It would have to be The Doors' 'Break On Through (To The Other Side),' right?"

Many nod in agreement. While The Shaman weighs his options, Vanessa suggests the Talking Heads' "Once in a Lifetime." Hamish, the New Mexico hippie, offers Jimi Hendrix's "Are You Experienced?"

The Shaman is amused. "Those are pretty good. But for some reason I keep coming back to AC/DC, 'For Those About to Rock, We Salute You!'"

The group loves that our spirit guide is quoting Angus Young, but The Deuce isn't persuaded. "A solid effort, Doc, but I'm afraid that is incorrect. The only possible entrance music for you would be 'Welcome to the Jungle' by Guns N' Roses. 'You know where you aaaare? You're in the JUNGLE, baby... You're gonna DIIIIIIIEEEEEE!'"

We nervously laugh as The Shaman nods, whispering to himself, "Out, brief candle." Then he kills the light.

The nighttime jungle is a symphony of chaos but, in these initial moments of darkness, there is silence. Then I hear Ishy and The Deuce breathing beside me. I feel my own deep, labored breaths in my chest. It takes a while to adjust as I sort through which patches of darkness are shadows and which are spots of my imagination. Just when it seems nobody will ever talk, the darkness is shattered by a struck match. It illuminates The Shaman's face, flames flickering higher as his Mapacho cigar crackles to life. He takes a few quick puffs, then billows smoke into a bottle of clear liquid. He and Don Alberto sip from this smoke-infused liquid, then spit it in a spray of mist all around their bodies. The air is tinged with camphor and garlic. The Shaman explains that he and Don Alberto use this concoction to protect themselves from the onslaught of evil spirits. I sense The Deuce's raised eyebrow.

Still seated, The Shaman readies himself like a boxer before a fight: eyes closed, rolling his head from side-to-side, muttering under his breath. He lets the silence decorate the night longer than is comfortable. At last, he says, "Everyone ready for a little ayahuasca?"

One by one, The Shaman calls us by name. The invitees slowly make their way to The Shaman, whispering their doubts and answering whether they want a half-cup or full. Last night, we asked about the taste. Though each person described varying degrees of repugnance, many suggested that they feared the rotting tamale leaf taste almost as much as the depths to which it would take them. As they return to their spot on the floor, each person's disgust is more marked than the last.

After all the other guests have taken their medicine, The Shaman motions for Ishmael. He rises on shaky knees and navigates through the tangle of people.

The Shaman looks him square in the eye. "You have that nervous, butterfly feeling in your stomach?"

"I do."

"Then you're ready."

The Shaman pours half a cup. Ishy peeks inside and then turns to us, waiting for a cue. The Deuce nods. Ishy closes his eyes and brings the cup to his lips, dry-heaving as he chokes back the first sip. The Shaman lets him know that it's okay. Ishy's eyes water and we all hear him proclaim, "It's fucking disgusting!" But he sucks it up and downs the remains, his face betraying something harrowing.

The Deuce is next. He struts up to The Shaman, saying, "Fill me up, Doc."

The Shaman laughs. "You're a rock star, my man."

The Deuce doesn't hesitate for a moment, every bit the tough guy archetype, slamming it back to chase his demons. It is dramatic and impressive, but I notice a twitch in his neck.

Knowing my time is nigh, I stare at the floor, searching for patterns in the wood grain. It is too dark to see, but I know they exist. When I look up, The Shaman is eyeing me. He nods. I struggle to my feet, the uneasiness a black pit in my stomach.

The Shaman doesn't even ask, whistling a beautiful melody into the overflowing cup.

I am terrified. "Any advice?"

"Just kick at the darkness 'til it bleeds daylight."

The drink is the same sediment and tannin brown as the river. It is thick and sludgy, tasting of feculent earth, as if the entire jungle—plants, bark, dirt, vines, feathers, leaves—were mashed and beaten and mixed with river water, then left to stagnate in a forgotten place. It is the taste of life spilling over into death.

I head back to my spot and lie on the floor. I don't know what to think but am doing everything in my power to keep the liquid from coming back up. I try to stay still, giving my stomach a chance to settle, waiting for the awful taste to subside.

The room is incredibly quiet as we wait for the unknown. A sign. A feeling. Our maker. The silence is boundless, and it begins to stretch out. Time and moments and the stillness take a less defined and recognizable form until everything is obliterated, the dried leaf rattle of the chakapa exploding in the darkness. Its presence weaves through the fabric of the night as The Shaman quietly sings his ícaro.

An intimate, indeterminate, infinitesimal, infinite chunk of time dissolves in which the world continues to roar through the universe while a dozen strangers occupy an intimate, indeterminate, infinitesimal, infinite space.

I notice that I'm spinning, but I don't know for how long. Through a tunnel. Into a black hole. Down the foggy ruins of time. I'm contemplating these paradoxical conditions as I slip away. I sit upright for a while, then lie on the floor with no recollection of how I'd gotten there. I am *mareado* without previously having been able to fathom the meaning of the word. When I close my eyes, I see dazzling colors. The entirety of the universe whizzes by in a blur of energy and brilliant life. I imagine this is what it's like to trip on acid while looking at Japanimation on a Lite-Brite... And that is what you see before you die.

The Deuce lies next to Ishy, unable to move. He is paranoid, self-conscious, and increasingly terrified. His mouth is wide open. It's impossible for him to understand or describe, but he swears that an aerial entity is being sucked out of him, moving away from him, settling somewhere in the ether. He tries to fight it but is helpless. Whatever it is or was, it is gone from him now, for better or worse, forever. He contemplates what it means but—just as the realization washes over him—it, too, is gone.

He snaps out of it, momentarily. He senses Ishy next to him. He doesn't see him, but he can feel him looking on; he discerns his concern. After what might be a lifetime, The Deuce manages to sputter, "Dude, this shit is no joke."

Ishy groans. He understands this to be the most ridiculous understatement in the history of the universe.

And then The Deuce is gone, sucked back in and under.

Ishy knows he's going to vomit, but he's doing everything to lock it down. He has no idea what a "cocoon of death" is, or whether he's in the process of inventing the concept, but he knows that he's immersed in one, shrouded and wrapped and ready to go into the cold, dark ground.

Except for that single puff from the joint aboard the Eduardo V, Ishy has never ingested a recreational drug in his life. But, even with his lack of experience, he knows there is nothing in this struggle that feels recreational. His body is completely cold, and he is shivering. Before he knows how, Ishy is on all fours, violently heaving and unleashing guttural, awful sounds. A fire-hose geyser spouts God-only-knows-what from his insides as he vomits into the bottomless pit of a filthy bucket.

He has no idea how long this goes on for.

The Shaman and Don Alberto restart the ícaros. Though the words are Spanish, the meaning of these spiritual songs transcends language, their essence distilled and embodied in the feeling that comes from the sounds absorbed by my body. They bring me joy, and they are the most beautiful songs I've ever experienced. I unconsciously keep the beat with my toes, my face aching from smiling so big. I become one with the ícaros, directing the music with my index fingers like a maestro. With purpose, the jungle walks to the stage and takes a seat with the rest of the symphony. A cricket's chirp shoots a lightning bolt of fluorescence through my world, bathing my mind's eye in a flash of electric green. A monkey's wail is the string section's laugh hitting the sky, and I swear on everything I've ever loved or known that the frogs croak in rhythm to Black Box's "Everybody, Everybody," da-na OW! Da-na-na-na-na-na-na-na-na OW!

I roll over and somehow communicate this to The California Kid lying on the other side of the room. We laugh because we recognize it, and it doesn't seem the least bit strange that we're sharing these observations telepathically.

Ishy's cramping and heaving are almost overwhelming as he continues to purge. Just when it seems it will never end, it does.

It is momentarily quiet in the ceremony house. Ishy sits back, holding his knees, a calm washing over. In the darkness, he makes out only shadows, then the fleeting glow of a Mapacho cigar. In the serenity of the moment, Ishy sends good vibes to Rosy and The Deuce. Prior to this, he's never considered sending vibes of any description beyond those unguarded moments where he finds himself singing along to The Beach Boys.

He is alive and well, but the same cannot be said for The Deuce. It is apparent to most everyone that The Deuce is going to a dark place. Gradually, and then suddenly.

Lucidity comes and goes for me, but I hear his primal sounds: the gagging and choking and him screaming, "GET THE FUCK AWAY FROM ME," as he gasps for air.

The Deuce's world is unravelling. Bad things are happening. Evil things. The sins of the father visiting the child. A demonic half-cartoon Dora the Explorer goes to work tormenting his daughter in the darkness above. Taunting her. Inflicting misery. Making her question her worth. Filling her with insecurities. Kids are so young that they don't know how to tell you. A little girl needs a dad in her life. I stand and turn away, trying to avoid the moment of clarity where the ever-present ache in a child's belly is revealed to its culprit, and that culprit is the father who has all but abandoned her.

The Deuce spasms as the medicine takes deeper hold. He confronts images of troubled adolescence. Lived, unlived, and yet-to-be lived. In the fog of chaotic clarity, it's so hard to tell. We see young people hurting themselves. Alcohol in a backpack. Drugs and a map. A wild child lashing out, vulnerable and afraid. She is shipwrecked. She is doing things she will regret. Committing acts that she's too young for, too innocent to understand the significance, too angry to consider the consequences. The boys take advantage and laugh. The pattern created; the pattern repeating. His daughter in the image of the lost souls he preys upon.

But then I'm gone. Away from The Deuce and the scene and everything in between.

A lizard that I can't shake runs up and down my left side. I try to remember what day it is, and if this is the first time that I've ever experienced ayahuasca. I can't fucking place it. At one point I was sweating, but now I'm shivering. The room is disjointed, people further away than I recall. Sounds come from places they shouldn't. I can't even tell if my eyes are open anymore, or whether the people I think I see milling about are people at all. Walking obscurities, strutting and fretting their hours upon the stage. There is a waif-like wraith. A headless giant. I rub my nose incessantly.

The Deuce bashes his head against the floor, trying to kill something inside of him. He squeals, "WHAT THE FUCK DID I DO TO DERSERVE THIS?" He babbles in tongues, possessed and demented and demonic. It is the screaming of the pigs.

The California Kid calls out for the black jaguar ícaro, whatever the fuck that is. The Shaman immediately begins in on it, the song singing itself. It makes sense in a way that speaks to its significance long before we arrived or realized. The guy from New Mexico stands to turn ever so slowly, 360 degrees, confoundedly pointing his finger at the world, as if just now recognizing the condition of his existence. There is screaming and wailing and retching and laughter. It is complete and utter pandemonium.

In the midst of it all, Ishy heads to one of the toilets in the back. The bathroom looks like that scene in *Trainspotting* with shit caking every conceivable surface. The door hangs from its hinges and the seat is ripped off, leaning against the toilet at a perverse angle. Ishy doesn't think twice, sitting down and having at it with savage ferocity. Without the audacity to have ever even passed wind in mixed company, it now seems like the most natural thing in the world for him to expel these foul and disgusting sounds within earshot of everyone. He finds himself laughing about his current place in the universe.

Vanessa is in a catatonic state. She has been silent the entire ceremony, unable to move as she stares into the infinite perimeter of the Koch snowflake. It's the vision and understanding and ever-present moment she came for. She is transfixed and awestruck and hypnotized, only partially aware that this image, in its timeless, frozen form, is tattooed on her shoulder.

She is inside the truth. She is inside the darkness and the brooding colors and geometric architecture of life, swirling in mesmerizing waves as she ventures deeper. Time disappears as she slips further down the infinite plane, always moving, always closer, just out of reach, never there, the depth and the meaning eluding and inducing, always, never, forever... Somewhere within the dissolving time-space continuum, the abyss and the ceremony house become one. She's here, but she's not. She's *there*, but also everywhere. She's numb but feels it all. She's paralyzed, but she is boundless and completely free.

After a long time in the bathroom, Ishy returns to the floor, feeling that the physical purge is over. A weight lifts, and he is unchained. The axis tilts ever so slightly. He envisions the future: not simply as he wishes, but as it will actually unfold. It is manifesting for him, right here in this jungle hut and right here in his head. All at once, and without any shadow of doubt, Ishy understands precisely what's required to make his love for Lucia real, what it will take to make it flourish: the time and commitment and investment of everything in himself to get her attention and have her fall irrevocably in love with him the way he's fallen so impossibly for her, his *Peruana perfecta.* The understanding is both a fabrication of his own devices and the inarguable truth, but he knows it to be as real as if it already happened. Lying there on that jungle hut floor, the chaos swirling around him, he is filling in the blanks.

The heart is a force of nature, the brain even more so. And when the two hum in synchroneity, the line is blurred between ourselves and omnipotence. He is unafraid. He is unwavering. He is undaunted.

He is alive.

The Deuce fights it all night but seems to come through the worst of it. He's on all fours, a bucket resting precariously close to his nose. He sweats something fierce. His voice is ragged, and he sporadically squawks, "I'M TIRED! FUCKIN' TIRED!"

I can't explain why, but I find the repetition hilarious. Beyond his lament, the ceremony house is quiet. And then The Deuce begins to vomit. Viciously. Years of rot expel from every organ as he retches horrific quantities of indescribably black matter. We see it all in the darkness. It doesn't go on for long, but the purging takes on a frightening intensity. It is so loud and painful that I wonder if he will survive. I watch him convulse as he buries his head in the bucket. The smell is sickening, but I can't turn away.

As The Deuce finishes, he feels three large, maggoty worms slither from his throat, flopping into the bucket in a way he doesn't even try to explain. He sits back and wipes his eyes, shaking his head. He quietly sobs. It is the only sound in the night. We give him his peace as he works through it, accepting and reckoning with a great number of mistakes and regrets and shortcomings that make him who he is. I love him for it. We all do. He laughs through the tears and apologizes for being such a "fuckin' pussy."

He lies back down and sleeps almost immediately.

I am under the impression that time is passing but am unable to wrap my head around the concept. I can't locate the arrow or direction. It feels like I'm stuck, or that the earth is no longer spinning. As if everything ceases to click, or it never did and I'm just now realizing it.

There's something awful building inside me. It feels like I'm dying. My body is fighting to sever ties with me, rejecting everything I am. The agony of existence in this moment is beyond my understanding. It is awful, painful, nauseating, and I am on my knees, willing to give anything to vomit it out, get it over with. But my body won't allow it.

Vanessa throws up from somewhere unrecognizable. She's in the ceremony house, but I can't place her. If it's possible for someone to vomit in a delicate, adorable way, she is. Maybe I'm the only one who hears it. She periodically retches, and despite my internal strife, I smile. In a moment between heaves, I call out to her in the darkness, "Vanessa... Is that you?"

She tries to whimper.

"You sound glorious."

Most everyone laughs. But not me.

When Vanessa finishes, she returns to her spot and the same catatonic paralysis overtakes her. The storm is coming, she knows it. There is nothing to stop it. She has no idea how long it lasts, but it does, interminably. She climbs inside her fears and fights to break down her defenses, all within the labyrinth of her subconscious, all while lying still. She is terrified and heartbroken and ecstatic and grateful, all in one undefinable moment.

I have no idea how long the battle rages within her, and neither does she. Time losses all form. We fade in and out of it. Ishy is here and then he isn't. The Deuce is alive, but I feel like he's dead. I don't know who I am and believe I never will.

When Vanessa's struggle ends, she is incredibly still next to me. I sense tranquility within her, as if she has accepted all things as they are and herself as she is.

Vanessa takes a deep breath. She exhales slowly. At the tail end of that breath, she feels her heartbeat. And when she feels her heartbeat, she feels it in a way she has never felt before. She feels the beating from within her heart, as if *she is* the beating. There is nothing but this beating-from-within for a long time.

And then, softly, she feels the blood in her veins, the gentle warmth of sunlight moving through her, embracing and empowering and comforting. The happiness and love is all-consuming.

And then without noticing how or when, she becomes acutely aware of her lungs. She takes in air so sweet and saccharine and amazing, every breath deeper than the last, the fragrant taste of every plant on earth on her tongue. The effect is so invigorating yet calming that it lulls her to something like sleep.

Ishy fades in and out of a state not quite tangible, feeling the energy in the room and everything that led him to this exact moment. The Shaman senses this and tiptoes over. He whispers, "Can you believe this stuff exists?"

They both giggle like children.

I don't know how to describe what I'm feeling. Restricting the sensation to words is inadequate and likely insane as I begin to feel the planes of reality unhinge. I'm freaking out and I'm freezing and I'm terrified... and then, all at once, the structure of everything I've ever known is blown to bits. A trillion pieces obliterate as the tiny shards disappear into the ether.

Just as softly as it came for Vanessa, sleep slowly withdraws. She blinks in the darkness. Open-close... Open-close ... Open-close. A hundred times until she can think of nothing but her tongue. The hugeness of it fills her mouth and reaches down her throat, so far back that if she thinks about it anymore, she might choke. The Shaman senses her panic and kneels to whisper something, spraying camphor mist around her. She is numb again. Alone in the darkness.

After what could be hours, she feels a follicle on her arm tingle, the energy manifesting so the hair begins to rise. Then another follicle, a tiny, invisible hair on the small of her back; the same tingle of energy, the same slow standing on end. Then another on her calf. Then another. And another. Every hair on her body transmits an unknown energy and stands on end until every extremity is supercharged and receptive, reaching out, channeling the electricity from the world around her, thrilling sparks dancing in the night, the energy transfer undeniable. The world around her, the celestial beauty, the love, the darkness, the breathing, the beating, and the being... She feels it all.

Vanessa remains in this state both forever and an instant.

A realization: This is the life force. She has it within her.

A warmth envelopes her, inside and out, as she begins to understand the indescribable beauty of life. Her eyes fill with tears as the truth washes over her, recognizing that all living things, by the very nature of their *being*, have this life force within them. She realizes that she will forever be able to look within herself to glimpse this life force, to feel it again, to be it forever.

She is overwhelmed with happiness and gratitude. It is the single most important realization of her life.

I have no idea who I am. I don't know what I am. I don't know if my family exists, but I'm desperately searching my shattered memory to piece them back together. I can't determine if the time I've spent in Iquitos is real or imagined. Do I have a job? It is impossible to contemplate sitting on an airplane. The game of hockey seems utterly absurd. I don't know if my arm is real, or if it's even attached to my body. Slices of energy leave my body.

Nothing exists except for this fucked-up scene I've awoken to: darkness and chanting and the shaking of dried leaves. I am paralyzed. My life is disappearing. I have no idea how I got here or what happened to everything I knew.

I am being sucked down long tunnels of memory, falling through the snowflake's edge of space and time. At the end of each tunnel are chunks of my life playing out from beginning to end, in real time, in no particular order: I am at my parents' house. I am sitting on the front porch with my mom, drinking lemonade and talking about how I'm not enjoying seventh grade. The sun is getting low in the sky, but the light is warm on our faces. The conversation is not a memory; it is happening this very moment, familiar, but for the first time. It doesn't *seem* real. It *is* real. Then just as quickly as I arrived at the scene, I am sucked back up the tunnel, through the spiraling fissure of memories, only to find myself deposited back in this indecipherable room in the middle of the jungle, hot and dark and sweaty with Mapacho smoke and ícaros and strangers. The songs are supposed to be comforting but I would give anything to stop their whinnying cries.

I want someone to hold me.

And then I am sucked back down the tunnel again, but this time you are all here with me, crossing into another plane, tumbling down the infinite perimeter of the finite figure. We are driving through the Pennsylvania night, my 12-year-old self in the front seat, the glow of the dashboard before us and Steve Earle in the tape deck as we eat up the interstate miles, the smell of fresh cut grass and warm asphalt and the feeling that summer will never end... You are with me when we stash the *Playboy*s in a tree fort in the woods... We all walk into a sleepy house in the small hours of the morning... You can see it with me, plain as day: the way I pick up the injured butterfly to put it in the old, wooden wagon I pull along that quiet street at dusk.

We are sucked back up the tunnel again, into the ceremony house with the haunting whistling of The Shaman and the shaking of chakapas. The Shaman assures us that we are right here, that we have always been right here, that we always will be right here. It is tormenting. I claw the floorboards. I hear a woman vomiting and I swear it's my mom. The tunnels are infinite, the night interminable. I am desperate for something real, for something to prove that the memories happened and existed somewhere outside my head. That they are more than just snapping synapses. That there is more to life than lying in the dark with strangers in an incomprehensible room.

People are concerned for my safety and sanity. I want water, but don't know how to ask. I plead for help, but The Shaman tells me I need to do this on my own. He assures us that life will push us to our limits, but it will not push us *past* them. That transcending fear makes you stronger. None of this is spoken.

It suddenly becomes evident that I will die here. That I will expire in this room without ever having lived. That my entire life is nothing more than falling down these tunnels of memories that aren't memories, but visions and dreams that never existed.

I have taken the red pill. I am already dead. I never actually lived.

I am sucked under again. Falling to a place I don't remember. A high school party that feels familiar but somehow different. I look around the room. There are too many people, and bottles everywhere, red cups littering the kitchen table.

And Katrina.

In the time before I knew her.

She is young and beautiful and carefree. But she is not herself. She is talking too loud and laughing too easily, knocking things over and making people uncomfortable. I stand back and watch with the feeling that things will go wrong. I am hoping that one of the neighbors will call the police, or that one of her friends will take her home, or that one of the kids will trip and crash into the fish tank, shattering glass and screaming as the living room carpet stains with blood and dead fish.

But none of that happens. What happens is far worse. There is a man I have never seen before. He is older than everyone at the party and looking at Kat in a way that telegraphs it all. It isn't long before he corners her in the kitchen. He talks closely and she hangs on his words. He pours her another drink. Something strong. He kisses her and she lets him. She laughs and he gives her another drink. Everyone can see what I'm seeing, but no one stops it. He grabs her by the wrist and pulls her up the stairs. Katrina is only half-willing as she falters.

The bedroom is dark and thick with the musk of adolescence and alcohol, cheap perfume and crushed cigarettes. There is no talking. She is falling asleep but not quite. She tries to say no but not quite. She doesn't want her first time to be this way and we know it unequivocally.

The arc of my relationship with Katrina melts and reshapes before my eyes as her pants are pulled down but not off. And it isn't exactly violent, but it isn't exactly consensual, and it doesn't last more than a minute, but it is a lifetime and costs as much.

It's years later. I've been here before. Last night's episode was the final straw. I thought I'd seen it all with Kat: throwing chairs, slamming doors, the sobbing B-movie routine. But this was something else entirely. My jaw still aches from the clean shot she took, and my head still throbs from the aftermath. My groin is raw from a year of pent-up desire that had come to a head in one raucous, forbidden hatefuck of a night in Jasmine's tiny apartment.

I despise myself but I don't. I'm standing at the door, deciding how to put the key in the lock. I take a deep breath.

The lock clicks over.

I slowly open the door.

It is startlingly quiet.

I step inside.

I climb the sixteen steps to our apartment.

I walk into the kitchen. I open the refrigerator and stare into the white brightness.

I walk into the living room and sit on the couch. I check my phone. The missed calls are an implication.

I go back to the refrigerator and stare into the empty light.

And then the sound: dripping, slowly. Like a weeping faucet. But not.

Knowing before I know.

Walking down the hall, long and dark in the late afternoon. Photographs on the wall.

The moment before. When life is different.

Standing with my hand on the door. Bowing my head. It opens itself.

Time stops.

The deep crimson is as breathtaking now as it was on that day, as alarming as it will always be. The gleaming white of the bathroom tile. The instantaneous understanding that her last act before *the* act was to scrub the bathtub with bleach.

My engraved Swiss army knife on the floor.

The quantity of blood is staggering. It smears the walls. Streaks her arms. Pools on the floor. Her eyes are open, yet she is astoundingly lifeless. She is naked and snow white, the black diamond between her legs like a shiv in the back. There is an unsmoked cigarette in the soap dish.

And my reflection in the mirror.

The moment lasts a lifetime. My lifetime. Hers. It endures.

We stare into the mirror.

It is my reflection and yours. It is her reflection and ours.

It is two mirrors reflecting one another, sharing the same existence. Forever.

The chanting, the chakapas, the ícaros, the love, the energy, the spirits, the jungle, the night, the memories, the river, the pain, a lifetime faster and faster birth and death and good and bad and right and wrong and experience live your life love yourself liveyourlifeloveyourself blood faith water light trustintheuniverse backyard icicles sex arms fear waiting crowd dreams fingernails future tears disease hope moments godpleaseforgivemeyouonlyneedtoforgiveyourself the color of your skin whistling shattered freedom devastation north everythingyouneed breathing hair circle shame lakes hands full moon surrendertotheuniverse guilt feeling trees regret home laughter beyond chalkboard unknown autumn leaves later loss vacancy future truth cold tongue mother streets time redemption dog sunshine why... perfectthewayyouare... life is all we have it's all we ever will it's all we have itsallwehaveitsallitsallallallall... I am blasted from the infinite, sucked back up the tunnel one last time and into the electric hum of the night's warm stillness.

I feel the breathing of the people around me. The ceremony house is sticky with silence. My body twitches. The dancing candlelight is sweet-talking reality. And then a moment of utter clarity, as The Shaman quietly says, "Take a deep breath. It's just a little bit of life... It's just a little ayahuasca."

The Shaman stays with me long after the others retreat to their mosquito-netted beds. He is there as I struggle to come out of it, as I try to confront a shattered life and an obliterated understanding of who I am. He sits nearby, singing ícaros and bringing water. He touches my forehead and whispers reassurance as I crawl from the ashes.

Sometimes the epiphany takes time to process, the revelation only revealing itself in the comfortable distance that comes with the circle more fully unbroken. I climb from the floor and nod to The Shaman. It is the best I can do, the closest I can come to giving thanks.

I drag my ragged carcass out of the ceremony house, unable to keep my balance as I stumble down the dirt path carved from the jungle floor, the plants snickering as I meander back to the place where Ishy and the Deuce lie sleeping.

The stars are the most brilliant I have ever seen.

25

Saturday: Amazon, Peru

A hypnotic fog hangs low to the ground as Ishy creeps from his hut, through the mist to the main lodge. He is thirsty for someone, anyone, to share his experience from the night before. He pours hot water into a mug, gently spoons some tea leaves, then finds a place to sit so he can reconcile the world now that the doors of perception have been nudged open. He's thinking about his life: about what matters, and what's just noise. He's thinking about the people he wants to spend his time with now that he better understands what he's always taken for granted: that this is the only life we have.

He's thinking that his mission to obtain six figures before 30 can take a backseat for a while, that maybe there's a difference between the road to happiness and the road *of* happiness.

As the early morning sun burns off the mist, guests trickle in. Ishy is grateful for the company, telling and retelling his visions to all who'll listen. The others have seen this morning-after enthusiasm before—in themselves, in fact. They smile as they sip green tea, their ad hoc cross-referencing making the most real experience of their lives feel even more so.

In the midst of animated conversation, The Deuce manages to sneak into the main lodge. Unable to look anyone in the eye, he takes a seat near the back to chain-smoke in silence. Ishy doesn't notice him for quite some time. Once he does, The Deuce gives a slow nod as if to confirm he's okay but needs space.

It is even later when Ishy notices Hamish, the weathered New Mexico hippie, with his hand on The Deuce's shoulder, speaking with quiet, unwavering earnestness.

While Ishy and The Deuce are out, I wallow in the cocoon of my mosquito-netted bed. My inability to sleep exceeds only my inability to face anything else. My mind is a whirr of fear and reckoning and dread. It is crippling. Painful. Hopeless. I know I will have to find a way to crawl out of it, but I don't have the strength.

It is mid-morning when I hear Ishy come back to the hut. I sense his indecision as he stands by the door. He eventually makes his way over to my bed, asking if I'm okay. The only response I can muster is to shake my head. I feel it in my throat and know if I try to talk, I'll break down and cry. When he asks if I want something to eat or drink, I roll over and stare at the wall. Five minutes later, he returns with a cup of water to place beside my bed. Then he leaves me alone.

An hour later, I hear The Deuce and Ishy speaking in muted tones. There is a disagreement about what they should do with me, but they eventually just disappear.

Ten minutes later, I hear the door creak open, then register Vanessa's presence at my side. She opens the web of my mosquito net, eyeing me with profound concern. She puts her hand on my forehead and doesn't say a word. I manage to keep it together for about fifteen seconds.

Vanessa remains silent, words unnecessary and inadequate anyway. She doesn't try to tell me that everything will be alright, or that I'm strong enough to get through it, or that everything happens for a reason. Instead, she crawls into bed and holds me while I cry.

Ishy and The Deuce return to the hut and begin packing our gear. Twenty minutes later, Gustavo appears at the door. He informs us that the supply boat has arrived to take us back to Iquitos. Ishy and The Deuce let him know we'll be at the dock in a minute, and then they stand in the doorway for a long time, gazing out at the jungle and shaking their heads.

Vanessa looks deep into me with soft and loving eyes, conveying that it's time to compose myself. I take a deep breath. She wipes the tears from my eyes as I watch them well in hers.

By the time we reach the dock, The Shaman and most of the guests have gathered to see us off. It is dead flat between here and the Atlantic, but the water moves swiftly, churning and effervescent.

For the briefest moment, I remember something I came across in a book at The Hideout. It described a time when the

Amazon flowed *west* from the highlands in the east, meandering across the central plain, emptying into the cool waters of the Pacific. This was the river's existence for millions of years until— seemingly overnight—the mountains appeared in the west, ruthless in their incontrovertible truth as they imposed their will to choke the river unrecognizable. The central plain became an oozing mire, a wasteland of water, silt, and sulfur that nearly consumed the continent, remaining stagnant and lost and dying for eons, perpetually indefinite, irrefutably eternal, a river no more.

And then one day, and for millions of immeasurable days, sediment from those westerly mountains began to erode in breathtaking patterns, altering the basin of the swamp. Reality shifted in deep time as what destroyed the river breathed life back into it: fragments of rock and dirt and death and decay settling infinitesimally beneath the water and inexplicably-always transforming the wasteland mire. The thing that was once a river struggling to become a river once again, breaking through and beginning to flow anew—this time to the east—a river to the sea forevermore.

We step onto the dock.

Infinite moments lay in wait. Moments we can see coming. Moments we can hope for. Moments we can dream.

There will be the three-hour boat ride back to Iquitos, and the time spent in the gringo hamburger joint overlooking the Plaza de Armas, the endless barrage of mototaxis rushing past as we sit in silence. There will be the short flight back to Lima, and the five hours spent in Jorge Chávez Airport as we alternate between the Duty Free Shop and our belongings spread across seats at the gate. There will be Ishy and The Deuce secretly discussing my fragile state. There will be me disappearing into the airport gift shop, consumed by the guilt and uncertainty of what a vanished son should bring home to his broken mother.

There will be the overnight flight to Miami, followed by another lengthy stopover, the flight back to Toronto, and our arrival in the granite darkness of November Sunday night.

There will be The Deuce and his daughter at the zoo, laughing for hours at the monkeys and kangaroos. The Deuce watching as Clara romps through the playland at McDonald's on a Tuesday night. There will be sleepovers in the living room and flashlight puppet shows. Him sitting in a lawn chair as she runs around the soccer field on a perfect summer evening. There will be skating at Nathan Phillips Square, sometimes with a lady-friend in tow, but mostly just the two of them. Kindergarten artwork hanging on the refrigerator and *My Little Pony* figurines in a box under his bed. Exchanges with her mother that will come to be respectful and occasionally even pleasant.

Not a perfect father. Maybe not even a good father. But a better one.

There will be Ishmael getting on a plane two months from now to fly back to Lima, hopelessly in love. Him giving Lucia the *wayruro* earrings he fashioned in the jungle, and her handing him back the sweatshirt she'd slept in every night since he'd left.

There will be Spanish lessons and discovering new cultures. There will be learning and marveling. There will be emotions once unfathomable.

There will be a quiet marriage service *en la oficina de distrito*, followed by a raucous party at The Happy Llama Hostel, complete with poutine and Steam Whistle and a Limean salsa band playing mambo-infused numbers by Sloan.

There will be Ish bringing Lucia to Canada, and that first night back at The Cloak and Dagger with The Deuce, me, and a host of others, laughing our asses off and unable to wrap our heads around the idea that the girl from the hostel in Lima is now in our little Toronto bar—with Ish! There will be children in quick succession, and Ishy buying a place in Miraflores that overlooks the Pacific so they can spend their winters in summer.

And there will be other moments. The ones we don't see coming.

And there will be the moment of confusion when I believe I've walked into the wrong room, unable to recognize the shriveled figure in the hospital bed: my mom withered and drained of everything, the slope of life slippery, the fall more precipitous than we ever imagine possible. There will be me breaking down into a deluge of regret and self-loathing and denial, time collapsing as I crumple inconsolably at her bedside.

And my mother's slow, cold, consoling touch.

It will be during these interminable vigil nights that pass in the blink of an eye, that the understanding will begin to set in. On those nights, sitting there and holding her head, trying in vain to make her more comfortable. In those lost hours giving her tiny sips of water. When I am with her and pouring my life out and pouring my heart out and never leaving, trying to wrap my head around the truth of it, never leaving, the tide of being and living and dying rising to engulf me night after night, and never leaving, and never leaving, and never leaving, never, never never.

It is impossible to comprehend an existence without my mom. She has always been there, the one constant for every breath and thought and miserable failure. She is the heartbeat of my existence, touching everything, meaning everything, being everything. How do you go on when the life force all-encompassing and all-loving ceases to exist? How do you breathe? How do you remain?

In those weeks by her side, late at night, I will crawl into the hospital bed with her and softly rub her back. In those quiet moments, I will be consumed by the recognition that this is all we have. That this is all we will *ever* have.

And then the moment.

It is impossible to understand the soul until its departure. The sudden, undeniable nothingness that slides in and supplants that which was before. The cold, fathomless emptiness in the room. The crippling, unforgettable stillness.

The soul is the opposite of its absence.

In that fleeting moment, after it has eternally departed, it is impossible to deny its existence.

And there will be this moment sooner as our plane rests on the purgatory tarmac: Ishy sound asleep, his future already manifesting in his head, and The Deuce studying the broken man in the seat next to them.

"Hey, cuz. I know it fuckin' sucks how it all went down. It'll probably keep you fucked-up for a long time. I don't know what to say, other than that it needed to happen this way."

I won't know what to do. The lost look I return will be one of hurt and uncertainty. My voice will be that of a child. "Why?"

"Because that's the way it happened."

I will bite my lip and turn away.

An indefinite interval will pass. The Deuce won't need to look at me to understand. "Hey, cuz. Everything's gonna be alright, okay?"

And the long silence. I will take a deep breath and slowly face him, my tear-soaked eyes looking into his. "I don't think it will. But I appreciate it all the same."

And then the plane climbing out of Iquitos at sunset, the impossible green of the jungle and the serpentine river appearing beneath us then falling away, the infinite tributaries revealing their archetypal beauty.

There will be all these moments and more, moments too innumerable to count, too complex and important to be bound by words and distance and time.

But in this particular moment, we are saying goodbye.

The river sparkles in the late morning sunshine while we stand on the dock, all of us, water licking the planks underfoot as the boat knocks against the posts to which it is tethered.

Ish is the first to make a move, thanking The Shaman by offering a handshake that transitions into an awkward semi-embrace, his clumsy sincerity heartfelt.

The Shaman looks him in the eye. "When you ask from the heart, you will always receive. The universe sees to it."

It's like a memory of something to come.

The Deuce extends his hand. "It's been a fuckin' trip, Doc."

"Full cup regret, into the light, over the top..."

"You said it, my man. It's a strange, shadowy path we lead ourselves down."

The Shaman smiles big and warm. "Keep listening to the trees, Stanley."

"Oh, yeah? What's the timber timbre?"

"*Tranquiiiiiilo.*"

I've barely spoken all morning.

The Shaman knows, and understands, and looks me in the eye for 10,000 years. "You can never live a better life than the one you're living. Let go of everything you no longer want to feel, Roosevelt. Life is all we have."

I take a deep breath and nod.

Vanessa moves closer and wraps her arms around me, tears in her eyes. I hold her tight and desperate as the ache in my throat consumes me. I can't begin to explain the noise it makes. Maybe the sound of heartbreak.

It is time for her to let me go. To let me go so I can get on the boat and go back to the life I have run away from; the life I have abandoned; the life I am terrified to live; the life I don't want but is the only one I have.

It is time for her to let me go.

But she won't. And I won't let her.

I hold her close, and I don't dare kiss her, not even on the cheek, but I need to tell her something. And it isn't that I love her even though I do, and it isn't to thank her for saving me even though she has, and it isn't that I will find her one day soon even though I will.

Before she lets me go, I close my eyes and hold her so close that, in the warmth of the sun shining down on us, it is possible— just for a moment—to forget who I am and where I am and when I am and even that we are two people instead of one.

Before I let her go, I whisper, "It's the soul."

It isn't until she is standing beneath a streetlight amidst the glittering flakes of that first Harlem snowfall that she understands.

Thanks for reading! Find more transgressive fiction (poems, novels, anthologies) at: Outcast-Press.com

Twitter & Instagram: @OutcastPress

Facebook.com/ThePoliticiansDaughter

GoFund.Me/074605e9 (Outcast-Press: Short Story Collection)

Amazon, Kindle & IngramSpark

Email proof of your Amazon/Goodreads review to OutcastPressSubmissions@gmail.com & we'll mail you a free bookmark!

Author Acknowledgements:

It all starts with Bob and Isa coming to Canada. Sure, it's the magic of family.

To Hamilton Souther for taking in this stray.

To Hamish Guthrie, Ed Lobb, Jed Rasula, Rob McCallum, and Mike McCallum for showing me how transcendent and powerful great fiction can be.

To Kevin McCallum for the gift of the hockey locker room, where all the best stories are told.

To Hilary McMahon for the hard truth on an early draft, and to Geoff Cole for teaching me to embrace the grind.

To The Point Hostel for setting the stage; to Liam and Gino for making the drinks; and to Andrea and Patty for bringing her back.

Gracias a Rolando, Carlos y Alicia for always taking me off the gringo trail.

A Century Club's worth of drunken toasts to The Lads for a lifetime of friendship and an endless supply of source material.

Thanks to Ronnie for believing that, like Gordie Lachance, I could be a real writer someday.

Endless gratitude to Lis for believing in this work more than I ever did. This book never sees the light of day without your unwavering support.

In the day we sweat it out on the streets... Dad, thanks for teaching me everything I could ever want to know about music, and for vowing to never read my work until the day I got it published (old school parenting!)

Mom, I will never be able to thank you enough for reading to me long before I knew what stories were, and for stomaching my writing long before it was ever ready for prime time.

To Sebastian Vice for having the guts to take a chance on an unknown writer; to Paige Johnson for her vision and her gentle edit; and to Emily Woe for getting it on the shelves. It's been a dream.

To LuLu and Liam for being the light; for making me smile every single day; and for making this whole "getting older" thing worthwhile.

And lastly, Thank You to Claudia for inspiring me to go the Whole Wide World. *Vale la pena.* Without you, none of this exists. *Te amo, mi Gatita.*

About the Author

Twitter: @Sean42McCallum

Sean McCallum lives outside of Toronto, Canada, with his wife and two children. *The Recalcitrant Stuff of Life* is his debut novel, and he is no stranger when it comes to Peruvian adventure; the stories come from experience and months spent backpacking around South America.

Interview on *The Recalcitrant Stuff of Life's* inspiration

I wanted to read about the main character from *Bright Lights, Big City* making terrible decisions in Iquitos. I wanted to read about the guys from Meatball Mulligan's lease-breaking party in *Entropy* (by Thomas Pynchon) trying to make their way across the Andes and down the Amazon. I wanted to explore the unanswerable questions surrounding the meaning of life and the origins of the universe in a way that my buddies and I might if we'd eaten some great mushrooms and were laying out on a dock, looking up at the stars in Northern Ontario.

In the end, I wanted to write a story my buddies would get a kick out of, that people travelling to South America would want to read while down there, and that would help me explain this inexplicable thing that happened to me…

For starters, I met this English dude who'd just gotten back from spending a few days down the Amazon River with a shaman. At that time, I never heard of ayahuasca, but I remember him telling me he drank this crazy medicine and began puking his brains out and shitting all over the place, that he was tripping balls and legitimately thought he was going to die. I couldn't imagine anything worse.

Fast forward two years, and by some coincidence I came across an article in *National Geographic* by Kira Salak (KiraSalak.com/Peru.html) about her ayahuasca experience. It was a stunning read about overcoming depression. Dark and terrifying, but completely unforgettable and moving. I had to check it out, so I made my way to Iquitos to track down that same shaman. I wound up spending 10 days deep in the Amazon and participated in five separate ayahuasca ceremonies. To say that those ceremonies changed my life would be an understatement. The experience changed my outlook on everything.

The stops in between changed my life, too.

I took an unforgettable three-day cargo boat ride down the Amazon. The boat was loaded so far past capacity, it was comical. There was an election going on, and the Peruvian government implemented new abstention fines, so everyone living along the river was desperate to get back to Iquitos to vote and avoid this fine. There were literally people racing out in speedboats and leaping into cargo boats to get back in time.

I was staying at a great party hostel in the Barranco district of Lima, Peru. A thousand different places to stay and I chose the one where this beautiful girl was working her first shift on the night of the Halloween party. During the party, in the midst of *waaay* too many Jägerbombs, I absolutely hit it off with my terrible Spanish. Problem was, I was flying to Iquitos the next day, so I told her I'd be back to see her in two weeks. As promised, I was able to reconnect with her for one more perfect night in Lima before leaving.

But here's the one thing I will never be able to explain. When I was in the jungle with The Shaman, everyone else was there to work through trauma, or sickness, or addiction, but I was simply curious, looking for inspiration as an aspiring writer who wanted to take a peek behind the curtain. Regardless, the Shaman took me aside and informed me that I probably didn't know why I was there, but he knew the reason. He assured me that the spirits had been calling me (I tried not to laugh when he said this), and that it would all make sense in a year's time.

Wouldn't you know it, I married that girl from the hostel a year to the day. Twelve years and two kids later, I think he might have been on to something!

The universe works in mysterious ways, and maybe the spirits really have been calling us all along.

Writing *The Recalcitrant Stuff of Life* has been the most rewarding experience of my life, and I hope it brings as much joy to readers as it has me.

CPSIA information can be obtained
at www.ICGtesting.com
Printed in the USA
BVHW072028190522
637465BV00001B/1